MINORITY
REPORT

MINORITY REPORT

WHAT HAS HAPPENED TO BLACKS, HISPANICS, AMERICAN INDIANS, AND OTHER MINORITIES IN THE EIGHTIES

EDITED BY

Leslie W. Dunbar

PANTHEON BOOKS
NEW YORK

Library of Congress Cataloging in Publication Data

Main entry under title:

Minority report.

  Includes index.
   1. Minorities—United States. 2. Discrimination—
United States. 3. Racism—United States. 4. United
States—Economic policy—1981–   . I. Dunbar, Leslie.
E184.A1M547 1984   305.8'00973   84-42670
ISBN 0-394-72513-1

Manufactured in the United States of America

Design: Robert Bull

  3456789

Justice William O. Douglas, writing his autobiography, spoke a truth to which we dedicate this book.

Only through the individual is our real quality of life revealed. That quality is improved by the tensions we remove, by the frictions we reduce, by the prospect of true equality of opportunity for every human in our midst.

From planning to final copy, Wendy Wolf of Pantheon made this book hers. It seems almost an act of presumption to express our thanks, but we nevertheless do, and they are warm and deep thanks, enough to extend to her assistant, Jeffrey Faude, as well. In preparation of copy for the publisher, James Skofield and Gisela Traugott were of special help.

CONTENTS

FOREWORD

The United States has been wrestling with its "minority question" nearly as long as our history itself has run. The injustice that minorities have endured has been the gravamen of the most sustained criticisms of our republic, both from outside and from within, for more than two centuries. We have in this book tried to depict the contemporary, and future threatening, nature of the old malignancy, lying deep at the core of our national existence.

We have not reviewed here the histories of blacks, Mexican Americans, Indians, Puerto Ricans, Chinese, and Japanese; nor the experiences of those European groups who came in the last century and early years of this one—the Irish, Italians, and Poles prominent among them—and were put into long struggle against several forms of discrimination; nor of Jews, whose American story is an extraordinary saga of dazzling achievements coupled with often brutal anti-Semitism. With varying degrees of accuracy, comprehension, and self-delusion, all Americans know those histories, well enough at least to locate themselves within them. Almost every American can, in fact, find some minority to identify with, and it is striking how natural and consoling it seems to us to do so whenever we feel a grievance, not merely contending that "I" have been wronged, but "we" have been discriminated against. A necessary task today is to begin to record the shorter histories of certain newer and significant minorities—the war refugees from Southeast Asia and poverty refugees from Central America and Mexico—for they seem to foretell that the American experience with minorities may be unending in its complications and unpredictable new factors.

That experience has been a compound of all the large currents of our national life—political, constitutional, economic, moral, and literary. Gunnar Myrdal, in his classic 1940s study of the Negro condition, put emphasis on the moral, on the "dilemma" within the national conscience arising from divergence between professed ideal and actual practice. In doing so, he signified how deeply and painfully we have always internalized black-white issues; much the same could be said regarding Indian-white issues (though those affecting Hispanics and Asians, possibly because they had been neither enslaved nor indigenous, seem not so wreathed in moral awareness).

For Americans, racial relations became a struggle with our own values, although not solely Yeats's "quarrel with ourselves," which he had said expressed itself in "poetry" rather than in the "rhetoric" of "quarrel with others."[1] Rhetoric about race has been among our plagues. But our novelists, poets, better essayists, and folk singers have spoken, too, and during long years and with few exceptions their voices have been a lament over the mangling of human spirits, of whites as well as nonwhites, that has gone on.

This book has little poetry to it, and if we have succeeded, not much rhetoric either. I hope that the moral drive, the poetic vision, that powered the civil rights movement of our day can be sensed beneath its surface; most assuredly, there is here more of the "uncertainty" Yeats ascribed to poets than of his rhetoricians' "confidence." Essentially, our thought is that what in the past had been for the United States a problem first of all moral, or first of all constitutional, is now primarily political and economic, in a tight mingling of the two. We see no disadvantages of American minorities likely to be much relieved without economic advance; we see no strong likelihood of that without enlarged political participation.

In saying that politics and economics are now primary we do not at all intend to ignore constitutional and moral questions that, in the nature of things, are and will remain strong, nor do we overlook the way they interact with political and economic policies. As Taylor suggests in his essay, however, all Supreme Court decisions regarding race since 1954 are at bottom applications of that year's great ruling in *Brown* v. *Board of Education.*[2] Much the same could be said for later holdings regarding voting and representation as being derivative of *Baker* v. *Carr*[3] in 1962, and the preceding series of "white primary" cases.[4] We once had a Constitution that sanctioned discriminatory classification by race and that severely restricted federal protection of the franchise. We emphatically have such no longer. Those great decisions gave force to—it may be said, released from captivity—the Fourteenth and Fifteenth amendments, appropriately referred to as the Civil War amendments. The courts have been engaged since then in what has surely been one of the grand enterprises of American constitutionalism, that of explicating and enforcing their meaning. No other service of the independent judiciary to the republic has been greater or more unsullied.

There are undoubtedly still open questions, and quite important ones. There are narrowly decided Supreme Court decisions that bear all the signs of having left issues unsettled. These include the series of "affirmative action" cases beginning in 1978 with *Bakke* v. *Regents of the University of California* [5]; the metropolitan school desegregation controversies left unclear since *Milliken* v. *Bradley* [6] in 1974; perhaps most important of all, the issue of equitable school financing, which in *San Antonio School District* v. *Rodriguez* [7] (1972) the Court turned away from; and the harsh problem of capital punishment which, as Gordon describes in her essay, the Court has struggled with so unsatisfactorily from all points of view. On another front, there is the question of women's constitutional status, and the Court's refusal to date to extend to gender classification the same "strict scrutiny" and almost automatic disapproval it gives to racial classifications. Hard questions, and one hopes good law, lie ahead on all these matters.

Nevertheless, the fundamental contours of the Constitution have been defined and accepted. Nor is there among those issues or their like any which could not be as well disposed of to the satisfaction of minorities, and quite possibly better so, by legislative action, federal or state: the Constitution no longer prevents, as once it was contended it did, an active legislative role. Legislatures are as free in this area as, since the "revolution" of the late 1930s and early 1940s, they are in the regulation of the economy. The one possible exception to that statement relates to the affirmative action area and the balancing of individual rights inherent in it; but even there, broad scope for legislative, executive, and private action has been repeatedly recognized by the courts, and it is hard to imagine drastic withdrawal.

Moral injunctions certainly lie heavy still upon us, and do indeed permeate every political contest. Perhaps also the most we can rightly claim is that a smug moral self-satisfaction has now replaced the old tormented conscience that Myrdal and others so perceptively described. But though it may be difficult for some of us to remember or younger generations to imagine, as recently as the early 1960s even church bodies (white ones, that is, and especially, but not exclusively, in the South) held back from condemning segregation as a moral and religious wrong, instead couching their appeals to their people simply in terms of citizens' obligation to obey the law. The nation sorely needs a moral consciousness that invigorates its political will, and this book's essayists are not hesitant in saying so. But America has progressed at least to the point where one no longer needs to argue that white supremacy and segregation are moral iniquities.

As with so much of the historical experience of racial minorities, there is a tragic dimension to their present American (and, in like ways, worldwide) situation. It lies in the coincidence that they have come to levels of self-assertion during an era of vast technological and demographic upheavals and international instability, disturbances that make all solutions more difficult and chancy. We have tried to be mindful of all that. Taking it into account has, for us, clearly pointed to the necessity of active government, shaping the economy in ways that could make the elimination of poverty a realistic possibility. We see governmental acts of that resolute quality not likely to come about unless there is substantially greater political influence among minorities, especially black and Hispanic. I don't know that all or any of this book's contributors go as far in analysis as did Mr. Justice Douglas, but all face in the direction he once did: ". . . we now know that no matter what the growth rate of our GNP, the private sector will not be able to take care of employment needs. Technological advances ('technological unemployment,' as it used to be called) are so great that disemployment will mark our future. In other words, by the end of this century the public sector and government largesse [he included Pentagon contracts in that term] will be the mainstay of most of our people—if we survive."[8] All the courtroom victories imaginable would not take the country far toward economic realism of that quality; only political policies could.

Since the civil rights movement days of the 1960s and 1970s blacks have sought to build their direct political influence. Hispanics were not slow to do the same. Numerous voter registration drives in the South have added black voters in numbers sufficient by now to have critical weight in several states and congressional districts and to win mayoralty elections in principal southern cities. Many of these drives have been originated and coordinated by the Voter Education Project, based in Atlanta. Blacks outside the South have done likewise. One result has been the capture of the mayor's office in one after another large city; another is the slow but steady increase in congressional seats held. A notable result of that has been a "black caucus," providing a reliable nucleus of congressional support for economic liberalism and consistent opposition to foreign interventions and military expansion.

Just as the black surge began in the South, the Hispanic political awakening began in the Southwest, where the Southwest Voter Registration Education Project has provided direction. In contrast to the early black political stirrings, which sought leverage on national issues, especially the passage of civil rights legislation and diligent federal enforcement and sympathetic administration, initial Mexican American interest was on local problems. Success came to voter registration drives when people began to see voting as a means toward getting their streets paved, their water cleaned up, their schools made respectful to their Spanish language, the police more careful of their rights. It has been a process of learning to make use of politics. It was also a process of discovering faith in the practical value of a democratic system to those who organize their strength. In California and Texas, where about 85 percent of all southwestern Spanish-surname people live, registration grew between 1976 and 1980 by at least 35 percent and 65 percent respectively. There are now nearly a million Mexican American voters in California, over 800,000 in Texas, and those two typically closely contested slates hold 76 electoral votes, better than a fourth of the number needed to elect a president. Other southwestern states have shown comparable advances. Mexican American mayors have been elected in San Antonio and Denver (where the candidate won with the appealing slogan, "Imagine a Great City").

As their base has expanded and grown more secure, Mexican American voters and leaders have looked beyond the Southwest and beyond local issues to the pockets of their fellow ethnics elsewhere (such as Illinois), to Puerto Ricans of the East, and to working alliances with blacks. Across the nation, there are now an estimated 3.5 million Hispanic voters out of perhaps six million eligible. Every survey indicates that they bring to national politics economic concerns that parallel those of blacks. They have their own other strongly held viewpoints—such as bilingual schooling—and may on the contemporary spectrum be conservative on social issues (such as abortion); but American politics has never been without its intricate multiplicity of opinions. What does seem unmistakable is that a growing Hispanic vote joins a growing black one in pressing for national economic policies that include a clear concern for their needs, and these are voters the majority of whom are very low on the economic scale. As Hamilton argues in his essay, vigorous governmental intervention in the economy is both a need of the newly politicized minorities and something they will and can effectively insist upon.

They can do so, in very large part, because their own protests plus the constitutional issues won since World War II have freed and empowered them. They have acquired the strength to register their wills, their interests, in the social calculus. In this year, which is the thirtieth anniversary of *Brown* v. *Board of Education*, that represents the fundamental achievement to be celebrated. Where their influence weighed little before, it is strong now. Minorities have joined in the determining of national policy, and their power will undoubtedly increase in the future. That is this book's optimistic counterpoint to our more pessimistic reading of present conditions.

One result of this empowerment is the possibility of transferring some vitally important controversies from courts to the political realm. The Constitution's Thirteenth Amendment outlawed slavery and peonage and its Fifteenth, Nineteenth, Twenty-Fourth, and Twenty-Sixth forbade denial of voting rights on grounds of race, sex, nonpayment of poll tax, or age if above 18. The Constitution is silent about other specific forms of discrimination, and the constitutional vacuum—as it came to be perceived—was filled by the federal courts largely under the Fourteenth Amendment's command: "nor shall any State deny to any person within its jurisdiction the equal protection of the laws." Few people, lay or lawyers, would have two or three decades ago read those words as, for example, authorizing federal judges to prescribe school bus routes in localities, even after compulsory segregation had ceased or had never been. The explanation has been that such orders are remedies intended to ease segregated patterns of the past where found still to deny children equal educational rights. The ensuing controversy is not merely the ordinary one over contested rulings—too far for some, not far enough for others—but of divergent views, of what a nondiscriminatory society is or should be. Does it require the attainment of integration (defined in some quantifiable ratios) or only the prevention of overt exclusion and denial?

I believe that the answer of this book is that American democracy could live healthily with either of those poles—and the distance between them might not be or stay very great—but that the choice, or, more likely, the choice of variants within them, must come from the working out of acceptable accommodations through consensus; and that only economically and politically self-assured people can do that. Action often produces its own truth, and that is especially so of democracy's searchings for the rights and wrongs of its social relationships.

This book accordingly concentrates on how well or how poorly American society today affords realistic opportunities for its racial minorities to participate in—to give their consent to—the decisions that determine their place within it; and consequently to the nature and guiding principles of our society.

One of the imperatives declared by the civil rights movement was integration. That is a concept hard to define, a goal hard to know when reached. Its beginning point must, however, be access. The first three essays of this book are devoted to ascertaining to what extent our politics and our economic and educational practices have been opened to minority participation. By the time this book is in print, all can now know better than we do now the outcome of Jesse Jackson's entry into the presidential campaign. That it will have been significant is hardly to be doubted. A leading black civil rights lawyer once remarked that in his experience even one black juror made a difference in what went on in the courtroom, in the jury room, and in the result. Mr. Jackson's candidacy is like that, as have been the candidacies of other minority persons for lesser offices and as has been the appearance of minority individuals on educational and economic ladders where they were not traditionally to be found. A new presence, a new awareness of possibilities, suddenly arrives to shake old patterns. Minorities entering the mainstream alter its flow.

The essays which follow discuss those left out—or not yet brought into—the mainstream. They treat, in other words, what are the most painful areas of contemporary American society: persistent urban poverty; the nexus between crime and the administration of criminal law; and the rural poor. The book concludes, as in our opinion all constructive thought on such problems must conclude, with considerations about proper governmental actions. There is, as there should be, some overlap among the articles, for in the final analysis, all the problems are one, which is how to further the cause of equality. Remarkably, there were hardly any disagreements among us, none of any substantial import.

Regretfully we scarcely touch here upon the problems of native Hawaiians and Alaskans, of recent Asian immigrants, illegal entrants from south of our borders, and of political refugees from all over, but we believe their essential concerns, if not the specifics of them, are like those we do discuss. As two remarkable reports in *The New York Times* last December 20 and 22 about Oak Park, Michigan, and the Elmhurst section of New York City reminded us, the United States is still a rich broth of a variety of national groups, clinging to their distinctive ways while pursuing personal and material goals not much dissimilar.

We think that to be, now as in the past, a badge of national honor and hope. If our pages reflect worry and apprehension over the country's drift and politics, we take those as seriously as we do because we are deeply conscious of the magnitude of the American search for equality and the opportunities uniquely here. There is hardly a fault this nation does not have, nor a sin it has not committed. Yet now as in all its history there is more and better besides, and that is due, more than to any other cause, to the ceaseless renewal of ideas and values brought to the fore by all the many minorities within our social order. Movement and dynamism in America have always drawn their most intense life from the nation's new and restless arrivals, from those, as it were, on the social margin. If in a time when all of us teeter on the brink of planetary suicide it may seem irrelevant to examine once again the cause of America's minority poor, their desire and ripening power to summon us to saner politics and national purposes—ones devoted to what the Constitution called the "general welfare" and not as is now the case to the aggrandizement of national power and corporate wealth—is justification enough.

Justice, or the want of it, is an idea at the center of all this book's essays. It would be only appropriate, therefore, to ask what is meant. Though seven persons can hardly be called on for one philosophically agreeable concept, I think the authors all share a few firmly held particulars.

Justice requires, in a society that perceives itself as a democracy, that each citizen must count proportionately in public decisions; the "one person, one vote" dictum expresses for us a necessary value. When individual preferment (including power) is bestowed by society, in order to be just it must derive from and be accountable to a "decision" in which all have had opportunity to contribute.

A second particular would be this, that justice requires—in whatever society a person may live—a reasonable opportunity to a large enough share in that society's wealth to make possible one's good health and dignified status. A third would be that it is unjust to require or ask anyone to serve policies opposed to those precepts. The nation made more progress toward those three standards of civil decency in the past three decades than ever before, though least of all toward the second. For each, a troubled road winds ahead.

L.W.D.
April 1984

NOTES

1. W. B. Yeats, *Mythologies* (New York: Macmillan, 1959), p. 331.
2. 347 U.S. 483.
3. 369 U.S. 186.
4. Especially, *U.S.* v. *Classic*, 313 U.S. 299 (1941) and *Smith* v. *Allwright*, 321 U.S. 649 (1944).
5. 438 U.S. 265.
6. 418 U.S. 717.
7. 411 U.S. 1.
8. William O. Douglas, *International Dissent* (New York: Vintage Books, 1971), p. 151.

MINORITY
REPORT

POLITICAL ACCESS, MINORITY PARTICIPATION, AND THE NEW NORMALCY

CHARLES V. HAMILTON

In the mid-1980s, it is difficult to say very much about minorities and politics that does not summon a sense of *déjà vu*—the subject has gotten more than its due of attention from analysts, activists, and just plain amateur observers in recent years. But some of us persist in addressing the subject, not because we immodestly suspect we have a new interpretation or unique insights but because these remain some of the most important unresolved issues for the American republic. We keep returning in the hope that there might be some different way to understand the complex problems, one that might then lead to a more viable way to alleviate some of them.

In many ways, American politics has always promised more than it can produce, and more than a few observers have noticed this contradiction or dilemma.[1] This country has seen fit, for any number of reasons, to pronounce grandly its goals and aspirations of political freedom and individual opportunity. In doing so, it has not necessarily been hypocritical, it has only been boastful. In practice, it certainly has deviated from its theory. The record here is sufficiently undisputed not to require elaboration.

I propose to take this discrepancy for granted, and am even

3

willing—for sake of argument—to concede that many Americans are genuinely disturbed by the divergence. Or, if necessary, I am prepared to accept the contrasting notion that there is no basic dilemma about the discrepancy between creed and practice, that in matters of race, especially, Americans have acted and pretty much continue to act very much as they truly believe.[2] Both views have been argued persuasively, and it is certain that we have not heard the final statement or rebuttal of either.

My focus is different: it is on the opportunities and limitations of political participation for our racial minorities, keeping in mind that such participation includes much more than voting periodically for candidates. Admittedly, elections are the most prominent form of political participation, but neither the very influential nor the very weak have the luxury of relying solely or even substantially on that process.

THE POLITICAL VALUE SYSTEM

It is important to establish the operative value system in which this discussion is occurring. I suggest that there is a very strong ethic in American society that clearly predates the current conservative mood and was not obliterated by the New Deal, the Fair Deal, the New Frontier, the Great Society, or any other movement of liberal reform. This ethic is in favor of minimal government. The embedded value of the maxim, "That government is best which governs least," is no idle ideological preference, held only by a hard-core right-wing holdover from Adam Smith. It is, for example, a notion that stems from ideas clearly if not initially articulated in *The Federalist*. We find it assumed by James Madison in No. 51, where he admonishes that "Ambition must be made to counteract ambition." We find it in the conviction that government is the main threat to individual liberty, and that therefore, in order to guard against "tyranny" (meaning governmental abuse of power), the Constitution should construct a political system that provided internal checks on the rulers. Thus an elaborate, sometimes unfathomable system of checks and balances was built into the governmental process. We find the founding framers devising a federal system of government, seeking to limit the national government to delegated powers and reserving "all others not delegated" to the people or the states. Without question, we find some escape clauses in the Constitution such as Article 1, Section 8, paragraph 18: "To make all laws which shall be necessary and proper. . . ." This clause and the broadly phrased language of other provisions have permitted courts, Congress, and the president from time to time to accomplish preferred governmental actions.

On the interstate commerce clause (Article 1, Section 8, paragraph 3), one is reminded, to cite one of many examples, of the Supreme Court's decision in *Wickard* v. *Filburn* (317 U.S. 111, 1942) which permitted the federal government to regulate the amount of corn a farmer grew on his farm *for sole use on his farm.* One is also reminded of Chief Justice Earl Warren's language in *Brown* v. *Board of Education* (349 U.S. 483, 1954), where he, for the Court, simply declined to be bound by whatever social conditions existed in 1868 or 1896, held that *Plessy* v. *Ferguson* (163 U.S. 537, 1896) could not be controlling in mid-twentieth-century America, and thereby gave the federal courts an active role in local school administration. But the relevant point, however, is that wherever government has been extended it has been against the background of caution and reluctance.

In the matter of economic activity, this is particularly evident, more so perhaps than in the realm of civil and political rights. This distinction is a critical one, because the thesis of my argument will be that, as minorities have moved the concentration of their struggle from rights to economics, they have confronted not merely discrimination and self-interest but the normalcy of the social system. If government is viewed as a potential force for evil (and by some as a *certain* force, if not tightly reined in), then it will be allowed to extend its operation in the economic sphere under only the most dire circumstances, and it will be monitored closely at each step. Objectively speaking, this need not be detrimental. But the problem is aggravated by the persistence of the value system. For in the American ethic of minimal government, there is not only preference for a limited governmental role, for doing only what is absolutely essential under the circumstances—usually the circumstances of an economic or political crisis—but there is also the quite strong desire for such governmental action to be *temporary,* for the government to intervene *if it must* only to set the disorder aside, to deal with the crisis, and to extricate itself as quickly as possible in order to leave the market forces to function again. There is, in other words, a decided orientation in the value system to "return to normalcy."

What constitutes that "normalcy" varies, of course, from one period to another, but there are some basic characteristics: minimal government as a guarantee against abuse of individual liberty, and the operation of the market economy with as few constraints as possible from government in the way of regulation. These are the "norms" by which much of what government does is measured. That they are disregarded time and again, and often in the interests and at the behest of the economic leadership itself, does not seem to detract from their creedal authority. Americans *want* to believe; and that will to believe can be and has been a strong barrier to minority advance.

Even in the depths of the Great Depression and the New Deal's response to that economic crisis, there were more than a few pro-New Dealers who recognized and characterized that response as essentially "conservative."[3] Granted there were major innovations, and David Truman has suggested that the New Deal brought about a profound alteration in American thinking about the role of government.[4] The fact remains that the country came out of that episode with its less than enthusiastic support for an activist state reasonably intact. There were some things that would not be reversed—social security, securities and exchange regulation, for example—but there were other measures that were clearly perceived to be temporary, ones that ought to recede, it was felt, once the crisis had subsided.

NORMALCY AND STATE INTERVENTION

The problem with the preference for a return to normalcy is that it cannot be recaptured precisely, because it cannot be recreated. Every time government is called upon to intervene to deal with a crisis, new interests are created and vested, new institutions are established, invariably the base of political participation is broadened and made permanent, and new groups are politicized who bring into the political system their felt needs and expectations. This is true whether we are discussing Jacksonian democracy, Reconstruction, the Populist period, the Progressive era, the suffragette movement, the Depression of the 1930s, the civil rights movement, or the environmentalist movement. The political system may not adopt radical new forms as a result of these phenomena, but it would be a mistake to fail to see in each of them lasting impacts as a function of their having occurred.

However the political system responds to its successive challenges, it is never again the same as it was. Government intervention takes several possible forms and has differing consequences. One phenomenon is, however, invariably true: when the economy expands, there is a corresponding expansion of government. Sometimes that is in response to immediate crises; sometimes it is to protect or regulate activity in an effort to fend off an impending crisis. As the term is used here, crisis refers to circumstances that threaten (or promise to threaten) established societal values, interests, and norms. Crisis can come from an external source (an oil embargo, for instance, imposed by OPEC), or it can be internally caused (strikes, racial violence, etc.).

Historically, as economic enterprise has grown from the local village shop to regional dimensions to national structures and, now, to multinational corporations, we find government's role expanding. This expansion sometimes occurs, for example, to protect private enterprise from foreign competition (protective tariffs); at times to regulate competition and to guard against unfair practices (antitrust laws); at times to protect consumers (food and drug laws). State intervention is then rationalized as in the national interest. Its purpose is to protect basic societal values. At the core of those values are a viable market economy and the sanctity of private property; so we have the familiar pattern of state power summoned to protect but not to plan and direct the free market. The state is seen as a partner (usually a junior partner). Certainly there will be those critics who will allege excessive and unnecessary intervention, but the government's role is generally understood as simply supportive of the private-sector economy.

Whatever the particular cause for government activism, the fact is that the "old normalcy" is usually altered in ways that make a return to the *status quo ante* virtually impossible. The rhetoric of the old normalcy may linger (be it free enterprise or states' rights or rugged individualism), but the reality of the "new normalcy" cannot be denied. The old ethic will survive, however, as a sort of nagging (almost nostalgic) reprimand, and the old normalcy will, as it does today through the Reagan administration, fight back.

ACCESS AND EARLIER ETHNIC POLITICS

It is commonplace to compare present-day black and Hispanic politics with that of other ethnic groups in the nineteenth and early
twentieth-century years. The generally accepted understanding regarding them is that those European immigrants came to this country, became involved in the political and economic systems at the
lower levels, and gradually worked themselves into a more as-
similated status. Initially, they manifested a high incidence of ethnic
solidarity, but as their socioeconomic status improved they began to
behave pretty much like their Anglo-Saxon counterparts. That is,
they became less sensitive to ethnic and nationality appeals and more
concerned about class or "mainstream" issues.[5]

A sizable amount of literature has developed over the last two
decades examining this ethnic development thesis[6] and I suspect the
weight of empirical evidence ultimately proves it more accurate than
not. There will remain, however, the important question of its relevance to understanding political access and influence for later groups.
Before we look at the black and Hispanic situation, it is useful to see
the context in which earlier ethnic politics in this country developed.

Those groups began arriving in America when industrial expansion was taking off. They could not have been more timely. Periodic
depressions notwithstanding, there was a continually growing private-sector economy that could accommodate, indeed welcomed,
growing masses of unskilled labor. That labor came. It was met by
urban political structures that mobilized it into machines, and votes
were exchanged for favors. The classic patron-client relationship
ensued. The local party bosses could give benefits to those who
supported them. The need was mutual and the relationship mutually
beneficial.

Benefits, in one formulation, are of two kinds: divisible (those
going to individuals, such as patronage jobs, a contract, a pushcart
license); and indivisible (those shared by the collectivity, such as
clean streets, good schools, national defense).[7] The party bosses were
able to dispense both, but in the nature of things, it was always better
(in the sense of being cheaper) to give divisible benefits. The party
had a certain amount of perks and patronage jobs to hand out at its
discretion, and it could do so to maximize loyalty and support. In

addition, the party could recommend its supporters to those local businesses that were favorably disposed to hire someone from the local clubhouse. A favor rendered would likely be returned in time through various means at the disposal of local officials.

Thus, the local political party could serve as a temporary bridge for the new arrivals, easing their entry into a new society. And these immigrants did not need to look to the political system for satisfaction of all their economic needs. There was a private-sector economy waiting to receive them, albeit at times for exploitative wages and under sweatshop working conditions. But a pushcart license here, help with naturalization papers there, a basket of food at Christmas, and the like could serve specific temporary functions until the family and subsequent generations could move into and up the private-sector economic ladder. The public sector did not have to provide vast indivisible benefits—these could come later with a move to better neighborhoods and higher incomes—and it need not see its clients as permanently dependent on the public largess. There was for decades a constant flow of second-generation children and new immigrants, replenishing the supply of political supporters and clients.

This classic relationship had other important ramifications. The clients became politicized in ways that led them to respect "politics." There was no reason to conclude otherwise. The precinct captain delivered, in tangible, nonideological ways.

This meant that the political environment was consistent with the economic environment, and that both operated to reinforce the societal values of minimal government and the dominance of a market economy. Even if the ethnic immigrant could not realistically hope to advance much beyond his or her present station, there was always the great likelihood that the children's lives would be substantially different, and better. In many ways, the system—economic and political—worked, at least for some. It had its defects and imperfections, to be sure, but these could be modified by incremental changes and modest reforms.

When the situation is combined with the following observation by Robert Lane, the point becomes even clearer:

> For the most part, the immigrant came to America not for political liberty but for the economic opportunities said to exist here,

and because he was said to be welcome. Yet when he came, he entered a slum and found the living precarious and the welcome less than cordial. He was uprooted, and sought to protect himself by reinstituting the institutions and practices of the old country. He banded together in colonies of fellow-ethnics, sought to re-establish the Church as he knew it back home, and organized associations of fellow nationals who held the same loyalties and faced the same problems. He was pitifully conservative, seeking amidst so much change to maintain some traces of what he had known.[8]

Such people had particular orientations and expectations which could be reasonably accommodated by the political system, aided by an available private economy.

NEW GROUPS AND DIFFERENT NEEDS

The post-World War II story of the struggle of black Americans to close the gap Myrdal described as an American dilemma has been recounted often. The struggle has been joined by still other groups —Hispanics, women, the elderly, homosexuals, antinuclear activists, environmentalists—who have been politicized by the civil rights movement, the Vietnam War and general cold war milieu, and the awareness of gross poverty within an affluent society. Their specific agendas overlap in many places, and essentially they can be regarded as liberal on economic and civil liberties issues. They have had their opposites, obviously, on the other side of the political spectrum; namely, tax-revolters, anti-ERA proponents, the Moral Majority, antiabortionists, and a variety of hard-line defense advocates.

It is the liberal group, however, that constitutes the thrust of a newly politicized (and in the case of blacks and Hispanics, recently enfranchised) cadre. This is the force that has mobilized over the last three decades and presented demands calling for increased govern-mental activity, which has meant increased governmental expendi-tures. These demands related to domestic social issues and have had to contend with competing demands, since the Vietnam War, for funds for military spending.

The circumstances surrounding black and Hispanic politiciza-tion are important to understand at the outset. If the earlier European immigrants came seeking economic opportunities and rather immediately immersed themselves in existing political structures, such was not the case with blacks. The latter had to devote a substantial amount of time and energy simply to establishing their claim to political citizenship. While the earlier ethnic groups could launch careers as precinct captains and political bargainers, blacks had to spend time as plaintiffs and protesters. The early years of black contact with the political system consisted of intricate constitutional and other legal arguments in courts interpreting the Fourteenth and Fifteenth amendments of the U.S. Constitution. For decades, the struggle concentrated on efforts to break down the barriers imposed by *de jure* segregation and discrimination.

Occasionally there were mass protest movements (against segregation on city streetcars in Atlanta in 1908; against discriminatory hiring in Harlem in the 1930s; A. Philip Randolph's proposed March on Washington for fair employment in 1940; and the Montgomery bus boycott in 1955 led by Martin Luther King, Jr., to name a few prominent examples). Always, the goal was to direct attention to the blatant inconsistencies between theory and practice in regard to race relations in this country. For obvious reasons, such a struggle could and did have a very heavy moral overtone. And there were many Americans who supported the struggle precisely because they felt it was morally right. In that sense, one might even suggest that such a movement was not political in the narrow sense of the word. It was about human rights, decency, and justice. Politics surely ought to be concerned with such matters, but the case to be made for a patronage job simply is not put in the same terms as one to be made for voting rights. Taking a southern county registrar to court for violating the Fifteenth Amendment is not the same as dealing with a ward boss in a back room for a political favor.

What is the significance of this for our immediate concern? It relates to politicization. A group learns about the system from its accumulated experiences. People who have experienced positive results (albeit limited in many instances) as a function of mobilization and bargaining are much more likely to have respect for that process —indeed, to participate in it—than those who have been thwarted at every step in trying to enter that process. If the process paid off somewhat for the earlier immigrants, that process had a decided negative impact on blacks. If they had to respond laboriously to the legal manipulations of local party officials who devised "grandfather clauses" and "white primaries" and the like, it was only to be expected that alienation would set in. The very legitimacy of the political system would likely be called into question. One is reminded of the observation of Seymour Martin Lipset:

> Legitimacy involves the capacity of the system to engender and maintain the belief that the existing political institutions are the most appropriate ones for the society. The extent to which contemporary democratic political systems are legitimate depends in large measure upon the ways in which the key issues which have historically divided the society have been resolved. . . .
>
> Groups regard a political system as legitimate or illegitimate according to the way in which its values fit with theirs.[9]

Over time, one of the country's most dramatic stories developed. Through a combination of court decisions, congressional legislation, executive decrees, and mass mobilization, the barriers slowly crumbled. *De jure* segregation was overturned. The *legal* foundation and justification for racial subordination was rejected. People began to register and to vote; they began to enroll in schools previously closed to them; they began to patronize public places that once barred their entry. In some instances, old practices of exclusion and subterfuge persisted, but they no longer had the cover of official authority.

Perhaps the most visible signs of dramatic change were manifested in the electoral arena. In 1982, the Joint Center for Political Studies reported that there were 5,160 black elected officials, certainly a vast increase over fewer than 200 in 1965, the year the Voting Rights Act was signed. The most widely heralded ones, of course, are those black elected mayors of big cities such as Gary, Cleveland, Los Angeles, Newark, Atlanta, Washington, D.C., Detroit, New Orleans, Birmingham, Chicago, and Philadelphia. The largest proportion of black elected officials is in municipal and educational positions—48 percent and 25 percent respectively. In 1982, there were 1,081 black women officials—21 percent of the total. Figure 1 indicates the voter registration trend of the voting-age population by race over two decades as reported from a survey done for the Joint Center.[10] The sharp increase of blacks in the late sixties corresponds with the heightened activity of civil rights organizations when concerted efforts were made, supported by the national government, to register people previously denied the ballot. The upward trend levels off after 1970 when it was generally perceived that vigorous federal enforce-

Figure 1. Voter Registration in 11 Southern States
by Race of Respondent, 1960–1980

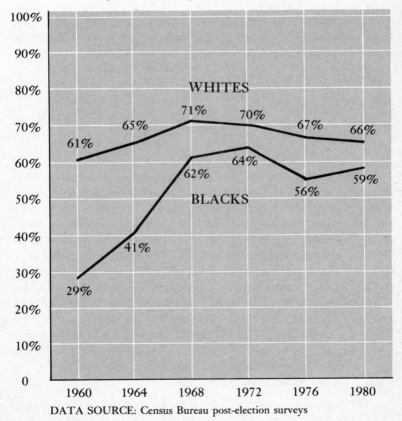

DATA SOURCE: Census Bureau post-election surveys

ment of voting rights was not a high priority of a new administration.

In recent years we have confronted problems of vote dilution. That is, there have been legal and political objections raised by civil rights advocates to the possibility that although blacks have indeed secured the right to vote, that vote can well be minimized by a series of structural mechanisms. These include such things as at-large elections, multimember districts, and annexation. "At-large elections embody the idea that there is a city-wide public interest. Because the majority voting bloc can control all of the seats in the city or county, at-large elections serve to suppress particularistic interests, including those of ethnic and racial minorities."[11]

The requirement for a run-off election if no candidate receives a majority vote is considered by some observers to be still another means of diluting the minority vote.

In 1981 a study of 239 metropolitan-area central cities also found that

> . . . The level of black representation was highly related to electoral arrangements: at-large elections meant less black representation than district elections when blacks constituted as little as 10 percent of a city's population.[12]

Some civil rights lawyers are not optimistic that the current Burger Court will be especially sympathetic to efforts to do away with multimember districts. But where a history of racial exclusion can be shown, there is a greater likelihood that a subsequent adoption of multimember districts or at-large elections will be overruled. Overall this is, however, a difficult area in which to fight, and one can speculate that it will possibly result in a "generation of litigation" in the way we witnessed earlier efforts to subdue the white primaries.

It is important to point out here that there *are* sometimes quite immediate positive consequences resulting from the exercise of the vote. Understandably, there is a reasonably cautious (one is tempted to say cynical) view about the utility of the electoral process. How much difference *can* be made through the exercise of the vote? A 1979 study of Alabama concluded:

> When they were excluded from political participation, southern blacks experienced group-targeted, legally sanctioned exclusion

from equal educational and employment opportunities and were denied adequate housing, health, welfare and other benefits by local officials. Once enfranchised, the new voters sought to use their political influence to expand the supply of these goods and met considerable success in their efforts. Paired comparisons among counties with substantial black electorates support a causal relationship between growth and black political participation and policy change: the greater the change in political mobilization, the greater the change in social welfare policy. . . . The presence in the county of black elected officials increased the likelihood of program expansion, particularly in public housing and AFDC (Aid to Families with Dependent Children) coverage.[13]

A recent study of Newark under eight years of leadership of a black mayor, Kenneth Gibson, reached the conclusion that the mayor was "very successful in expanding the universe of those engaged in the political system. More blacks were appointed to higher offices as well as employed throughout the city government."[14] There was also a strengthening of the city human rights commission and the forceful implementation of affirmative action policies.

And there have been other similar findings—that blacks tend to have a greater sense of political efficacy and trust in the government when a black is at the governmental helm, that there is an understandable feeling of pride when a black occupies a position of high influence. This is no different from the feeling of other groups toward "one of our own who made it." Such attitudes are bound to exist in a pluralistic, heterogeneous polity. And it likely serves no useful purpose to assume, without deeper examination, that these views are chauvinistic or harmfully divisive. They could be, but they need not be. At any rate, they are likely to exist in this historical time and especially in this place.

More important to note are the implications of these developments. As indicated earlier, people are politicized frequently by their real experiences. One relates to what I shall characterize as the 3-P proposition: Process, Product, Participation.

The proposition is a reasonably simple one: to the extent that the *process* is perceived as related to the *product* desired, then *participation* will increase. There is nothing complicated about this. If people believe that if they vote or march or write letters or strike (the *process*), they will very likely get good housing or clean streets or good schools (the *product*), they will then *participate* in the particular endeavor.

The converse is clear: if certain processes are deemed irrelevant or ineffective, they will be rejected. Therefore, when we see low voter turnout or low participation in other activities, we should not be too quick to conclude apathy. An apathetic person is not necessarily alienated; he might simply be overburdened by personal concerns. But this is not to be confused with an attitude of alienation, which is far more judgmental. The alienated person does not participate because he or she has given up on the processes offered. He sees them as altogether unlikely to yield a desired product. Such a person is still concerned, but sees no *viable* means for effectuating that concern. Such a person is far more likely to be a recruit for destructive deviant activity than one who is simply apathetic; or if appealed to convincingly, a recruit for activity in behalf of high ideals.

Therefore, the system has, one would think, a decided self-interest in maximizing the perceived utility of its processes. But that maximization comes from linking process with product—*in fact*, not only in theory.

When blacks struggled for years to gain the right to vote, one has to assume that that struggle was a serious one. It was not waged for purely symbolic or casual reasons. If the long-sought victories to participate in the process turn out to be Pyrrhic, the *system* becomes the potential loser.

Thus, through a variety of objective experiences, people develop needs and expectations. They constantly assess the validity of the structures and processes in which they are involved in terms of the capacity and willingness of the system to respond to their needs. There are enough studies on political socialization not to have to elaborate this point exhaustively. Most of that literature has focused on black Americans, but we are beginning to learn more about other minority groups.

A recent study of political efficacy among American Indian children made the following observations:

Although children do not have participatory roles in any political systems, their sense of political efficacy is a reflection of the kinds of political socialization they have received from such competing agents as schools and family. . . .

White children were more willing than the native American children to express efficacy toward the state and federal governments, both with regard to the measure of personal influence on the governments and the measure of governmental influence toward them personally. As was also expected, native American children were more likely to express feelings of political efficacy toward the tribal government than toward the white-dominated state and federal governments.[15]

The study concluded: "These children . . . share in [the] heritage of white control and manipulation, and native American powerlessness. While it is encouraging to note that these native American children express some level of political efficacy, especially with regard to the tribal government, it is less encouraging to see that they do not overwhelmingly express a strong belief in their influence on the tribal government either."[16] From which one might deduce that they have an accurate sense of where actual power over their situation lies, that it is in the distant white government beyond their reach, not in the nearby tribal government.

There are, however, analyses that draw a political distinction between those Indians who remain on reservations and those who have moved to the cities and formed urban organizations.

There developed a division between the reservation leadership generally and the urban leadership. The leaders of tribal councils on the reservations represent a conservative position. . . . On the other hand, the urban and student leaders view themselves as having much in common with minority groups in the United States generally; they espouse civil rights causes and have been influenced by the viewpoints of blacks and Mexican Americans. . . . A new set of ideas about their place in the United States was injected into Indian life as a result of the rise of the urban leadership.[17]

The various minority groups have had different experiences in the American system. American Indians are aware of the many broken treaties. Hispanic populations have had to confront numerous barriers associated with language as well as low skills. Black Americans, as already noted, have an extended history of legal struggle to overcome *de jure* segregation. These experiences influence the ways the groups perceive the system and its responsiveness to their needs and demands. But if there have been frustrations, disappointments, and, indeed, alienation, there has also been the recognition that governmental action is necessary to correct abuses.

Invariably, such groups have had to rely on government to solve many of their social, economic, and political problems. In a 1982 study of Hispanic political behavior and attitudes in East Los Angeles and San Antonio, we find great concern about issues of jobs and socioeconomic matters.

> In general, Chicanos felt that we as a society were spending too little on crime, health care, education, Hispanics and Bilingual Education. . . . There was also strong consensus that we were spending too much on foreign aid and space exploration.[18]

In San Antonio, the problems of jobs, drainage, discrimination, education, and crime were uppermost on the minds of the respondents—in that order. They were also "more supportive of the Equal Rights Amendment than the general population of the country."

Another recent study of the Mexican American electorate has reached similar specific conclusions:

> The consensus shared by Mexican Americans on government spending priorities and policy makes it relatively easy for organizers and politicians to mobilize and serve this electorate. With few exceptions, regardless of age and education, Mexican Americans speak with one voice. They think the government should spend more on domestic and social programs and less on international programs. They also support civil rights issues, though they are divided by age on abortion. Candidates desirous of Mexican American votes should therefore make explicit their agreement on these issues. Furthermore, these findings refute any suggestion that Mexican Americans as an electorate will respond positively to conservative political appeals, i.e., appeals calling for reduced government spending on social welfare programs.[19]

There is consistency here with views held by black Americans. Anyone even casually familiar with voting records and policy preferences will know that blacks clearly are in the liberal category on socioeconomic issues. When focusing on the issue of government spending, we find blacks decidedly favoring more, not less, and by substantial margins over their white counterparts. For example, survey data over a seven-year period from 1973 to 1980 indicated the following results:

> 69% of nonwhite respondents felt "we are spending . . . too little . . . on improving the nation's education system."
>
> 53% . . . felt "we are spending . . . too little . . . on solving the problems of big cities."
>
> 68% . . . agreed that the government in Washington ought to reduce the income differences between the rich and the poor, perhaps by raising the taxes of wealthy families or by giving income assistance to the poor.[20]

This clear pattern of preference has persisted over the decades.

POLITICAL ACCESS AND THE NEW NORMALCY

If there was a convenient coincidence between earlier ethnic politicization and a receptive economic environment, the same cannot be said for the post-1960s. At precisely the time many blacks, Hispanics, and issue-oriented groups were coming into their own politically, the economy was beginning to undergo quite drastic changes. And blacks and Hispanics turned out to be as "issue oriented" as were the other newly politicized groups, and as the old ethnic groups were not, at least to the same extent.

The juxtaposition of the following words with contemporary outcomes makes the point in a most concrete way. On May 17, 1957, Dr. Martin Luther King, Jr., delivered a speech proclaiming:

> Give us the ballot and we will no longer have to worry the federal government about our basic rights. Give us the ballot and we will no longer plead to the federal government for passage of an anti-lynching law. We will by the power of our own vote write the law on the books of the South and bring an end to the dastardly acts of the hooded perpetrators of the salient misdeeds

of bloodthirsty mobs into the calculated good deeds of orderly citizens. Give us the ballot and we will fill our legislative halls with men of good will and send to the sacred halls of Congress men who will not sign a Southern Manifesto because of their devotion to the manifesto of justice. Give us the ballot and we will do justly and love mercy. And we will place at the head of the southern states governors who have felt not only the tang of the human but the glory of the divine. Give us the ballot and we will quietly and non-violently, without rancor or bitterness, implement the school decision of May 17, 1954. Give us the ballot and we will help bring this nation to a new society based on justice and dedicated to peace.

This was an ambitious claim for the promised potential of the franchise, even allowing for oratorical excess. In some ways, it has not fallen too far off the mark. There *has* been a definite change in pronouncements and practices of many white southern politicians who recognize that they must now be mindful of the new black votes in their districts.[21]

There is, however, another side. Fifteen years after King's 1957 speech, the *Wall Street Journal* ran a front-page story that ostensibly was not related to civil rights, voting, or even politics, but is precisely related to the general concern of this chapter. That 1972 article stated, in part:

The realization that companies can operate effectively with far fewer employes than they dreamed possible back in 1969 may be comforting to top corporate brass and shareholders. But it's not particularly good news for job-hunting graduates, former middle-management executives, technicians and other salaried employes. Nor is it very happy news for factory hands. . . . Many companies can increase output substantially without adding to the work force.[22]

And that, too, became a basic fact of the "new normalcy." The question quickly became a different one. If the newly enfranchised blacks could now vote to alleviate some of the more blatant forms of segregation and discrimination, could they mobilize electoral resources for purposes of achieving definitely needed economic ends? King's speech did not speak to this point directly, only implicitly, but it would not be long before such matters were put on the political agenda.

That agenda would come to include demands for a meaningful full-employment policy that understood full employment to mean jobs at decent wages for all persons able and willing to work. That agenda would insist on the national government exerting an active role to stem the runaway cost of health care and at the same time assuming the responsibility for protecting people from the devastation of unavailable adequate medical services. And that agenda would include the national government committing considerably more resources to the basic educational needs of children locked into inequitable property-based financial systems for supporting local school needs.

The facts are clear, and the implications manifest. The new agenda is a liberal-progressive one, and it cannot be met by neoclassical theories of a market economy.

Newly politicized minority groups are making demands on the economic and political structures that can only strain the capacities of those structures in ways quite unprecedented. Whereas in earlier times the local political parties could mobilize votes, dispense relatively minimal divisible benefits, and serve as *temporary* providers of assistance until supporters got a foothold in the private economy, that role has been dramatically and permanently transformed. The private-sector economy simply is no longer able to accommodate the vast economic needs of many people. As the capital economy becomes more efficient in production, it presents serious problems of inequitable distribution. Hence, the public sector *must* become a coequal, not junior, partner in rectifying this dilemma. To be sure, some segments of the minority communities can and will succeed in the market economy. But too many are left behind through no fault of their own, and this reality must be faced.

Notwithstanding this reality, there is still a strong, lingering attachment to old values and norms. We still find deeply embedded notions supporting minimal government and predominantly market-economy solutions to chronic problems, such as structural unemployment, health care, and decent, affordable housing. There is still a longing to "return to normalcy." And that normalcy is expressed in various ways, such as rejection of Great Society programs which, it is said, merely "sought to throw money at problems"; or, at another breakout point, in rejection of governmental regulations of certain industries, such as airlines and aspects of banking. In 1980, the simplistic phrase, "Get government off our backs," summed up this nostalgic yearning and seemingly captured at least enough support to usher in a decidedly conservative administration and United States Senate.

But the old normalcy cannot be recaptured. Automation, the development of much more competitive foreign producers, and the move generally toward more, rather than less, capital-intensive activities, make the essentially junior partnership role of government of an earlier time an anachronism.

New groups are making demands that call for *more*, not less, government intervention in the economy. And typically, up to now, for *less*, not more, United States intervention abroad. Typically, too, the Republicans of the Reagan administration and the 1980s Congress are for the opposite: *less* intervention in the domestic economy, *more* in world politics. Republicans desiring of making inroads in the minority vote are blocked by this disparity of values. But national Democrats, who at this time need less to fear minority shifts to the other party than minority nonvoting because of the 3-P calculation, must also contend with it.

The new demands are not only or even largely for patronage jobs for a few party faithfuls, or contracts—not, that is, for divisible benefits, but for indivisible benefits. Thus, the government is pressed to deliver more—and for a longer period of time. The implications for tax policy and monetary policy are clear. This means that it is not possible to talk about politicization of blacks and Hispanics without also understanding the necessity of discussing the structure and policies of, for example, the Federal Reserve System. It is not possible to talk about extending the right to vote to previously excluded groups without understanding that, if used, that vote would likely ultimately be concerned about energy policy, "industrial policy," environmental issues, as well as defense policy. The new normalcy requires a much more coherent, coordinated look at public policies and private activities. Intelligent planning for the short and long term is mandatory, as much as that process strikes fear in the hearts of advocates of the old normalcy. It raises fears of government usurpation of power and abuse of liberty. But it can also be a modern acceptance of new realities and used in ways to liberate, not enslave, the total society. This proposition would not be too difficult to accept, if there is the recognition that a society where the schism between the haves and the have-nots, between the comfortable and the destitute, is growing and becoming permanent becomes itself increasingly less viable.

The new normalcy, in other words, has led to a situation whereby the criteria for measuring access and influence have changed substantially. The issue is not simply or even substantially electing "one's own" to offices and being reasonably satisfied with the symbolic rewards of such achievements. The issue is not a matter of showcase appointments that conceivably further the individual careers of the appointees and provide largely vicarious gratification to a mass constituency.

If one is to understand the meaning of the new normalcy and its impact on assessment of access and influence, then one is required to understand the basic challenges posed to old values and norms. The outputs that served well the politicization of earlier groups are no longer sufficient. Current and future economic and social conditions require fundamental altering of political values, structures, and processes.

On reflection, there are signs that permit more than a modicum of optimism. We have become familiar with different kinds of tally sheets showing progress in some areas, retrogression in others. The statistical data are relatively easy to compile and analyze; this is an ongoing enterprise of activists and policymakers. We count the growth of black elected officials; we note the population growth of Hispanics; we carefully watch employment figures and relative income data; we chart educational achievement scores; etc. Data, not exposés of gross and degraded white conduct, are the material of contemporary minority demands. The figures are voluminous and understandably subject to varying interpretations.

Perhaps a useful way to assess the future is to look at the way the earlier civil rights movement developed beyond a primary emphasis on rights to include a broadened agenda focusing on economic equity. In the process, this development has brought along other groups who see their fate tied to the achievement of an inclusive liberal-progressive agenda. At times this is discussed in terms of a coalition of similar interests. In a democratic polity, this is as it should be. As more people come to see their needs as inextricably bound to those of others, they will likewise see it to their advantage to coalesce to achieve their common goals. There is nothing mystical about this; it is pluralist politics in a democratic society. But neither is there anything inevitable about the outcomes. The democratic struggle for equity and justice is, of necessity, a protracted one, and victories and defeats are never in perpetuity.

NOTES

1. Gunnar Myrdal, *An American Dilemma* 20th anniv. ed. (New York: Harper & Row, 1962); Samuel P. Huntington, *American Politics, The Politics of Disharmony* (Cambridge, Mass.: Harvard University Press, 1981).
2. Charles E. Silberman, *Crisis in Black and White* (New York: Random House, 1964).
3. William E. Leuchtenberg, *Franklin D. Roosevelt and The New Deal* (New York: Harper Torchbooks, 1963).
4. David B. Truman, *The Governmental Process,* 2nd ed. (New York: Alfred A. Knopf, 1971).
5. Robert A. Dahl, *Who Governs?* (New Haven and London: Yale University Press, 1961).
6. Michael Parenti, "Ethnic Politics and the Persistence of Ethnic Identifications," in *The Ethnic Factor in American Politics,* ed. Brett W. Hawkins and Robert A. Lorinskas (Columbus, Ohio: Charles E. Merrill Publishing Co., 1970); Raymond E. Wolfinger, "The Development and Persistence of Ethnic Voting," *ibid.*
7. Dahl, *Who Governs?,* chapter 5.
8. Robert E. Lane, *Political Life* (New York: The Free Press, 1965), p. 244.
9. Seymour Martin Lipset, *Political Man* (Garden City, N.Y.: Doubleday & Co., Anchor Books, 1963), p. 64.
10. Kenneth H. Thompson, *The Voting Rights Act and Black Electoral Participation* (Washington, D.C.: Joint Center for Political Studies, 1982), p. 5.
11. Stephen L. Watsby, *Vote Dilution, Minority Voting Rights, and the Courts* (Washington, D.C.: Joint Center for Political Studies, 1982), p. 5.

12. Richard L. Engstrom and Michael D. McDonald, "The Election of Blacks to City Councils: Clarifying the Impact of Electoral Arrangements on the Seat/Population Relationships," *American Political Science Review* 75 (June 1981): 344–354.

13. Elizabeth M. Sanders, "New Voters and New Policy Priorities in the Deep South: A Decade of Political Change in Alabama" (Paper presented at the annual meeting of the American Political Science Association, Washington, D.C., August 1979).

14. Kathryn Yatrakis, "Electoral Demands and Political Benefits: Minority as Majority, A Case Study of Two Newark Elections 1970, 1974" (Ph.D. diss. Columbia University, 1981), p. 305.

15. Margaret Maier Murdock, "Political Efficacy Among Native American Children Toward Federal and Tribal Governments" (Paper presented at the annual meeting of the American Political Science Association, Chicago, Illinois, September 1983).

16. *Ibid.*

17. *Harvard Encyclopedia of American Ethnic Groups*, ed. Stephan Thernstrom (Cambridge, Mass.: Harvard University Press, 1980), s.v. "American Indians," by Edward H. Spicer. pp. 58–114, at p. 113.

18. Andrew Hernandez, "Hispanic Political Behavior and Attitudes in East Los Angeles and San Antonio: A Preliminary Reading of the Data" (Paper presented at a meeting of the National Association for Chicano Studies, San Antonio, Texas, February 1982).

19. Rodolfo O. de la Garza and Robert R. Brischetto, *The Mexican American Electorate: Information Sources and Policy Orientation* (San Antonio, Texas: Southwest Voter Registration Education Project, 1983).

20. "NORC: Portrait of America, The Government's Role," *Public Opinion*, October/November 1980, pp. 22–25.

21. Mark Stern, "Southern Congressional Civil Rights Voting and The New Southern Demography" (Paper presented at the annual meeting of the American Political Science Association, Washington, D.C., August 1979).

22. "Companies Find They Can Operate Effectively With Fewer Employes," *Wall Street Journal*, March 8, 1972, p. 1.

ACCESS TO ECONOMIC OPPORTUNITY

Lessons Since *Brown*

WILLIAM L. TAYLOR

The Supreme Court's 1954 decision in *Brown* v. *Board of Education*, striking down school racial segregation laws as unconstitutional, opened the modern civil rights era. All of the cases, laws, and policies mandating equal treatment and opportunity that came after are traceable in one way or another to *Brown* and stand in stark contrast to policies of racial separation and inequality that preceded. Thirty years seems a reasonable period for an accounting of the effectiveness of the post-*Brown* period. A full generation has passed; black and white children born in 1954 are now adults, and many have children of their own.

Any fair accounting will yield a mass of contradictions. For those meant to be the beneficiaries of new civil rights policies, there have been both increased affluence and deepened misery. For the country as a whole there have been major changes in behavior and attitudes, accompanied by persistent prejudice. The story has been one of striking success and abject failure. Such contradictions are difficult to comprehend and accommodate, yet understanding and coming to grips with them is the key to the hope of future progress.

In some ways the children of the 1980s are growing up in a

society not very different from the one that confronted their parents three decades ago. Racial isolation, division, and tension persist. Few would contend that the life chances of black and white children have become equal, and there still exists little consensus as to measures appropriate or effective for dealing with the legacy of discrimination.

Yet a fundamental difference between the 1950s and the 1980s should not be obscured: the official caste system that held sway for more than two centuries before *Brown* has been eliminated. Under that system, black people in large areas of the country were treated as a subject class, experiencing daily indignities solely because of race. Blacks were relegated to the back of the bus, refused food and lodging at restaurants and hotels almost everywhere, addressed by their first names in government offices and court proceedings, denied common courtesies, and threatened with physical and economic repercussions if they stepped out of line. They were segregated in all public institutions, provided inferior public services of all sorts—from higher education to garbage pickup—and widely denied the right to vote freely. While this system of subjugation was legalized and all-encompassing primarily in the South, large parts of it applied unofficially in the North and West as well.

Today that caste system is gone. Black people who have the means can move with confidence in everyday society, in restaurants, hotels, theaters, public beaches, tennis courts. And blacks, whatever their socio-economic status, generally can expect civil and even-handed treatment at the polls, the courthouse, on buses, and at other public facilities. They command the respect routinely denied in the past because they have demanded and won it through their efforts in the courtroom and in the streets.

These changes in the public face of America reflect the political power of blacks, unleashed by the enforcement of the laws that finally ended racial disenfranchisement. In Birmingham, where Commissioner Bull Connor once set hoses and police dogs on Martin Luther King, Jr., and his adherents, a black mayor now presides. In the state capitol, a governor whose "segregation forever" speeches once provided the model for racist politicians now clings to power by making promises to blacks. In Washington, in 1982, Senators Strom Thurmond (R., S.C.) and John Stennis (D., Miss.), once champions of the old order, cast reluctant votes for an extension and strengthening of the Voting Rights Act, a silent tribute to the effectiveness of the 1965 law in compelling attention to the needs of black constituents.

To a degree also, the change in the public face of the nation stems from a recognition of the foothold that black people collectively have gained in the economy. Black faces on television commercials and in the front office are testimony to the business creed that no segment of the marketplace should be neglected.

The explanation for the disappearance of outward manifestations of the old caste system, however, goes beyond the pull of political and economic self-interest. Experience has proven President Eisenhower wrong in his prediction that law (specifically the *Brown* decision) would not "change the hearts and minds of men." Law, once it was enforced, did change behavior patterns and the attitudes that underlay them. Recognizing this, the Reagan administration, intent on undoing many of the remedies for discrimination that have been forged over the past two decades, does not base its primary appeal on the old code words, but on an effort to persuade the public that it desires to be "fair" to all and seeks only to find more effective policies. More important, the strong resistance that the administration has encountered to its proposals, from school boards solicited to join in efforts to end busing and from employers invited to abandon affirmative action, suggests that the institutional and attitudinal changes that have occurred since *Brown* have durability. Whether or not people are ready to extend the gains made in racial justice, there is no overpowering nostalgia for the "good old days" of enforced segregation.

These differences in the race relations of the 1950s and 1980s might be taken as a given were it not for the lack of historical perspective that seems to be an American trait, and the current conventional wisdom that governmental efforts to solve social problems are doomed to failure. Most Americans under the age of 35 appear to view the regime of "separate but equal" as a foible, easily dispensed with once people focused on its irrationality. Few recognize how deeply entrenched were the roots of the system, not just in emotional but in economic terms, and at what cost in blood and effort the elimination of the old order was purchased. A deeper historical perspective might make people more pessimistic about the possibility of eliminating racism, but might also encourage the belief that even seemingly intractable problems can yield to citizen action through government.

Brown, however, was not just about removing the stain of white supremacy from the nation's lawbooks and its public dealings. Undergirding the decision was a belief that government has an affirmative obligation to afford its citizens equal opportunity to succeed.

> Today [the Court wrote] education is the most important function of state and local governments. . . . It is required in the performance of our most basic responsibilities, even service in the armed forces. It is the very foundation of good citizenship. Today, it is a principal instrument in awakening the child to cultural values, in preparing him for later professional training, and in helping him to adjust normally to his environment. In these days, it is doubtful that any child may reasonably be expected to succeed in life if he is denied the opportunity of an education. Such an opportunity, where the state has undertaken to provide it, is a right which must be made available to all on equal terms.

An opportunity "to succeed in life." Not a guarantee of success, but not a merely formalistic concession either. Rather, a genuine chance to develop one's skills and to reap the rewards of using those skills. Not far beneath the surface of the *Brown* decision was the belief that segregation laws were not only a device for isolating and humiliating black people, but also a set of shackles that restrained them from moving as far as abilities would carry. Whether or not the validity of that belief was essential to the decision,[1] the objective of *Brown* and of the cases and laws that followed dealing with schooling, jobs, housing, and other matters was to provide genuine opportunity; to extend something once said by Jefferson, "to bring into action that mass of talents which lies buried in poverty"—*and racism* —"for want of means of development."

Thus, in judging the success of the civil rights laws and policies that began with *Brown* and their serviceability for the future, a fair though tough measure is whether they have resulted in tangible economic and educational progress. If, in the words of the familiar saw, blacks can now sit at the lunch counter but still do not have the price of the meal, the victory, if not Pyrrhic, is at least hollow.

Therefore, we have to recognize both progress and the lack of it, to recognize that some people may be worse off now than they were 30 years ago. This chapter will attempt to describe that dual experience, how many blacks are prospering while many others are not. There are undoubtedly complex causes for this, and not all of them are associated with what the federal government has or has not done. But the history of blacks and of other minorities in the United States has been, for good or for ill, inseparable from governmental acts and policies. I shall, therefore, after looking at its successes and failures, suggest how government has been involved in each. The chapter will conclude with some thoughts about more adequate governmental policies.

BLACK GAINS: 1954–1982

While numbers are an inadequate way to tell of changes in human lives they do have utility in determining movement. By familiar and accepted gauges, a significant segment of the black population, particularly people who have come to maturity in the post-*Brown* era, has made striking progress.

One key measure is the movement of black workers into more skilled and remunerative occupations. From 1961 to 1982, the proportion of black people in the labor force in professional and technical jobs increased from 4.6 percent to almost 10,[2] in executive, managerial, and administrative jobs from 2.5 percent to more than 5 percent.[3] While these gains reflect in part a general upgrading of the occupational status of the labor force, their significance is suggested by the fact that the gains for white workers during the same period were more modest.[4]

When attention is directed to the younger minority groups in the population, even more encouraging indications of mobility emerge. As recently as 1968, only 12.4 percent of all black women in the 25–34 age category were employed in professional jobs. By 1977, the proportion for the same group (by then in the 35–44 age category) had increased to 18.8 percent.[5]

This movement of black people into the professions and other higher-status occupations is reflected in income gains. In 1982 almost one quarter of all black families had incomes over $25,000, compared to only 8.7 percent in 1960 (measuring income in constant dollars).[6] While the income gap between blacks and whites for the entire population has not narrowed over the past two decades, *for those subgroups who have gained some occupational mobility it has closed appreciably.* Thus, when considering only families where there are two wage earners, black income in proportion to white rose from 73 percent in 1968 to 84 in 1981.[7] For younger and more educated blacks, the income gap has closed even more significantly. In 1976 blacks in the 25–29 age group who were college graduates earned 93 percent as much as their white counterparts, a gain of about 12 percent in 12 years.[8]

The improved occupational status and growing income of a segment of the black population reflect important changes in educational attainment. As recently as 1966, the number of black students attending college was only 340,000. By 1974 black enrollment had risen to 814,000 and by 1982 to more than one million.[9] By 1980, 80 percent of black students attended predominantly white institutions, a move away from the rigidly segregated character of higher education in the past. Changes in expectations and prospects for minorities are suggested by the rise in the proportion of black students majoring in business, from 5 percent in 1966 to 18 percent, while concentration in occupations traditionally reserved for blacks declined.[10]

Significant change also has taken place in the enrollment of minorities in professional schools, particularly in medical and law schools which have had serious affirmative action efforts. Law schools as recently as 1969 had a black enrollment of 3 percent. By 1979 it had risen to 4.2 percent and total minority enrollment, including Hispanic Americans, Asian Americans, and American Indians as well as blacks, was at 8.1 percent.[11]

Medical schools, many of which excluded black students until after World War II, had only a 2.7 percent black enrollment in 1968. By 1980 black enrollment had risen to 5.7 percent and minorities were 7.9 percent of the total medical school population.[12] The magnitude of change is illustrated by the fact that 3,000 black students were enrolled in medical schools in 1974 at a time when there were only 6,000 black physicians in the nation.

Studies show that significant numbers of advanced minority students come from families of lower income and job status. This indicates that rising enrollments reflect increased mobility, not simply changing occupational preferences among middle-class families.[13] These striking gains in higher and professional education are evidence that improvements in the economic and occupational status of blacks are the product of their own efforts to acquire education and skills and to break down discrimination barriers, not of preferential treatment by government. Further refutation of claims that advances are not based on merit may be found in the improved performance of many black students on tests commonly accepted as measures of educational ability. At a time when there is justified concern about stagnation and decline in achievement of public school students, the National Assessment of Educational Progress reported encouraging gains in cognitive skills by black students. The greatest gains between 1970 and 1980, black or white, were made by black elementary students in the public schools of the Southeast.[14] And while maintaining educational progress through high school has often proved difficult, the generation of black students who came through school in the 1970s has also managed to narrow the black-white gap on college entrance examinations.[15]

For those black people who have broken through in the past two decades to better education, more skilled jobs, and higher pay, there have been the rewards of middle-class status. They are far more likely than in the past to own their own homes, to be part of families that never suffer the tragedy of infant death,[16] and to live to become senior citizens.[17]

In sum, for a substantial segment of the black population, *Brown* has fulfilled its promise not only of eliminating official racism, but of providing genuine opportunity. The status of some may not be secure, and there are often galling reminders of prejudice—the classic example being the black executive who still has trouble flagging down a taxi—but a substantial segment has joined the mainstream. While the ranks of the black middle class remain small compared to whites, the story of the past two decades is one of individual and collective progress exceeding that made by blacks in any other period in American history.

THE LINK BETWEEN FEDERAL CIVIL RIGHTS POLICY AND BLACK PROGRESS

The breakthroughs to opportunity made by black people have come through a complex process not easily attributable to any single law or court decision. Victories by civil rights organizations in legal forums were a kind of self-empowerment for black citizens. From success in legal, political, and community efforts flowed heightened aspirations and increased confidence, confidence that was reinforced when people discovered they had the inner resources to withstand attacks on their rights. None of this is susceptible to calibration by social scientists.

Nevertheless, it is possible to identify certain policies and programs resulting from those efforts that have made important contributions to minority progress. Chief among these measures are:

1. affirmative action policies aimed at increasing minority participation in higher education and employment;
2. court decisions and government enforcement action to reduce racial isolation in the public schools; and
3. "Great Society" programs designed to upgrade the educational and job skills of poor people, particularly minorities.

Interestingly, these are precisely the policies and programs that have come under the heaviest attack from the Reagan administration.

AFFIRMATIVE ACTION

In various ways, federal laws and policies require or encourage the use of race as a remedial device in allocating employment and educational opportunities. The basic rationale is that decades of discrimination and exclusion of minorities can only be overcome effectively through affirmative action that seeks out qualified minority applicants for enrollment in colleges and professional schools and for hiring and promotion in public and private employment.

Proponents of affirmative action policies, while continuing to espouse the goal of a color-blind society, believe with Justice Harry Blackmun that:

> In order to get beyond racism, we must first take account of race. There is no other way. And in order to treat some persons equally, we must treat them differently.[18]

Thus, Title VII of the Civil Rights Act of 1964, the major expression of national equal employment policy, has been construed by the Supreme Court to prohibit practices that operate to deny opportunities to minorities even when the practices were not intentionally discriminatory.[19] This has meant that where intelligence tests that businesses use to screen applicants disproportionately exclude minorities, employers have had to seek out other selection devices that meet their needs for an efficient and trustworthy work force without disadvantaging minority applicants.

Title VII also has been interpreted to permit employers and unions to enter into voluntary agreements to make conscious use of race to eliminate "old patterns of racial segregation and hierarchy."[20] In the *Weber* case, the Court approved an agreement between the Kaiser Aluminum Company and the United Steelworkers to raise the level of black participation in craft jobs by establishing a new on-the-job training program that reserved 50 percent of its openings for black employees. Where voluntary agreements are not reached, and courts find that employers have engaged in pervasive practices of discrimination, they have sometimes ordered stiff remedies, restraining the employer from hiring new white employees until proportionate numbers of qualified minority employees are hired.[21]

Similar regulatory policies have governed the employment practices of contractors who do business with the federal government. An executive order issued by President Kennedy in 1961 provided the first modern articulation on a national level of the concept of affirmative action.[22] When the steps called for by that order (e.g., visits to black colleges and contacts with minority organizations and media) failed to stir significant movement in many industries, the Johnson and Nixon administrations instituted a requirement of "goals and timetables," first applied to the construction trades and later to all contractors.[23] The rules call upon employers to compare their utilization of minorities and women to the available labor pool and, where a gap exists, to develop concrete plans for tapping the market of minorities and women who possess the needed skills or who could acquire them through training programs. The goals are objectives, not fixed requirements, since no penalties are imposed for failure to reach if the contractor can demonstrate that he has made good-faith efforts to comply. Nor are employers compelled to hire unqualified people or to compromise valid hiring standards.[24]

These policies, and similar measures governing the federal civil service, minority business enterprise under federal contracts, and admission to colleges and universities have formed the core of the federal equal employment effort since the 1970s. There is no doubt that affirmative action has produced results. Economist Bernard Anderson reported substantial gains in the employment of black workers in managerial and skilled craft positions in the huge Bell Telephone system after the company entered into a consent decree in 1973 calling for the initiation of goals and timetables.[25] Similar progress has been reported in the employment of minorities in skilled positions in the steel industry following a consent decree in 1974.[26]

In Philadelphia, where the concept of goals and timetables was first applied, minorities constituted only one percent of skilled construction workers in 1969 but 12 percent by 1981.[27] In law enforcement, which has been a special target of litigation and other affirmative action efforts, the number of black police officers throughout the nation has increased from 24,000 in 1970 to 43,500 in 1980.[28]

With the exception of Thomas Sowell and a few others who have argued that affirmative action policy is ineffective, the basic claim of opponents is that the policy has been too effective, that it subverts the ideal of a color-blind society. But in the Reagan administration's assault on affirmative action, no explanation has been provided by it of how a society that has inflicted wrongs on a class of people solely because of race can suddenly become "race neutral" and still furnish redress to those who have been the victims of discrimination. In the words of Richard deLone, the argument "assumes that history is something that ended yesterday (through passage of a few anti-discrimination laws) and that it has no palpable consequences in the present or future."[29]

Since the Reagan assault is premised on the belief that race-conscious action is morally and ideologically reprehensible, simply correcting abuses that may be discovered (such as instances in which employers have been forced to hire unqualified workers) will not satisfy their objections. Nor does it matter to the administration that the law has sought pragmatically to balance and protect the interests of white workers by assuring that they will not be displaced from positions they already hold, even if discrimination helped to get them there.[30] Neither course will appease a firm conviction that the philosophy of affirmative action itself is unacceptable.

Fortunately, many employers have taken a more practical and humane view of the issue. Experience has taught them that minority applicants who do poorly on paper and pencil tests because of inferior schooling can still be productive workers if given a chance. They have learned also that goals and timetables for equal employment are techniques not very different from the setting of business goals in other areas, useful tools for holding middle management accountable for implementing company policy and for measuring progress.[31]

Affirmative action is a temporary policy to be pursued until minorities gain a secure foothold in the economy. That time has not arrived. Some sectors of industry still have done little to encourage minority employment. Even where progress has been made, the gains may be fragile. The managerial positions secured by black workers are located disproportionately in the public sector, an area which, after many years of expansion, is now shrinking. In private industry, minorities are still found in the lower-skill range of most occupational categories and many of the management positions they hold are not regarded as central to the work of the company. In times of recession, the application of seniority principles can have a devastating effect on newly hired minority workers. Affirmative action policies have produced much progress, but that amounts to saying only that there is now a toehold where there was none before.

SCHOOL DESEGREGATION

Although the *Brown* decision is approaching its thirtieth anniversary, massive resistance by government officials in the South prevented its effective enforcement for almost half of those years. It was only when Congress endorsed the decision in the 1960s and the executive branch indicated a readiness to enforce it through lawsuits and by withholding funds from noncomplying school districts that the Supreme Court deemed it time to spell out the remedial obligations of public school systems that had engaged in deliberate segregation.

So it was not until 1971 that the Court determined that pervasive, mandatory segregation practices could only be redressed by thorough mandatory desegregation including, if necessary, the use of busing.[32] And it was not until 1973 that the Court first dealt with segregation in the North and West, holding that similar thoroughgoing remedies were called for where evidence showed that segregative practices, though not official or blatant, were nonetheless deliberate and pervasive.[33]

Accordingly, in much of the nation, experience with school desegregation is a decade or less old, and many areas, principally metropolises in the North and West, still maintain largely segregated systems. Despite the brevity of experience, however, the results are encouraging. As noted earlier, the most impressive gains on reading tests in the seventies were registered by black elementary students in the Southeast, the area in which school desegregation efforts were focused most intensively.

Fortunately, school desegregation experience to date has been carefully studied and evaluated by social scientists, and it is possible to point to some strongly indicated outcomes. These include the following:

1. Many case studies show linkage between desegregation and academic achievement. In most situations where desegregation came about through court-ordered busing, the achievement levels of minority students have risen significantly while those of white students have held or even risen slightly.[34]

2. The best gains have occurred in those systems where desegregation began at kindergarten or first grade; and where comprehensive programs were instituted that included diagnostic and compensatory services for students and in-service training for teachers.[35]

3. Metropolitan and county-wide plans, plans that often entail substantial busing, invariably show the strongest gains for black students.[36]

4. Consistent with that finding is the conclusion of other research that shows disadvantaged children faring better in schools and classrooms where they are in a minority, rather than being isolated with others of the same background.[37]

5. Black children attending desegregated schools are more likely to complete high school, to enroll in and graduate from four-year desegregated colleges, and to major in subjects nontraditional for minority students, ones that lead to more remunerative jobs and professions. This is so not only because of academic gains but from the social strengthening, the contacts made and the vistas opened.[38] Graduation from high school, as D.W. Brogan observed years ago, often signifies that "lessons in practical politics, in organization, in social ease have been learned that could not have been learned in factory or office."[39] When minority youngsters have been given opportunities to function in a wider community, they have learned practical as well as academic lessons in how to live (and succeed) in America.

6. Finally, there is evidence that area-wide desegregation helps foster residential stability. Such plans tend to be stable, unaffected by the trend toward white suburbanization that continues in most cities, and to be accepted by the community. Thus, in Tampa-Hillsborough County, Florida, Charlotte-Mecklenburg County, North Carolina, and other places where courts have ordered systemwide desegregation, parents have accepted the plans, retaining their residences and keeping their children in the public schools, despite extensive busing.[40] And beyond avoidance of "white flight," areawide desegregation appears to promote black suburbanization and breaking down of discriminatory housing barriers.[41] Once schools are no longer perceived as white or black, racial barriers in housing begin to lower. That process may be accelerated by plans, such as in Louisville, that exempt desegregated neighborhoods from busing requirements.

In sum, strong evidence is accumulating that major reductions in racial isolation in the public schools, particularly when on a metropolitan basis, lead to increased educational, occupational, and residential mobility for minorities.[42] The major difficulty lies in implementation, principally because where urban areas are divided into several school districts, the Supreme Court has demanded rigorous proof from the plaintiffs in order to claim the right to adopt metropolitan remedies.[43] In large parts of the South, school districts (such as Charlotte-Mecklenburg, Tampa-Hillsborough, and Nashville-Davidson, Tennessee) are organized on county lines and no legal barriers were posed to metropolitan desegregation. In other places, such as Indianapolis and Wilmington, Delaware, the Court's conditions have been met or (as in St. Louis, Hartford, and Rochester, New York) some metropolitan desegregation has been accomplished on a voluntary basis. But in the biggest cities of the country where black and Hispanic students are concentrated in large numbers, little, if any, desegregation has taken place.

"GREAT SOCIETY" PROGRAMS

Affirmative action has contributed to economic mobility by altering structures that have excluded minorities in the past and by giving people who may lack paper credentials a chance to prove their worth. School desegregation has contributed by providing an educational environment more conducive to achievement and by opening windows on a wider world. And gains have also come about from a variety of federally assisted programs, targeted to the disadvantaged and designed to upgrade their education and skills by preventive and remedial measures. These principally originated in or grew from the Johnson administration.

Here evaluation is difficult. Programs may fail, and many have, for a number of reasons: because maladministered, or, to note another and more usual reason, because too narrow, too inadequately funded, to provide genuine opportunity. Even when effective on a pilot basis, some programs are not successfully replicated because resources are insufficient or the talented and committed people who operate the programs are stretched too thin.

Nonetheless, some programs have been successful in promoting access to opportunity. Head Start and other early childhood education programs have sought to implement findings that children are ready to learn long before enrollment in the public schools. By beginning the teaching process early, by involving parents in the education of their children, by providing basic health and nutritional services, they have sought to start poor children off on as even a footing as possible with their middle-class peers. Using performance on aptitude tests as the measuring rod, most evaluations have concluded that the programs are initially successful and that while some children lose the gains as they grow older, others sustain them.[44]

Efforts to make up for skill deficits already incurred are more difficult than preventive measures, and government, business, and trade union leaders have struggled for more than two decades with the problems of devising effective job training. Some programs have records of success. Since the 1960s, the Jobs Corps has sought to meet the needs of economically disadvantaged teenagers, particularly minorities and others who have dropped out of high school with low reading skills and no employment record. Jobs Corps graduates do better than other similarly situated young people in returning to school to obtain their diplomas, in securing and keeping jobs with higher pay rates, in avoiding criminal activity and welfare dependency.[45]

A more recently initiated program, "supported work," jointly financed by government agencies and private foundations, has had an important measure of success in meeting the skill and job needs of people thought even harder to reach: mothers on welfare and ex-addicts. As with the Jobs Corps, the guiding principle is to provide comprehensive assistance over a long term, assistance that includes jobs, training, and counseling designed to break bad habits, provide marketable skills, and instill self-confidence. The payoff has been in the movement of program participants into "unsupported" jobs where they diminish or escape entirely their previous dependency on welfare.[46]

A few preventive or remedial programs to provide education and skills, even effective ones, do not add up to a national strategy for overcoming discrimination and securing access to opportunity. They do demonstrate, however, that the gains made by black people in the past two decades have not been limited to those who already had some advantages. And they refute suggestions that government efforts to assist people in helping themselves are doomed to failure.

FAILURE: 1954–1982

If the civil rights revolution has brought genuine access to opportunity to large numbers of black people, a greater number find their situation unchanged or even worsened.

The statistical evidence for this conclusion is by now depressingly familiar. For almost all of this period, in good economic times and bad, the unemployment rate for blacks has been approximately double that for whites. During 1983 when white unemployment reached 10 percent, black unemployment was more than 20 percent, the highest point it had ever reached in the three decades since *Brown*. In part, this worsening situation reflects the failure of national policy and of the economy to produce jobs for a growing black population. During the period from 1960 to 1982 the black male population over the age of 16 almost doubled, from 5.6 million to 10.73 million.[47] But the number of employed black men increased only from 4.15 million to 5.94 million, adding 3.4 million black men to the ranks of the unemployed. As a result, the proportion of black males over the age of 16 who were employed dropped from 74 percent in 1960 to 56 percent in 1982.[48]

One major consequence of the crisis in black unemployment is the persistence of the wide gap between black and white family incomes. In 1981 the median income of black families was 56 percent of that of white families, hardly different from the 55 percent ratio that existed in 1960. Real income for black families rose during that time from a median of $9,919 to $13,266; but, as indicated previously, the gains were reaped largely by some subgroups (e.g., younger, two-income families) while others were left mired in poverty.

The human impact of joblessness and low income may be assessed in various ways, but one important gauge is its impact on children. In 1959 two of every three black children under the age of 18 were growing up in poverty. In 1981 45 percent of all black children under the age of 18 still were living in poverty.[49] While the change represents some progress, the fact that in the 1980s almost half of all black children, compared to 14.7 percent of white children, grow up in impoverished circumstances is striking commentary on the status of the quest for access to opportunity.

Moreover, the characteristics of poverty have changed in recent years in ways that place additional barriers in the way of these children. In the 1950s and 1960s, although very large numbers of black children were born into poverty, they at least were usually raised in households where both parents were present. By 1981, of all the black families in the nation, 47 percent were headed by women who were responsible for raising children without the presence of a spouse.[50] A very high proportion of these female-headed families were poor. Indeed, in female-headed black families two of every three children under the age of 18 and three of every four under the age of six live below the poverty level.[51]

All told, about three million of the nine million black children in the nation are growing up in impoverished single-parent households, with mothers who are responsible both for raising them and bringing income into the homes.[52]

In addition, poor black children are tightly concentrated in the poverty areas of central cities.[53] While black families who have acquired middle-class status have gained some residential mobility, the poor have not. In the ghetto areas of big cities, black children living in poverty increasingly are isolated from other children in their schools and neighborhoods by income as well as race. The risk is great that they will be afflicted with nutritional and health problems, that they will become involved with drugs, that they will emerge from school without basic skills, that they will become victims or perpetrators of crime. Some, by dint of extraordinary talent or effort, will surmount their environment, but the odds against most are very high.

THE LINK BETWEEN POVERTY AND NATIONAL POLICY

The critical issue is how to diagnose the persistence of black and Hispanic poverty and deprivation. The black situation is better known but not unlike other urban minorities. One thesis, relying on the cessation of overt practices of racial discrimination and the success that many black people have had in gaining access to opportunity, holds that the plight of the underclass is now determined largely by socioeconomic factors such as the lack of education and skills, rather than by racial factors. This theory is wrong at least in part, it seems to me, because it fails to take into account two important facts: first, that a disproportionate number of black people are still in poverty as a direct result of the caste system and the barriers it imposes, whose effects are both heritable and real even if the system itself has ended; and second, that people still suffer from racial discrimination which, if less blatant than before, is no less damaging.

We have to see these connections if we are to address equality in a serious and effective way. Policies designed to ameliorate poverty may be largely ineffective if they do not recognize the combined effects of racism and deprivation. It is generally agreed, for example, that strong family structure is a key to social mobility. The model most deeply held to is that of the European immigrants (even some of the most recent) who have come to this country with very few resources and have moved into the mainstream when aided by strong family bonds and a commitment to education and hard work. Why, it is asked, cannot the black poor follow the same road? And, if they need support in developing stable families, is not aid more appropriately provided by private and community institutions such as the church than by the government? Even blacks themselves, persuaded by this model's "proof," look to entrepreneurship or political clout as the keys to societal power; if they can take control of city institutions in the way the Irish or Italian have, they will then get the power or influence those groups have as well.

Such an analysis overlooks the devastating impact of government policy, both past and present, on the black family. James Comer and others have argued persuasively that the most malignant effect of American slavery was its destruction of the familial and communal bonds of a people that, prior to their forcible removal from West Africa to the United States, had been quite powerful.[54] The duration of slavery, about 250 years, its impact on feelings of self-worth, and its replacement by a legalized caste system made it extremely difficult for black people to reestablish supportive cultural institutions after emancipation.

In the 1980s, when the official caste system itself has been ended, the effort to encourage family stability is thwarted not only by the persistent denial of economic opportunity, but by the operation of social welfare policies that in theory should support the family.

Welfare policy in the United States has been built in large part on a critical distinction between the "deserving" and the "undeserving" poor. Programs to serve those not deemed responsible for their own plight, e.g., the elderly and the disabled, are generally made available as a matter of right, without means tests or other conditions, and at relatively higher benefit levels. Assistance to others, in contrast, is usually regarded as a "privilege," subject to pre- and postconditions, and made available only at bare subsistence levels. The distinction is based upon a belief, difficult to prove but impossible to discount, that to do otherwise would be to encourage welfare dependency. If the needs of able-bodied people are met through government aid, the theory runs, a great many of them will lose the incentive to work.

This rationale for welfare policy is marred by difficulties of implementation and internal contradictions. To maintain consistency, welfare payments should continue to be made, albeit in reduced amounts, to people able through their own labors to earn a marginal income. Otherwise, according to the theory, there would be little incentive to work. Thus, when the Reagan administration, in the name of fiscal prudence and serving only the "truly needy" (or deserving), eliminates people with marginal incomes from eligibility for welfare, food stamps, or other aid, it runs counter to its own professed desire to discourage dependency.

Whatever the validity of the rationale, the devastating impact of current welfare policies on the black poor is clear. Black men who are jobless over a long term, for any reason, are discouraged by current welfare policy from maintaining stable family relationships. The presence of an "undeserving poor" person in the home would penalize the entire household since the family unit would be expected to survive on its own.

Black women with children under current welfare policy are in a sort of limbo status between deserving and undeserving poor. It is true that they are eligible for federal assistance under the Aid to Families with Dependent Children Program. But as the beneficiaries of that program changed from the 1940s, when many were widows and most were white, to unmarried, separated, or divorced women, almost half of whom are black, in the 1980s, the benefit levels began to drop.[55] In most states, the current benefit levels are far below the poverty line, forcing women to seek work if they are to provide a bare subsistence for their families.[56] But if poor women are expected to work while raising children, they will need support in the form of good-quality, low-cost day care that neither government nor employers have yet provided. And, if the object is to give women and their families an opportunity for mobility rather than dead-end subsistence jobs, then basic problems such as the need for training and the elimination of persistent sex discrimination in the workplace must be addressed by government. Moreover, if national policy now favors a division between work and child care for women who head their own households, other social welfare policies require reexamination. Systems such as unemployment compensation which enable people to become part of the "deserving" poor are based on the old model of male workers with a full-time and continuous work history, and do not allow the accumulation of credit by women whose work patterns necessarily may be part-time or sporadic.

In the lexicon of welfare policy, children might be thought to be among the deserving poor since they certainly cannot be held responsible for their own plight. But children are held hostage by government policy to a belief that payments that are adequate to meet their needs would encourage welfare dependency by their mothers. However that dilemma is viewed, it would appear to pose no bar to providing services to children, particularly preschool education, that would give them some chance to surmount their environment. As noted earlier, programs to develop the cognitive and social skills of children beginning as early as two have proved successful. Nor in most cases need the program drive a wedge between children and their parents since effective techniques have been developed (as in Head Start) for involving parents in the education of their children.[57]

In sum, efforts to promote family stability as a means for overcoming poverty cannot succeed without an understanding of the continuing impact of past practices of racial discrimination and of the barriers posed by current social welfare policies. What is needed in the 1980s is serious congressional, executive, and judicial examination of the racial impact of government welfare policies, one that parallels the examination of employment practices that in the 1970s, as in

Griggs and in the development of goals and timetables, sought for solutions, not culprits. The inquiry should not bog down on the issue of whether welfare policies are prompted by racial animus but rather should probe the question of whether they have an adverse impact on the minority poor; whether they are necessary to the achievement of proper government objectives, such as decreasing dependency and promoting family stability; and whether other policies might more effectively serve these objectives without visiting harm on the poor.

Similarly, any analysis of government policies on economic opportunity that relies on facile immigrant analogies and that discounts the continuing significance of race is faulty. European immigrant groups that arrived during the late nineteenth and early twentieth centuries achieved mobility through family entrepreneurship, banding together in the construction trades, securing federal land grants, or engaging in other enterprises that did not require a great deal of education and training. These opportunities were located primarily in the North and West and were not accessible to black people who remained concentrated in the rural South. Blacks who did live in industrial areas were faced with rigid racial barriers, such as near-total exclusion from the skilled construction trades.

When in the mid-twentieth century black people began arriving in large numbers in the industrial North, manufacturing companies, freed by the federally funded interstate highway system from dependency on rail and port facilities, were already relocating from central cities to suburbs and to other areas inaccessible to the new migrants. Now in the latter part of the twentieth century, the problem of access has become much worse. Whole industries, such as automobiles, steel, and textiles, that once were significant sources of job opportunity are now in decline because of foreign competition (based on low wages and better management) and the export of capital. Improvements in technology which might help to revive some of these lagging industries will not provide jobs.

At each stage of development, some government policies (from the Homestead Act to FHA programs that aided suburbanization to the interstate highway system) have facilitated economic change and expansion, while others (segregation, noninvestment in training and education) have prevented the black poor from gaining access to the abundance that government was helping to create. Whatever its role in the past, it is clear in the 1980s that government is inextricably involved in determining the shape of economic opportunity for the future. Despite the mythology of Reaganomics, government through its tax, trade, investment, regulatory, and monetary policies has, and will continue to have, a crucial voice in deciding which sectors of the economy will grow and which will shrink, where centers of opportunity will be located, and who will participate in them.

CONCLUSION

Without attempting a prescription for macroeconomic policy, some observations may be ventured. First, the kinds of limited and piecemeal efforts that have been made in the past to help disadvantaged people acquire skills are inadequate to serve the needs of the present and future. Workfare programs and short-term government efforts to train people for jobs which turn out to be nonexistent or dead-end will not provide access to opportunity. At most, these may give people a tenuous foothold in the secondary job market, where, as fast-food workers or keypunch operators, they will have little or no mobility.

Instead, what is needed is a kind of negotiated social contract involving the federal government, business, unions, and public school systems. Under such an arrangement, the business community would be encouraged to establish closer relationships with public school systems, identifying its manpower needs, helping to shape the curriculum to meet those needs, and motivating young people early by introducing them to the world of work. Some professional groups, notably doctors and engineers, have recognized that a successful program to improve minority representation requires identifying talent and offering encouragement to young people while they are still in high school or even earlier.

Business, which knows its own skill requirements far better than government, should take on the full task of training workers, along with a commitment to insure that minorities will receive a fair share of the opportunities. Government, rather than directly running training programs that companies often complain do not meet their needs, should limit its role to monitoring and enforcing the commitments made by business and providing the resources required to carry out that commitment.

Negotiated agreements, in which the responsibilities of the parties are defined with precision but the means for achieving the objectives are left flexible, may provide a more sensible approach to meeting national goals of fairness and productivity than methods that rely on detailed and rigid government regulation.[58]

Second, any strategy designed to provide access to opportunity for the poor undoubtedly requires that a larger share of the nation's wealth be used to meet public needs. This is so for a couple of reasons. One is the accumulating evidence that technological change in the private economy is redistributing jobs in ways that further limit mobility for the poor. With the tremendous loss of production work in manufacturing, some argue that the job market is increasingly being polarized into positions calling for very high or very low skills with little opportunity for advancement from the latter to the former.[59] If this is true, then it is through public investment that jobs calling for midlevel skills (e.g., construction work in building housing and repairing the infrastructure of deteriorating cities, or service jobs such as paramedical work) will be created. Even if concern about the redistribution of jobs in the private economy is overstated,[60] it remains true that increased public investment is needed to provide the basic services—education, child care, health, nutrition, housing —that poor people need if they are to help themselves into the mainstream of American society.

Concerns expressed by conservatives that public expenditures in the modern "welfare state" have had a stultifying effect on economic growth have little basis in fact. The portion of gross national product devoted to government expenditures (including defense) has declined in recent years and remains less than that of other industrial nations, including countries like Sweden and West Germany, which do not have so substantial a group of people in poverty and thus have even less need than ourselves to invest in the development of human potential. If economies are needed in expenditures for social benefits, it would be more sensible and equitable to use the tax system to recoup funds received under entitlement programs by persons who already have means than to cut back assistance to the poor.

Moreover, the slowdown in economic growth in recent years has masked the fact that millions of Americans have experienced a great increase in personal wealth and standard of living over the past three decades. The booms in international travel and the purchase of expensive jewelry and electronic gadgetry are partial testimony to the fact that lifestyles once reserved in the United States for the rich (and still accessible only to a wealthy elite in most other nations) are now widely enjoyed by the middle class. The issue is not whether the nation has adequate resources, but how the balance will be struck between policies encouraging private and public investment, and whether a larger commitment to developing the talents of the disadvantaged is not dictated by the national interest in improved productivity as well as by considerations of equity.[61]

Finally, no policy designed to provide access to opportunity is likely to succeed if it permits the minority poor to escape racial isolation only *after* they have become affluent. Poor people of all ethnic derivations have experienced a high degree of physical isolation in this country. But for no group other than black people was physical isolation the official policy of government over a long period of time. The devastating impact of the policy of apartheid on the aspirations and self-esteem of the victims is evident in the "pathology of the ghetto" that Kenneth Clark wrote about incisively in the 1960s and that persists today. The evidence is accumulating that measures to end social isolation (e.g., desegregation of public schools on an areawide basis, or the location of decent housing for low-income people outside ghetto areas) are among the most effective instruments for providing economic mobility.[62]

Integration policies remain difficult to implement because of the racial fears and misunderstandings on both sides that have been engendered by so many years of separation. But the success achieved thus far warrants persistence. And no one has yet demonstrated that it is possible to give the minority poor access to society's economic and social opportunities while keeping them in physical isolation.

Almost 40 years ago, Ralph Ellison wrote that out of the black struggle for equality could come the creation of "a more human America."[63] Certainly, there is much objective evidence that Ellison's vision has been at least partially attained. Lynching, racial disenfranchisement, the humiliation imposed by the caste system, and the most blatant restraints on access to opportunity have all but disappeared from the American scene. The movement for black civil rights also has played an important role in spawning similar legal and political movements that have asserted the rights of women, disabled citizens, older people, Hispanic Americans, and other minority groups. Progress has been made by all of these groups. Legal strategies to protect the health of coal miners and the safety of industrial workers and to restore the environment have also been derived from the civil rights movement.

Most of us have become more aware in the past decade of some of the unjust limitations that government and society have imposed on the lives of minority people or women or disabled people or others and how our own prejudices and stereotypes have contributed to these barriers. Once aroused, this new consciousness of injustice does not fade easily, even under the prod of regressive political leadership. Thus it seems reasonable to say, even in difficult times, that the civil rights movement has helped to create a more human America.

But Ellison also wrote: "What is needed in our country is not an exchange of pathologies, but a change of the basis of society."[64] In the fervor of the civil rights movement there were those who believed that success in the immediate objectives would bring broader changes in "the basis of society." Somehow, it was thought that the ascendancy to leadership positions of women, blacks, and others who had known underdog status would alter the character of that leadership, that they would bring with them qualities of compassion that would modify the tendencies of a world power toward belligerence, competitiveness, and exploitation.

While the thesis has yet to be tested by the full enfranchisement of women and minorities in political and corporate society, there is little evidence so far to support it. People who have tasted discrimination may tend as a group to be more responsive to those who are still in need, but race and sex are not invariably linked with particular political and social values. Indeed, it well may be that the governing ethos of society is having as important an impact on the civil rights movement as vice versa. Although the strain of egalitarianism in the movement remains strong, it is at times submerged by demands for greater power-sharing with the elites of each group. Such claims (e.g., for a woman vice presidential candidate, for more blacks on corporate boards) of course are rationalized by the need to secure a share of power if government and corporate authority are to be exercised more equitably and humanely. But that point at times is ambiguous or obscured, and the poor may wonder with justification who speaks for them.

What some of us may have underestimated is the capacity of this corporate state to resist fundamental change even while making major adaptations to demands for more equity. The United States after the civil rights revolution remains a toughly competitive nation of "winners" and "losers." It is of great significance that blacks and women in far larger numbers than in the past have genuine opportunities to be winners. But this does not alter the fact that many losers still are determined by accidents of birth and circumstance including, most prominently, the legacy of discrimination. Nor does it mitigate the harsh consequences of being a loser in this society.

As for the future, current trends contain the seeds for either progress or decay in the struggle for economic and social justice.

In the rapid growth of industrial technology there is the threat that larger numbers of people will become "disposable," their labors and contributions viewed as unnecessary to the efficient operation of the economy. But technology may also liberate resources for use in education and human development.

In the revolution in communications there are the seeds of a society so "privatized" (e.g., by the ability to transact business through computers in the home) that we isolate ourselves from most human contact and shared concerns. But there is also the promise of breaking down through wider communication the barriers of misunderstanding that have long set people apart.

In the new wave of immigration to the United States, there is the threat that the ranks of a permanent underclass will be swollen by economic and political refugees who will compete in an atmosphere of racial animosity with blacks and others for the most menial work at the lowest wages. Yet in the arrival of new groups of people seeking jobs and political freedom lies also the possibility that the nation will be reinvested with some of its original sense of purpose, as a land that offers opportunity to all and recognizes diversity as an asset.

The answers no doubt will emerge from the warring instincts of hope and fear, of generosity and meanness, that reside within all of us and in the quality of political leadership that appeals to those instincts. If there are hopeful signs to be gleaned from the experience of the post-*Brown* era, they are that this society has not lost its capacity for constructive change, that in facing the future we need not be prisoners of the wrongs of the past.

NOTES

1. The *Brown* decision has been attacked as an inappropriate expression of sociological or educational opinion by the Court rather than a legal judgment. My own view is that the decision was solidly grounded in the Fourteenth Amendment's fundamental purpose of exempting black people from legislation hostile to their interests. See William Taylor, "*Brown* in Perspective," in *Effective School Desegregation*, W. Hawley, ed., (Beverly Hills, Calif.: Sage Publications, 1981).
2. The current figures appear in Center for the Study of Social Policy, *A Dream Deferred: The Economic Status of Black Americans* (Washington, D.C.: Center for the Study of Social Policy, 1983), p. 22, and in Bureau of the Census, *America's Black Population, 1970–82* (Washington, D.C.: Government Printing Office, 1983), p. 11. Though both are based on census data there are some slight variations in the figures in the two reports. The statistics for earlier years are reported in Malveaux, *Shifts in the Employment and Occupational Status of Black Americans in a Period of Affirmative Action* (New York: Rockefeller Foundation Working Papers, 1979), pp. 148 ff.
3. *Ibid.*
4. Comparing the Malveaux statistics to the Bureau of the Census, *Current Population Reports* for May 1982, the comparable figures for whites were from 12.3 percent to 17.3 percent over a 20-year period in the professions and from 11.6 percent to 12.2 percent in managerial and administrative jobs.
5. Malveaux, *Shifts in Employment*, p. 153. For black women in the 25–34 age category in 1977, the proportion was 18.6 percent.
6. *A Dream Deferred*, p. 6.
7. *Ibid.*, p. 8.
8. William Julius Wilson, "The Declining Significance of Race: Myth or Reality," in *The Declining Significance of Race*, ed. Washington (Philadelphia: University of Pennsylvania Afro-American Studies Program, March 1979), p. 8.
9. *Ibid.*, p. 7.
10. The proportion of black education majors dropped from 45 to 26 percent in the same period.
11. Statistics are drawn from figures cited by the U.S. Commission on Civil

Rights in *Equal Opportunity: Affirmative Admissions Programs at Law and Medical Schools* (Washington, D.C.: Government Printing Office, June 1978), pp. 74–75, and from Department of Education's Higher Education General Information Survey. Since law school enrollment burgeoned during the 1970s, the numerical increase in minority students may be even more noteworthy. In 1969 there were only 2,933 minority students, including 2,128 blacks, enrolled in approved law schools. By 1979 there were 10,008 minority students including 5,257 blacks. See also American Bar Association, *A Review of Legal Education in the United States,* Fall 1978 (Chicago: American Bar Association, 1979), pp. 60, 63.

12. Statistics are drawn from the *Journal of Medical Education* 51 (August 1976): 692, and 55 (December 1980): 1042; and *The New York Times,* November 9, 1980, p. 67:5. During the last decade, the increase in enrollment of women in medical and law schools has been even more striking. In 1971 only one medical student in 10 was a woman; in 1980 one medical student in every four was. These changes are less attributable to specific affirmative action programs than to the elimination of admissions barriers by professional schools and the revolution in perceptions of women's role in working society.

13. See Marcus Alexis, "The Effect of Admission Procedures on Minority Enrollment in Enrollment in Graduate and Professional Schools," in Malveaux, *Shifts in Employment,* pp. 52 and 59–60.

14. *Three National Assessments of Changes in Reading Performance, 1970–1980,* Report No. 11-R-01, National Assessment of Educational Progress (April 1981).

15. *Washington Post,* August 31, 1983, pp. A1, 6.

16. *A Dream Deferred,* p. 47. Black infant deaths, which numbered 44.3 for every thousand live births in 1960, decreased to 21.8 in 1979. White infant deaths were 11.4 per thousand in 1979.

17. *Ibid.,* p. 48. The life expectancy of black males at birth was 65.5 in 1979, an increase of more than four years since 1960, and 74.2 for black females, an increase of almost eight years since 1960. Life expectancy for white males and females in 1979 was about four years longer than their black counterparts.

18. Justice Blackmun, concurring in part, in *Bakke* v. *Regents of California,* 438 U.S. 265, 307 (1978).

19. *Griggs* v. *Duke Power Company,* 401 U.S. 424 (1971).

20. *United Steelworkers of America* v. *Weber,* 443 U.S. 193 (1979).

21. See, e.g., *Carter* v. *Gallagher,* 452 F.2d 315 (8th Cir.), *modified en banc,* 452 F.2d 327 (8th Cir., 1971), *cert. denied,* 406 U.S. 950 (1972).

22. In its current form, the provision is found in E.O. 11246, Sec. 203, 30 Fed. Reg. 12319.

23. 41 C.F.R. Part 60–2 (1974). This provision, known as Revised Order

No. 4 applies to nonconstruction contractors. A parallel set of require-ments (41 C.F.R. Part 60–4) applies to construction contractors.

24. The courts have upheld the validity of the contract compliance pro-gram, including its provisions for goals and timetables, against claims that it involves an impermissible use of race and preferential treatment. (See, e.g., *Associated General Contractors* v. *Altschuler*, 490 F.2d 9 (1st Cir. 1973), *cert. denied*, 416 U.S. 957 (1974).

25. Hearings before the Subcommittee on Employment Opportunities, House Committee on Education and Labor, 97th Cong. 1st sess. v. 1, pp. 219–220.

26. *Ibid.*, pp. 528–529, Statement of Phyllis Wallace.

27. *Washington Post*, April 11, 1982, p. A10.

28. *Ibid.*

29. deLone, Richard, "Creating Incentives for Change," 41 *Christianity and Crises*, no. 5 (March 30, 1981), p. 92.

30. Where a white person has been promoted to a job over a minority person who was more qualified, the ordinary remedy is to permit the white to retain the position, but require the employer to pay the minor-ity person the salary that the position calls for. The difficult cases arise in instances where the expectations of whites clash with the need to provide remedies for past discrimination. For example, in layoff situa-tions, the seniority accumulated by whites may lead them to expect that they will retain their jobs even at the cost of wiping out the gains of an affirmative action plan by laying off all recently hired minorities. The Supreme Court has yet to resolve this issue.

31. See, e.g., statements of Kaiser Aluminum Company executives, *Wash-ington Post*, April 13, 1982, pp. A1, 6.

32. *Swann* v. *Charlotte-Mecklenburg Board of Education*, 402 U.S. 1 (1971).

33. *Keyes* v. *School District No. 1 of Denver, Colorado*, 413 U.S. 189 (1973).

34. Robert Crain and Rita Mahard, *Desegregation Plans That Raise Black Achievement: A Review of the Research* (Santa Monica, Calif.: Rand Cor-poration, 1982). A substantially identical report, Crain and Mahard, "Minority Achievement: Policy Implications of Research," is published in *Effective School Desegregation*, ed. W. Hawley (Beverly Hills, Calif.: Sage Publications, 1981).

35. Crain and Mahard, *Desegregation Plans*, p. 35.

36. *Ibid.*

37. See, e.g., James Coleman *et al.*, *Equality of Educational Opportunity* (Washington, D.C.: Government Printing Office, 1966); U.S. Commis-sion on Civil Rights, *Racial Isolation in the Public Schools* (Washington, D.C.: Government Printing Office, 1967); Frederick Mosteller and Daniel Patrick Moynihan, *On Equality of Educational Opportunity* (New York: Random House, 1972). In schools consisting predomi-nately of advantaged children, the norms set by parents and teachers—

and by the students themselves—ordinarily are high; academic success and advancement to college are expected or demanded. Where schools fall short, middle-class parents are practiced in wielding influence to bring about change.

38. James McPartland, "Desegregation and Equity in Higher Education and Employment: Is Progress Related to the Desegregation of Elementary and Secondary Schools?" *Law and Contemporary Problems* 42 (Summer 1978): 110–113, 124, 131; McPartland and Joe Mills Braddock, "Going to College and Getting a Good Job: The Impact of Desegregation" in Hawley, *Effective School Desegregation*, pp. 141, 146–151.

39. D. W. Brogan, *The American Character* (New York: Time, Inc., 1956), pp. 170, 174–175.

40. Opinion polls show that most people in communities that have actual experience with busing for school desegregation react positively, more so than those who deal with busing only as an abstract notion. See the *Harris Survey* (New York: The Tribune Co. Syndicate, March 26, 1981); *CBS/N.Y. Times Poll,* January 1981.

41. Diana Pearce, *Breaking Down Barriers: New Evidence on the Impact of Metropolitan School Desegregation on Housing Patterns* (Washington, D.C.: National Institute of Education, 1980).

42. The potential gains of such desegregation may be limited if students, once assigned to desegregated schools, are resegregated in the classrooms. While courts are reluctant to intervene in educational decisions on such matters as ability grouping, they have dealt with arbitrary practices of classifying and stereotyping minority children. See, e.g., *Larry P.* v. *Riles,* 343 F. Supp. 1306 (N.D. Cal. 1972), *aff'd per curiam* 502 F.2d 963 (9th Cir. 1974).

43. *Milliken* v. *Bradley,* 418 U.S. 717 (1974). In that case, by a 5–4 margin, the Court rejected a metropolitan school remedy for Detroit.

44. Research on early childhood education is summarized in John Ogbu, *Minority Education and Caste* (New York: Harcourt Brace Jovanovich, 1978).

45. Frank Slobig, "Young Americans: Their Deteriorating Status in the Labor Market" (unpublished manuscript, April 1983).

46. See Stanley H. Masters and Rebecca Maynard, "The Impact of Supported Work on Long-Term Recipients of AFDC Benefits," *Final Report of the Supported Work Evaluation,* vol. 3 (New York: Manpower Demonstration Research Corporation, February 1981). See also Ken Auletta, *The Underclass* (New York: Vintage Books, 1983), pp. 220ff.

47. *A Dream Deferred,* p. 20. Despite the fact that the unemployment rate for black teenagers is often more than 50 percent, they accounted for only a small portion of the 3.4 million unemployed.

48. *New York Times,* July 18, 1983, A1, 8.

49. *A Dream Deferred,* pp. 25–27.

50. *Ibid.,* p. 29.

51. *Ibid.*, pp. 26–31.
52. *Ibid.* While the breakup of families is a phenomenon that affects all races, it is striking that only three million of the more than 50 million white children in the country live in female-headed households that are poor.
53. *Ibid.*, p. 27.
54. James Comer, "The Need for A National Racial Policy: America in the 1980s," *Journal of Public and International Affairs* 3 (1983): 137ff.
55. Diana Pearce, *Farewell to Alms: Women and Welfare Policy in the Eighties* (Washington, D.C.: Center for National Policy Review, 1982).
56. *Ibid.* The benefit levels set by states under AFDC run a range from 46 percent to 98 percent of the poverty line. A further clue that the niggardly benefits provided under AFDC stem more from a view that its recipients are undeserving than from simple budgetary constraints can be derived from a comparison of AFDC and foster care payments. The latter are much higher and the gap is growing.
57. Removal of children from their homes sometimes is necessary where the environment is destructive. Under current policy, however poorly or unevenly administered, children who are abused or neglected may be taken from the control of their parents. The law deems the interests of the child of higher priority than maintaining families "intact."
58. There is some useful precedent in other areas for this kind of approach. In the 1970s, local governments in Maryland and California adopted ordinances requiring builders of large subdivisions to set aside a portion of their units for sale or rental to low and moderate-income families. In return, the developers were exempted from some costly zoning requirements and could avail themselves of federal subsidies for low and moderate-income housing. During the period before interest rates skyrocketed, the ordinances were successful in providing decent housing for low-income people in far more suitable environments than the massive projects operated by public housing authorities. And the direct federal assistance involved was far more useful in reaching the objective than tax subsidies or credits which often reward businesses for steps they planned to take anyway.
59. Robert Kuttner, "The Declining Middle," *The Atlantic Monthly*, July 1983, pp. 50 ff.
60. Robert Samuelson, *National Journal*, June 25, 1983, p. 1348.
61. The issue also may be whether a political process so tainted by the influence of monied special interests has the capacity to respond. With the exception of Mr. Carter's sermons on the need to curb materialism to conserve energy (a challenge to which the nation *did* respond), no president or presidential candidate in the past decade has treated the American people as adult enough to make difficult choices of priorities among competing public and private needs. Instead, all have pledged themselves to the goal of producing more material wealth for the afflu-

ent, as well as everyone else, differing only on policies to achieve the goal.

62. See, e.g., McPartland, "Desegregation and Equity"; U. S. Department of Housing and Urban Development, *Gautreaux Housing Demonstration* (Washington, D. C.: Government Printing Office, 1979).

63. Ralph Ellison, *Shadow and Act* (New York: New American Library, 1966), p. 302.

64. *Ibid.*

AFFIRMATIVE
ACTION

HERMAN SCHWARTZ

The Reagan administration's assault on the rights of minorities and women has focused on the existing policy of affirmative action. This strategy may be shrewd politics but it is mean-spirited morally and insupportable legally.

The attack on affirmative action is only a small part of this administration's campaign against the hard-won rights of blacks, women, and other groups that suffer the inequities of society. Since 1964 this country has developed and refined a body of constitutional, statutory, and regulatory approaches designed to exorcise the existence and effects of the racism and sexism so deeply entrenched in our society. Until 1981 all of our presidents, to a greater or lesser extent, contributed to this effort, even when, like Richard Nixon, they were less than enthusiastic.

The Reagan administration has broken with this tradition. President Reagan's spokesmen—Assistant Attorney General for Civil Rights William Bradford Reynolds and Reagan's Civil Rights Commission appointees Clarence Pendleton and Morris Abram—declare their unlimited devotion to fighting discrimination and furthering civil rights, and in Abram's case is an honorable track record. But the administration's record has been one of across-the-board hostility to civil rights, and though the politically potent issue of affirmative action may have dominated rhetorically, it actually represents only part of the offensive.

Examples are numerous. The Reagan administration vigorously supported tax exemption for schools that discriminate against blacks. It crusaded for a specific intent rule that would have greatly handicapped both federal enforcement and private plaintiffs in voting rights and housing cases, and grudgingly surrendered on voting rights when Congress overwhelmingly declined to go along. It has consistently been permissive regarding voting law changes that blacks have questioned, as was the case in Louisiana and North Carolina. It has approved previously rejected proposals by Louisiana, Mississippi, and North Carolina regarding compliance with federal court orders to rid their higher education systems of racial discrimination; has held up as a model a school desegregation plan it negotiated in Bakersfield, California, which the *New York Times* called a "blueprint for evasion and for continuing the administration's lax approach to school desegregation"; and has intervened against black plaintiffs in school desegregation cases, with Mr. Reynolds in a South Carolina case instructing his trial attorneys to make "those bastards . . . jump through every hoop."

Judicial and other appointments have gone overwhelmingly to white males, even in the heavily black District of Columbia, where only 3 of 14 judges appointed by Reagan have been members of racial minorities.

Where women are concerned, the administration has urged sharp limitations on the nondiscrimination obligations of educational institutions receiving federal money, has opposed the Equal Rights Amendment, and has opposed equal pay for equal work. It has also refused to follow a congressional mandate that the Department of Justice intervene frequently on behalf of retarded, mentally disturbed, and other children and adults institutionalized in intolerable conditions. Neither has it enforced §504 of the Disabled Persons Civil Rights Act, which outlaws discrimination, but instead has tried to reduce the obligation of federal agencies and others to accommodate the handicapped.

All these acts and policies are in addition to the administration's position on goals and timetables and in most cases represent a 180 degree shift from the position of all prior administrations. Most revealing of this shift is the administration's corruption of the United States Commission on Civil Rights, transforming it from an independent conscience of the national community, committed to advancing civil rights and free from political interference, to an arm of the administration committed to promoting antiminority, antiwomen, and antihandicapped person policies.

All this is perhaps not surprising, given a president who as a governor and an opinion leader had opposed every major civil rights law enacted by Congress in the last 20 years, though now Mr. Reynolds has only praise for these same statutes, which he claims mandate "race neutrality."

Affirmative action has been defined as "a public or private program designed to equalize hiring and admission opportunities for historically disadvantaged groups by taking into consideration those very characteristics which have been used to deny them equal treatment.* The controversy swirls primarily around the use of numerical goals and timetables for hiring or promotion, for university admissions, and for other benefits. It is fueled by the powerful strain of individualism that runs through American history and belief. Insofar as affirmative action is designed to compensate the disadvantaged for past racism, sexism, and other discrimination, many understandably believe that today's majority should not have to pay for their ancestors' sins.

It is a hard issue, about which reasonable people can differ. But somehow we must undo the cruel consequences of the racism and sexism that still plague us, both for the sake of the victims and to end the enormous human waste that costs society so much. Civil Rights Commission Chairman Pendleton has conceded that discrimination

---

*Duncan, *The Future of Affirmative Action: A Jurisprudential Critique,* 17 Harv. C.R.–C.L. L. Rev. 503 (1982). Another description is Ann Fagan Ginger's: "Affirmative action means that someone who has the potential for being a good employee, apprentice, supervisor, or professional, but who lacks the formal, paper qualification customarily required, is nonetheless offered an opportunity to get into the classroom, apprenticeship program, or job, in order to enable the applicant to overcome the effects of past discrimination." Ginger, *Who Needs Affirmative Action,* 14 Harv. C.R.–C.L.L. Rev. 265, 268 (1979).

is not only still with us, but is, as he put it, "rampant." As recently as January 1984, the dean of faculty at Amherst College wrote in the *New York Times:*

> In my contacts with a considerable range of academic institutions, I have become aware of pervasive residues of racism and sexism, even among those whose intentions and conscious beliefs are entirely nondiscriminatory. Indeed, I believe most of us are afflicted with such residues. Beyond the wrongs of the past are the wrongs of the present. Most discriminatory habits in academia are nonactionable; affirmative action goals are our only instrument for focusing sustained attention.

The plight of black America not only remains grave, but in many respects, it is getting worse. The black unemployment rate—21 percent in early 1983—is double that for whites and the spread continues to increase. For black males 20–24, the rate—an awful 30 percent—is almost triple that for whites; for black teenagers the rate approaches 50 percent. More than half of all black children under three years of age live in homes below the poverty line. The gap between white and black family income, which prior to the seventies had narrowed a bit, has steadily edged wider, so that black family income is now only 55 percent of that of whites. Only 3 percent of the nation's lawyers and doctors are black, and only 4 percent of its managers, but over 50 percent of its maids and garbage collectors. Black life expectancy is about six years less than that of whites; the black infant mortality rate is nearly double.

Although the situation for women, of all races, is not as bad, women still earn only two-thirds as much as their male counterparts; and the economic condition of black women, who now head 41 percent of the 6.4 million black families, is particularly bad: a recent Wellesley study found that black women are not only suffering in the labor market, but they receive substantially less public assistance and child support than white women. So is that of female household heads of any race: 90 percent of the 8.4 million single parent homes are headed by women, and more than half are below the poverty line. Bureau of Labor Statistics data reveal that in 1983 women actually earned *less* than two-thirds of their male counterparts' salaries, and black women earn only 84% of the white female incomes. In his 1984

State of the Union address, President Reagan claimed dramatic gains for women during the 1983 recovery. A *Washington Post* analysis the next day charitably described his claims as "overstated," noting that the Bureau of Labor Statistics reports (on which the President relied) showed that "there was no breakthrough. The new jobs which the president cited included many in sales and office work, where women have always found work" and are paid little.

We must close these gaps so that we do not remain two nations, divided by race and gender. Although no one strategy can overcome the results of centuries of inequity, the use of goals and timetables in hiring and other benefit distribution programs has helped to make modest improvements. Studies in 1983 show, for example, that from 1974 to 1980 minority employment with employers subject to federal affirmative action requirements rose 20 percent, almost twice that of elsewhere. The employment of women by covered contractors rose 15 percent, but only 2 percent among others. The number of black police officers nationwide rose from 24,000 in 1970 to 43,500 in 1980; that kind of increase in Detroit produced a sharp decline in citizen hostility toward the police and a concomitant increase in police efficiency. There were also large jumps in minority and female employment among fire fighters, and sheet metal and electrical workers.

Few other remedies work as well or as quickly. As the New York City Corporation Counsel told the Supreme Court in the *Fullilove* case about the construction industry (before Mayor Edward Koch decided that affirmative action was an "abomination"), "less drastic means of attempting to eradicate and remedy discrimination have been attempted repeatedly and continuously over the past decade and a half. They have all failed."

What, then, is the basis for the assault on affirmative action? Apart from the obvious political expediency and ideological reflex of this administration's unvarying conclusion that the "haves" deserve government help and the "have-nots" don't, President Reagan and his allies present two related arguments: (1) hiring and other distributional decisions should be made solely on the basis of individual merit; (2) racial preferences are always evil and will take us back to *Plessy* v. *Ferguson* and worse. Quoting Dr. Martin Luther King, Jr., Thurgood Marshall, and Roy Wilkins to support the claim that anything other than total race neutrality is "discriminatory," Assistant Attorney General Reynolds warns that race consciousness will "creat[e] . . . a racial spoils system in America," "stifle the creative spirit," erect artificial barriers, and divide the society. It is, he says, unconstitutional, unlawful, and immoral. Midge Decter, writing in the *Wall Street Journal* a few years ago, sympathized with black and female beneficiaries of affirmative-action programs for the "self-doubts" and loss of "self-regard" that she is sure they suffer, "spiritually speaking," for their "unearned special privileges." Whenever we take race into account to hand out benefits, declares Linda Chavez, the new executive director of the Reagan Civil Rights Commission, we "discriminate," "destroy[ing] the sense of self."

The legal position was stated by Morris Abram, in explaining why the reshaped commission hastened to do Reagan's bidding at its very first meeting by withdrawing prior commission approval of goals and timetables:

> I do not need any further study of a principle that comes from the basic bedrock of the Constitution, in which the words say that every person in the land shall be entitled to the equal protection of the law. Equal means equal. Equal does not mean you have separate lists of blacks and whites for promotion, any more than you have separate accommodations for blacks and whites for eating. Nothing will ultimately divide a society more than this kind of preference and this kind of reverse discrimination.[1]

In short, any form of race preference is equivalent to racism.

All of this represents a nadir of "newspeak," all too appropriate for this administration in Orwell's year. For it has not only persistently fought to curtail minority and women's rights in many contexts, but it has itself used "separate lists" based on color, sex, and ethnic origin whenever politically or otherwise useful.

For example, does anyone believe that blacks like Civil Rights Commission Chairman Clarence Pendleton or Equal Employment Opportunities Commission Chairman Clarence Thomas were picked because of the color of their *eyes?* Or that Linda Chavez Gersten was made the new executive director for reasons having nothing to do with the fact that her maiden and professional surname is Chavez?

Perhaps the most prominent recent example of affirmative action is President Reagan's selection of Sandra Day O'Connor for the Supreme Court. Obviously she was on a "separate list," because on any unitary list this obscure lower-court state judge, with no federal experience and no national reputation, would have never come to mind as a plausible choice for the highest court. (Incidentally, despite Ms. Decter's, Mr. Reynolds's, and Ms. Chavez's concern about the loss of "self-regard" suffered by beneficiaries of such preferences, "spiritually speaking" Justice O'Connor seems to be bearing her loss and spiritual pain quite easily.) And, like so many other beneficiaries of affirmative action given an opportunity that would be otherwise unavailable, she may perform well.

This is not to say that Reagan should not have chosen a woman. The appointment ended decades of shameful discrimination against women lawyers, discrimination still practiced by Reagan where the lower courts are concerned since he has appointed very few female federal judges apart from Justice O'Connor—of 123 judgeships, Reagan has appointed no women to the courts of appeals and only 10 to the district benches. Of these judgeships, 86 percent went to white males. But the choice of Sandra O'Connor can be explained and justified only by the use of affirmative action and a separate list, not by some notion of neutral "individual merit" on a single list.

But is affirmative action constitutional and legal? Is its legal status, as Mr. Abram claims, so clear by virtue of principles drawn from the "basic bedrock of the Constitution" that no "further study" is necessary?

Yes, but not in the direction that he and this administration want to go. Affirmative action is indisputably constitutional. Not once but many times the Supreme Court has upheld the constitutional or statutory legality of considering race to remedy the wrongs of prejudice and discrimination. In 1977, for example, in *United Jewish Organizations* v. *Carey*, [2] the Supreme Court upheld a New York statute that "deliberately increased the nonwhite majorities in certain districts in order to enhance the opportunity for election of nonwhite representatives from those districts," even if it disadvantaged certain white Jewish communities. Three members of the Court including Justice Rehnquist explained that "no racial slur or stigma with respect to whites or any other race" was involved. In the *Bakke* case, [3] five members of the Court upheld the constitutionality of a state's favorable consideration of race as a factor in university admissions; four members would have sustained a fixed 16 percent quota. In *United Steelworkers of America* v. *Weber*,[4] a 5–2 majority held that private employers could set up a quota system with separate lists for selecting trainees for a newly created craft program. In *Fullilove* v. *Klutznick*,[5] six members of the Court led by Chief Justice Burger unequivocally upheld a congressional set-aside of 10 percent for minority contractors on federal public works programs.* All members of the present Court except for Justice O'Connor have passed on affirmative action in one or more of these four cases, and each has upheld it at one time or another. Although the decisions have been based on varying grounds, with many differing opinions, the legal consequence is clear: affirmative action is lawful under both the Constitution and the statutes. To nail the point home, the Court in January 1984 not once but *twice* rejected the Justice Department's effort to get it to reconsider the issue where affirmative action hiring plans are adopted by governmental bodies (the Detroit Police Department and the New York State Corrections system), an issue left open in *Weber* which had involved a private employer.

The same result obtains on the lower court levels. Despite the persistent efforts of Reagan's Justice Department, every one of the nine circuit courts of appeal that has dealt with hiring quotas has continued to sustain them.

Nor is this anything new. Mr. Reynolds told an audience of pre-law students in January 1984 that the Fourteenth Amendment was intended to bar taking race into account for any purpose at all, and to ensure race neutrality. "That was why we fought the Civil War," he once told the *New York Times*. If so, he knows something that the members of the 1865–1866 Congress, who adopted that amendment and fought the war, did not. Less than a month after Congress approved the Fourteenth Amendment in 1866 the very same Congress enacted eight laws exclusively for the Freedmen,

---

*The Reagan administration has nevertheless reduced the number of government contracts going to minority firms by almost 10 percent, reversing a 15-year policy. And in some cases where local governments have adopted minority set-asides, the Justice Department is trying to annul them as unconstitutional, despite the Supreme Court's decision in *Fullilove*.

granting preferential benefits regarding land, education, banking facilities, hospitals, and more. No comparable programs existed or were established for whites. And that Congress knew what it was doing. The racial preferences involved in those programs were vigorously debated with a vocal minority led by President Andrew Johnson, who argued that the preferences wrongly discriminated against whites.

All these governmental actions reflect the obvious point that, as Justice Harry Blackmun has said, "in order to get beyond racism, we must first take account of race. There is no other way." Our very conservative Chief Justice, Warren Burger, had made the point even clearer in a prophetic commentary on this administration's efforts to get the courts to ignore race when trying to remedy the ravages of past discrimination. Striking down in 1971 a North Carolina statute which barred considerations of race in school assignments, the Chief Justice said:

> The statute exploits an apparently neutral form to control school assignments' plans by directing that they be "color blind"; *that requirement, against the background of segregation, would render illusory the promise of Brown.* Just as the race of students must be considered in determining whether a constitutional violation has occurred so also must race be considered in formulating a remedy . . . *[color blindness] would deprive school authorities of the one tool [race consideration] absolutely essential to fulfillment of their constitutional obligation to eliminate existing dual school systems.* [6]

So much for "basic bedrock" constitutional principles. But this is hardly surprising from an administration in which a White House spokesman denied that the Justice Department was failing to enforce the law—"unless you call all of the decisions of the Supreme Court the law of the land," he explained.

But what of the morality of affirmative action? Does it amount to discrimination? Is it true, as Brian Weber's lawyer argued before the Supreme Court, that "you can't avoid discrimination by discriminating"? Will racially influenced hiring take us back to *Plessy* v. *Ferguson*, as Pendleton and Reynolds assert? Were Martin Luther

King, Jr., Thurgood Marshall, Roy Wilkins, and other black leaders against it?

Hardly. Indeed, it is hard to contain one's outrage at this perversion of what Dr. King, Justice Marshall, and others have said, at this manipulation of their often sorrow-laden eloquence, in order to deny a handful of jobs, school admissions, and other necessities for a decent life to a few disadvantaged blacks out of the many who still suffer from discrimination and would have few opportunities otherwise. No one can honestly equate a remedial preference for a disadvantaged (and qualified) minority member with the brutality inflicted on blacks and other minorities by Jim Crow laws and practices. The preference may take away some benefits from some white men, but none of them is being beaten, lynched, denied the right to use a bathroom, a place to sleep or eat, being forced to take the dirtiest jobs or denied any work at all, forced to attend dilapidated and mind-killing schools, subjected to brutally unequal justice, or stigmatized as an inferior being. Setting aside, after proof of discrimination, a few places a year for qualified minorities out of hundreds and perhaps thousands of employees, as in the Kaiser plant in the *Weber* case, or 16 medical school places out of 100 as in *Bakke*, or 10 percent of federal public work contracts as in *Fullilove*, or even 50 percent of new hires for a few years as in some employment cases—this has nothing in common with the racism that was inflicted on helpless minorities, and it is a shameful insult to the memory of the tragic victims to identify the two.

This administration does claim it favors "affirmative action" of a kind: "employers should seek out and train minorities," Linda Chavez told a *Washington Post* interviewer. Apart from the preference involved in setting aside money for "seeking out" and "training" minorities (would this include preference in training programs like the *Weber* plan, the legality of which Mr. Reynolds said was "wrongly decided"?), the proposed remedy is ineffectual—it just doesn't work. As the "old" Civil Rights Commission had reported, "By the end of the 1960s, enforcement officials realized that discernible indicators of progress were needed." Consequently "goals and timetables" came into use.[7]

Questions may nevertheless remain. Does affirmative action divide people? Is group thinking immoral? Dangerous? Where does it stop—aren't we all minorities, and aren't we all therefore entitled? If so, won't we wind up with claims totaling 200 percent of the pie? Why should a white policeman or fire fighter with ten years in the department be laid off when a black or a woman with less seniority is kept because an affirmative action decree is in force? Aren't those denied a job or other opportunity because of an affirmative action program often innocent of any wrong against the preferred group and just as much in need of the opportunities?

The last question is the most troubling. Brian Weber was not a rich man and he had to support a family on a modest salary, just like any black worker. A craft job would have been a significant step up in money, status, and working conditions. And *he* hadn't discriminated against anyone. Why should he pay for Kaiser's wrongs?

A closer look at the *Weber* case brings some other factors to light, however. Even if there had been no separate list for blacks, Weber would not have gotten the position, for there were too many other whites ahead of him anyway. Moreover, but for the affirmative action plan, there would not have been any craft training program at the plant at all, for *any* whites.

Furthermore, even with the separate list, the number of whites adversely affected was really very small. The Kaiser plan (adopted "voluntarily" to avoid employment discrimination suits by blacks and the loss of federal contracts) contemplated hiring only three to four minority members a year, out of a craft work force of 275–300 and a total work force of thousands. In the first year of its operation, Kaiser still selected only a handful of blacks, because it also brought in 22 outside craftsmen, only one of whom was black. In the 1980 *Fullilove* case, in which the Supreme Court upheld a 10 percent set-aside of federal public works projects for minority contractors, only 0.25 percent of the total annual expenditure for construction in the United States was involved. In *Bakke*, only 16 places out of 100 at one medical school were set aside for minorities. A new Boston University special admissions program for black medical students will start with three a year, with the hope of rising to ten, increasing the minority enrollment at the school by 2 percent.

The *Weber* case discloses another interesting aspect of affirmative action plans. Because they can adversely affect the careers of majority white males, creative ingenuity is often expended to prevent this from happening. In *Weber*, a new craft program benefiting both whites and blacks was set up. Although white employees and the union had been clamoring for such a program for many years, it wasn't until Kaiser felt it had to adopt an affirmative action program that it granted this request. In the lay-off cases, time sharing and other ways of avoiding the dismissals—including raising more money— can be devised. So much for Mr. Reynolds's worries about "stifling creativity."

Strains can and do result, especially if deliberately stirred up. But strain is not inevitable: broad-ranging goals and timetable programs for women and blacks were instituted in the Bell Telephone Company with no such troubles. The same holds true elsewhere, especially when, as in *Weber*, the program creates new, previously unavailable opportunities for whites. On the other hand some whites may be upset, even if, as the administration urges, the remedies are limited to specific identifiable victims of discriminatory practices. If a black applicant can prove that an employer wrongly discriminated against him personally, he would be entitled to the seniority and other benefits that he would have had but for the discrimination— with the administration's blessing—and this would give him competitive seniority over some white employees regardless of those employees' innocence. The same thing happens constantly with veterans and other preferences, and few opponents of affirmative action seem to be upset by that.

Among some Jews, affirmative action brings up bitter memories of ceiling quotas which kept them out of schools and jobs that could on merit have been theirs. This has produced a serious and nasty split within the civil rights movement. But affirmative action goals and timetables are really quite different. Whereas quotas against Jews, Catholics, and others were ceilings to limit and keep these groups out of schools and jobs, today's "benign preferences" are designed to be floors that let minorities *into* a few places they would not ordinarily enter, and with relatively little impact on others.

There is also a major confusion, exploited by opponents, resulting from the fact that we are almost all ethnic or religious minorities. Of course we are. And if it were shown that any minority is being victimized by intentional discrimination *and* that the only way to get more of that minority into a relatively representative portion of the work force or school is through an affirmative action plan, then these people would be entitled to such a remedy.

There is really nothing inherently wrong about taking group identity into account, so long as the person selected is qualified, a prerequisite that is an essential element of all affirmative action programs.* We do it all the time, with hardly a murmur of protest from anyone. We take group identity into account when we put together political slates, when a university gives preference to applicants from a certain part of the country or to the children of alumni, when Brandeis University restricts itself to Jews in choosing a president (as it did when it chose Morris Abram) or Notre Dame to Roman Catholics or Howard University to blacks, when we give preferences to veterans for jobs, promotions, and the like, when this administration finds jobs in government for children of cabinet members. Some of these examples are less laudable than others. But surely none of these seldom criticized practices can be valued above, or has the serious purpose of, undoing the effects of past and present discrimination. In choosing a qualified applicant because of a race preference we merely acknowledge, as Morton Horwitz has pointed out, "the burdens, stigmas, and scars produced by history . . . the injustices heaped on his ancestors and, through them on him. The history and culture of oppression, transmitted through legally anonymous generations, is made antiseptic when each individual is treated as a separate being, disconnected from history."[8]

In some cases, moreover, group-oriented choices are necessary for effective performance of the job. Justice Powell in the *Bakke* case noted the importance of ethnic and other diversity for a university, as a justification for taking race into account as one factor in medical school admissions. He did stress that the choice must be individualized, but his choice of the Harvard program as a model gave away the ball game because a key part of it (described in the appendix to his opinion but not in the excerpt he chose to quote) is a certain number of minority admissions as a goal.

One area where effective job performance almost mandates such

---

*Fifteen of the sixteen minority admittees in *Bakke* graduated from the medical school.

group consideration is precisely the area where the administration has chosen to make its stand against affirmative action in the courts: police departments. The confrontation of an almost all-white police force with an angry, socially depressed minority community has produced violence, police brutality (thoroughly documented by the pre-Reagan Civil Rights Commission), and inefficient police work. Those unhappy conditions were in fact a major reason for extending Title VII of the Civil Rights Act to state and local governments.

Such race-conscious selection within police departments has worked. In Detroit, a largely black city where racial friction between a nearly all-white police force and ghetto dissidents had been epidemic and bloody—one such incident sparked the violence in 1968 that led to the death of 34 people—the police department voluntarily instituted an affirmative action plan which, as the Justice Department itself has admitted, "was expressly made as a response to undeniable past discrimination against blacks that had created a police force that was largely unresponsive to the concerns of a substantial portion of the City's population." Since then, racial incidents and police/community frictions have declined.*

Affirmative action has, of course, not always been completely effective. No policy can be. Certain marginally qualified students have been unable to meet the academic demands of colleges and professional schools. Once these problems emerged, however, many schools set up special remedial programs which, like the Kaiser craft training plan, often benefited needy whites as well. Unfortunately,

---

*In New Orleans as well, the Justice Department is trying to turn the clock back and get the federal court to reverse itself and strike down goals and timetables for police promotion. The first black policeman in New Orleans was not hired until 1950, and the bathrooms were segregated as late as the mid-1960s. A black policewoman was running the department's community-relations operation but was not promoted to the appropriate rank, and of course paid far less than a similarly responsible white male. New Orleans agreed to a consent decree with promotional goals, which the Justice Department attacked. When the Equal Employment Opportunity Commission tried to file a brief in support of the New Orleans plan, Justice pressured it into not doing so, even though the brief had already been written and approved. Several civil rights organizations obtained a copy of the brief, which was widely available, and, adopting it as their own, brought it to the attention of the court.

the Reagan administration's cutbacks on educational programs (for all its talk of support for "affirmative action" in improving education and training) have decimated these programs, with the result that far fewer marginally qualified minorities are being admitted to colleges and professional schools.

The seniority layoff problem is undeniably the most troubling, for in this case people lose jobs they *have*, obviously a more serious matter than not getting a job you want but don't have. But layoffs on the traditional "last in, first out" basis will undo what little progress we have made toward racial equity.* And a layoff of whites is far more likely to result in quick rehiring than a layoff of blacks, as Boston and Memphis both showed: when the courts in those cases ordered whites to be laid off, money suddenly materialized and all the laid-off workers were promptly rehired.† Nevertheless, this is the one situation in which the Supreme Court has struck down an affirmative action plan. In the Memphis fire-fighters case, the Court ruled that the concern for seniority reflected in Title VII of the Civil Rights Act of 1964 barred federal courts from overriding minorities from affirmative action plans.[10]

---

* The pre-Reagan Civil Rights Commission found that fiscal cutbacks caused by the 1974–75 recession had a devastating effect on minorities in local government. "The recent recession has had a critical impact on minorities and women. Many had only recently obtained their first promising jobs. Increasing numbers had begun to penetrate employment areas of great importance in our society, such as state and local government. Because they have not had time to acquire adequate seniority, however, minority members and women have been affected disproportionately by the personnel cutbacks occasioned by this recession, and much of their limited progress has thereby been obliterated. In light of dismal predictions of slow economic recovery and continuing high unemployment, this recession threatens to lock these groups into place as a permanent, expendable economic and social underclass. . . . In New York City, layoffs in mid-1975 of 371 female officers appointed since January 1973 by the New York City Police Department ended their brief tenure with the previously overwhelmingly male police force. Over half of all Hispanic city workers in New York lost their jobs between July 1974 and November 1975.[9]

† The primary reason that white Boston police with ten years seniority were laid off was not that blacks were retained but because of the veterans' preference. In Memphis, the laid-off white fire fighters didn't have longer service than the blacks retained because of the affirmative action decree; both groups had equal seniority but the white workers had priority on an *alphabetical* list.

There are indeed problems with affirmative action, but not of the kind or magnitude that Messrs. Reynolds and Abram claim: problems about whether these programs work, whether they impose heavy burdens, how these burdens can be lightened, and the like. They are not the basis for charges that affirmative action is equivalent to racism and for perverting the words of Dr. King and others.

"Equal is equal" proclaims Morris Abram, and that's certainly true. But it is just as true that equal treatment of unequals perpetuates and aggravates inequality. And gross inequality is what we still have today. As William Coleman, secretary of transportation in the Ford administration, put it,

> For black Americans, racial equality is a tradition without a past. Perhaps, one day America will be color-blind. It takes an extraordinary ignorance of actual life in America today to believe that day has come. . . . [For blacks], there is another American "tradition"—one of slavery, segregation, bigotry, and injustice.

One final note. After so many years of invidious, cruel color-consciousness, of devastating "special treatment," and of harmful "group thinking," one cannot avoid suspicion about the sudden demand for color neutrality just as society begins trying to undo the harm wrought by hostile color-consciousness. Scepticism seems especially justified when some of those making the demand have in the past always been indifferent to color-hurt minorities and who now oppose the struggle for equal rights in almost every other sphere. This is, after all, an administration which does not include (unless Mr. Abram is considered an administration man) a single person with a record of leadership or even of supporting activity on behalf of civil rights and minority advance. That could not have been said of any previous administration of the past 50 years. It is an administration whose leader, when asked whether he agreed with Senator Jesse Helms that FBI files would show Martin Luther King, Jr. had ties to communists, replied with a grin, "We'll know in about 35 years, won't we?" Perhaps the most appropriate lesson from all this is what Hamlet learned: "That one may smile and smile and be a villain."

NOTES

1. *New York Times,* January 18, 1984.
2. 430 U.S. 144 (1977)
3. *University of California* v. *Bakke,* 438 U.S. 262 (1978).
4. 443 U.S. 199 (1979)
5. 448 U.S. 448 (1980)
6. *Board of Education* v. *Swann,* 402 U.S. 43, 45–46 (emphasis added).
7. U.S. Commission on Civil Rights, *Affirmative Action in the 1980s: Dismantling the Process of Discrimination,* November 1981, p. 19.
8. Morton Horwitz, "The Jurisprudence of Brown and the Dilemmas of Liberalism," *Harvard Civil Rights–Civil Liberties Law Review* 14 (1979): 599, 610.
9. U.S. Commission on Civil Rights, *Last Hired, First Fired: Layoffs and Civil Rights* (Washington, D.C.: Government Printing Office, 1977), pp. 60–61, 25–26.
10. *Firefighters Union Local No. 1784* v. *Stotts,* ____ U.S. ____ (June 12, 1984). The Court's opinion gratuitously went far beyond the layoff problem, however, and intimated disapproval of court-ordered quotas for hiring or promotion as well. If these intimations become law in a future case, efforts to improve employment opportunities for minorities and women will be devastated. Even without such a decision, the Court's language will probably deter lower courts from entering such decrees until further clarification, and will discourage settlements; also, the Department of Justice immediately announced that it would try to reopen and set aside the hundreds of such affirmative action decrees entered since 1969.

THE
URBAN
UNDERCLASS

WILLIAM JULIUS WILSON

The social problems of urban life in advanced industrial America are, in major measure, associated with race. Urban crime, drug addiction, out-of-wedlock births, female-headed families, and welfare dependency have risen dramatically in the last several years and the rates reflect a sharply uneven distribution by race. There has been a reluctance on the part of liberal social scientists, policymakers, and civil rights leaders to underline the close association between these forms of social dislocation and race. Often discussions of such issues as crime and out-of-wedlock births deliberately exclude reference to race, or attempt to conceal the racial factor, or acknowledge the racial connection but only as a way to emphasize the deleterious consequences of racial discrimination or of structural inequality in American society.

Indeed, in an effort to protect their work from the charge of racism or of "blaming the victim," liberal social scientists have tended

---

This chapter is based on a larger study, *The Hidden Agenda: Race, Social Dislocations, and Public Policy in America,* to be published by the University of Chicago Press.

to avoid describing any behavior that could be construed as unflattering or stigmatizing to particular racial minorities. Accordingly, the growing problems of black crime, family dissolution, out-of-wedlock births, and welfare dependency tend not to receive careful and systematic attention.

But this has been true only of the last several years. In the mid-1960s these problems were readily discussed and analyzed by scholars such as Kenneth B. Clark, Lee Rainwater, and Daniel Patrick Moynihan. They produced studies that examined in clear terms the cumulative effects of racial isolation and class subordination on life and behavior in the urban ghetto.[1] As Clark put it: "The symptoms of lower-class society afflict the dark ghettos of America—low aspiration, poor education, family instability, illegitimacy, unemployment, crime, drug addiction and alcoholism, frequent illness and early death. But because Negroes begin with the primary affliction of inferior racial status, the burdens of despair and hatred are more pervasive."[2] Whether the social and psychological dimensions of the ghetto were analyzed, as in the case of Clark's study, or ghetto family patterns were examined, as in the case of Rainwater's and Moynihan's studies, the conditions or realities of ghetto life "that are usually forgotten or ignored in polite discussions"[3] were both vividly described and systematically analyzed.

All of these studies closely tied their discussions of the experiences of inequality to their discussions of the structure of inequality. To put that in more concrete terms, they attempted to show the connection between the economic and social situations into which many blacks are born and their modes of adaptation to them. That included the creation of subcultural patterns and norms of behavior frequently taking the form of a "self-perpetuating pathology."[4] The works of Clark and Rainwater, especially, not only sensitively portrayed the destructive features of ghetto life but also comprehensively analyzed those structural conditions, including changing economic relations, that combined with race-specific experiences to produce these features.

If social scientists have lately shied away from this focus of research, they may perhaps cite the virulent attacks on the "Moynihan Report" on the Negro family in the latter half of the 1960s as one of the reasons.[5] There is no need here for detailed discussion of the controversy generated by the report, which like so many controversies over social issues raged in large measure because of misinterpretations and distortions.[6] I would like, however, to point out that there was nothing new in the report. Various aspects of Moynihan's arguments had been raised previously by people such as E. Franklin Frazier and Bayard Rustin as well as Clark.[7] As had Rustin, Moynihan argued that as barriers to black liberty are eliminated by antidiscrimination legislation, attention will shift from issues of liberty to issues of equality; in other words, from concerns of freedom to concerns for equal resources enabling blacks to live in material ways comparable to whites. The simple removal of legal barriers will not achieve this goal, he maintained, because the cumulative effects of discrimination have created circumstances that make it very nearly impossible for a substantial majority of black Americans to take advantage of opportunities provided by civil rights laws. He pointed out, in this connection, that "the Negro community is dividing between a stable middle-class group that is steadily growing stronger and more successful, and an increasingly disorganized and disadvantaged lower-class group."[8]

Like Clark, he emphasized that the deterioration of the family—as reflected in the rising rates of broken marriages among urban blacks, out-of-wedlock births, female-headed homes, and welfare dependency—was one of the central problems of lower-class blacks. And like Frazier, Moynihan maintained that the problems of the black family, which create major obstacles to black equality, stem from previous patterns of inequality that originated with slavery and have been maintained and reinforced by years of discrimination. He concluded his report by calling for a shift in the direction of federal civil rights activities to "bring the Negro American to full and equal sharing in the responsibilities and rewards of citizenship" and thereby to enhance "the stability and resources of the Negro American family."[9]

The vitriolic attacks on the "Moynihan Report," attacks which paid far more attention to Moynihan's description of the black family than to his policy recommendations for an equality of outcomes,[10] helped to create an atmosphere that discouraged many scholars from exploring certain aspects of the lower-class black experience. This atmosphere was enhanced by the emergence of a black solidarity movement in the latter half of the 1960s that, among other things, proffered a new definition of the black experience proclaimed as the "black perspective." This new definition was popularized by militant black spokespersons in the 1960s and was incorporated as a dominant theme in the writings of young black scholars and intellectuals by the early 1970s.[11] Although the black perspective represented a variety of views on matters of race, the assertions of black pride and black self-affirmation were characteristic features of the speeches and writings that embodied the intellectual component of the solidarity movement. Accordingly, the emphasis on the positive aspects of the black experience resulted in the uniform rejection of earlier arguments, which maintained that some features of ghetto life were pathological, in favor of those that accented black community strengths. And arguments extolling the strengths and virtues of black families replaced those that underlined the deterioration of black families. In fact, aspects of ghetto behavior described as pathological in the studies of the mid-1960s were reinterpreted or redefined as functional by some black perspective proponents because, they argued, blacks were displaying the ability to survive and, in many cases, to flourish in an economically depressed environment. Ghetto families were described as resilient and as adapting creatively to an oppressive racist society. In short, these revisionist studies, purporting to "liberate" the social sciences from the influence of "racism," effectively shifted the focus of social science writings away from a discussion of the consequences of racial isolation and class subordination to a discussion of black achievement.

Also, consistent with the dominant focus on racial solidarity in the writings of the black perspective proponents was an emphasis on "we" versus "they" and "black" versus "white." Since the accent was on race, little attention was paid to the social-economic differences within the black community and the implications this has for different public policy options; and little discussion was devoted to problems with the economy and the need for economic reform. Thus, the promising move to pursue programs of economic reform by defining the problems of American economic organization and outlining their effect on the minority community in the early and mid-1960s was cut off by slogans calling for "reparations," or "black control of institutions serving the black community" in the late 1960s. This is why

Orlando Patterson was led to proclaim in a later analysis that black ethnicity had become "a form of mystification, diverting attention from the correct kinds of solutions to the terrible economic condition of the group," thereby making it difficult for blacks to see "how their fate is inextricably tied up with the structure of the American economy."[12]

Meanwhile, during this period of black solidarity, significant developments were unfolding in ghetto communities across the nation that profoundly affected the lives of millions of blacks and dramatically revealed that the problems earlier described by Clark, Moynihan, and others had reached catastrophic proportions. To be more specific, one quarter of all black births were out of wedlock in 1965, the year Moynihan wrote his report on the Negro family, and by 1980 over half (55 percent) were; almost 25 percent of all black families were headed by women in 1965, and by 1980 41 percent were; partly as a result, welfare dependency among poor blacks has exploded. And perhaps the most dramatic indicator of the extent to which social pathology has afflicted urban blacks is crime, especially violent crime, which has risen sharply in recent years. Finally, these growing social problems have accompanied increasing black rates of unemployment and decreasing rates of labor-force participation.

Although these problems are heavily concentrated in urban areas, it would be a serious mistake to assume that they afflict all segments of the urban black community. Rather, these are the problems that are identified with the urban underclass—that heterogeneous grouping of inner-city families and individuals who are outside the mainstream of the American occupational system. Included in this population are persons who lack training and skills, and either experience long-term unemployment or have dropped out of the labor force altogether; persons who are more or less permanent public assistance recipients; and persons who are engaged in street criminal activity and other forms of aberrant or antisocial behavior.

THE TANGLE OF PATHOLOGY IN THE INNER CITY

When figures on black crime, out-of-wedlock births, female-headed families, and welfare dependency are released to the public without sufficient explanation, racial stereotypes are reinforced. And the tendency of liberal social scientists either to ignore these issues or to address them in circumspect ways does more to enhance than to undermine racist perceptions.

These problems cannot be explained simply in terms of racial discrimination or in terms of a culture of poverty. Rather, they must be seen as having complex sociological antecedents that range from demographic changes to problems of societal organization. But before turning to these explanatory factors, I should like to sketch the growing social problems of the inner city, beginning first with violent crime.

RACE AND VIOLENT CRIME

Only one of nine persons in the United States is black; yet in 1980 nearly one of every two Americans arrested for murder and nonnegligent manslaughter was black, and 44 percent of all victims of murder were black.[13] As Norval Morris and Michael Tonry point out, "Homicide is the leading cause of death of black men and women aged 25 to 34."[14] Furthermore, nearly 60 percent of all persons arrested for robbery and 36 percent of all persons arrested for aggravated assault in 1980 were black.[15] Moreover, the rate of black imprisonment in 1979 was eight and one-half times greater than the rate of white imprisonment.[16]

The disproportionate involvement of blacks in violent crime is most dramatically revealed in the data on city arrests collected by the Federal Bureau of Investigation. Thirteen percent of the population in cities are black, but, as reported in Table 1, blacks account for almost half of all city arrests for violent crimes. In particular, more than half of those arrested in cities for murders and nonnegligent manslaughter and more than half of those arrested for forcible rape are black, as are 61 percent of those arrested for robbery. The rate of black crime is even greater in large urban areas where blacks constitute a greater percentage of the population. In 1977, 28 percent of the population in central cities in metropolitan areas of 1,000,000 or more were black; and though the Federal Bureau of Investigation's *Uniform Crime Reports* does not provide data on arrest by *size of city and race*, the depth and social significance of the problems of violent black crimes in large urban areas can perhaps be revealed by examining data on murder rates provided by the Chicago Police Department.[17]

TABLE 1. City Arrest, Percent Distribution by Race

Percent Distribution*

Offense Charge	WHITE	BLACK	AMERICAN INDIAN OR ALASKAN NATIVE	PACIFIC ISLANDER
Murder and nonnegligent manslaughter	43.8	54.8	.7	.7
Forcible rape	45.0	53.5	.8	.5
Robbery	38.0	60.8	.5	.7
Aggravated assault	58.3	40.1	1.0	.6
Burglary	65.6	33.2	.7	.6
Larceny-theft	65.7	32.3	1.0	1.0
Motor vehicle theft	64.7	33.3	.9	.3
Arson	75.3	23.9	.4	.4
Violent crime†	49.9	48.7	.8	.6
Property crime**	65.7	32.5	.9	.9
Crime total index	62.6	35.7	.9	.8

SOURCE: U.S. Department of Justice, Federal Bureau of Investigation, *Uniform Crime Reports for the United States, 1980* (Washington, D.C.: Government Printing Office, 1981).
*Because of rounding, the percentages may not all total.
†Violent crimes are offenses of murder, forcible rape, robbery, and aggravated assault.
**Property crimes are offenses of burglary, larceny-theft, motor vehicle theft, and arson.

The 1970s was a violent decade for the city of Chicago. The number of violent crimes began to rise in the mid-1960s and reached record levels in the 1970s. The number of homicides climbed from 395 in 1965 to 810 in 1970. During the severe recession year of 1974, the city was rocked by a record 970 murders (30.8 per 100,000 population) and 4,071 shooting assaults. Despite the record number of homicides in Chicago in 1974, of the ten largest cities in the United States Chicago's murder rate was actually exceeded by those in Detroit (51.9), Cleveland (46.3), Washington (38.3), and Baltimore (34.1). In 1979, another recession year, 856 murders were committed in Chicago, the second highest ever, yet the rate of 28.6 per 100,000 placed Chicago only sixth among the ten largest urban centers in the country (see Table 2).

In Chicago, like other major urban areas, blacks are not only more likely to commit murder, they are also more likely to be murder

TABLE 2. Murder Rates and Ranks of 10 Largest U.S. Cities, 1974–1979

CITY*	Six-year Average†		1974		1975		1976		1977		1978		1979	
	RATE	RANK	RATE	RANK	RATE	RANK	RATE	RANK	RATE	RANK	RATE	RANK	RATE	RANK
Detroit	44.2	1	51.8	1	45.5	1	50.8	1	38.0	2	40.3	1	38.3	3
Cleveland	41.6	2	46.3	2	45.1	2	33.9	2	40.2	1	34.1	2	50.0	1
Washington	29.9	3	38.3	3	32.9	3	27.1	3	28.0	3	28.4	4	24.6	9
Houston	28.4	4	26.2	6	22.3	7	22.3	7	24.4	6	30.9	3	41.4	2
Baltimore	27.8	5	34.1	4	30.6	4	23.8	6	22.4	7	24.8	7	31.1	5
Chicago	27.5	6	30.8	5	26.4	6	26.5	5	26.9	4	26.0	6**	28.6	6
Dallas	27.1	7	22.5	8	27.4	5	26.7	4	25.5	5	26.0	5**	34.4	4
New York	22.4	8	21.4	9	22.6	8	20.9	8	21.7	8	21.8	9	25.8	7
Los Angeles	20.2	9	17.1	10	18.8	10	17.8	9	19.0	9	22.9	8	25.7	8
Philadelphia	20.1	10	22.8	7	19.4	9	17.5	10	18.1	10	20.1	10	22.9	10

SOURCE: *The Chicago Reporter: A Monthly Information Service on Racial Issues in Metropolitan Chicago,* Vol. 10, No. 1 (January 1981).

†Average of murder rates (murders per 100,000 population) for all years since 1974.

*Ten largest U.S. cities as of 1970 census.

**Chicago's rate was 25.98, Dallas's rate was 26.01.

victims. During the 1970s, eight of every ten murderers in Chicago were black and almost seven of every ten murder victims were black.[18] In 1979, 547 blacks, 180 Hispanics, and 120 whites (other than Hispanic) were murder victims; and 573 of the murders were committed by blacks, 169 by Hispanics, and 64 by whites. In 1970 only 56 of the murder victims were Hispanic as compared with 135 white and 607 black victims. Demographic changes in the Hispanic population accounted in major measure for their increased involvement in violent crimes (a matter that will be discussed later in greater detail).

It is significant to note that homicides in Chicago were overwhelmingly intraracial or intraethnic. In fact, throughout the 1970s, 98 percent of black homicides were committed by other blacks, 75 percent of Hispanic homicides were committed by other Hispanics, and 51.5 percent of white homicides were committed by other whites.

In examining the figures on homicide in Chicago it is important to recognize that the rates vary significantly according to the economic status of the community, with the highest rates associated with the communities of the underclass. For example, "In 1980, through mid-November, more than half of the murders and shooting assaults in Chicago were concentrated in seven of the city's 24 police districts. . . . These are areas with heavy concentration of low-income black or Latino residents. . . ."[19]

The most violent area is the heavily black Wentworth Avenue police district on the South Side of Chicago. Within this four-square-mile area an average of more than 90 murders and 400 shooting assaults occur each year; and one of every 10 murders and shooting assaults in Chicago occurred there during the 1970s. "Through mid-November of 1980, Wentworth saw 82 murders (almost 12 percent of the citywide total) and 309 shooting assaults (11.3 percent of the city total)."[20]

The Wentworth figures on violent crime are high mainly because the Robert Taylor Homes, the largest public housing project in the city of Chicago, is located there. Robert Taylor Homes includes 28 16-story buildings covering 92 acres. The official population in 1980 was 19,785, but, according to one report, "there are an additional 5,000 to 7,000 adult residents who are not registered with the housing authority."[21] In 1980, all of the more than 4,200 official households were black and 72 percent of the official population were minors. Ninety percent of the families with children were headed by women. The median family income was $4,925. Eighty-one percent of the households received Aid to Families with Dependent Children (AFDC).[22] Unemployment in Robert Taylor Homes was estimated to be 47 percent in 1980.[23] Although only slightly more than one-half of one percent of Chicago's more than three million people live in Robert Taylor Homes, "11 percent of the city's murders, 9 percent of its rapes, and 10 percent of its aggravated assaults were committed in the project."[24]

Robert Taylor Homes is by no means the only violent housing project in Chicago. For example, Cabrini-Green, the second largest, experienced a rash of violent crimes in early 1981 that prompted Chicago's former Mayor Jane Byrne to take up residence for several weeks to help stem the tide. Cabrini-Green consists of 81 high- and low-rise buildings covering 70 acres on Chicago's near-North side. In 1980, 13,626 people, nearly all black, were officially registered there; but like Robert Taylor Homes, there are many more who reside there but do not show up in the records of the Chicago Housing Authority (CHA). Minors were 67 percent of the official population; 90 percent of the families with children were headed by women. Seventy-eight percent of the 3,591 households were on welfare in 1980 and 70 percent received AFDC.[25]

In a nine-week period that began in early January 1981, 10 Cabrini-Green residents were murdered; 35 were wounded by gunshots, including random sniping; and more than 50 firearms were seized by the Chicago police, "the tip of an immense illegal arsenal," according to police.[26]

URBAN FAMILY DISSOLUTION AND WELFARE
DEPENDENCY

What is true of Robert Taylor Homes and Cabrini-Green is typical of all the CHA housing projects. In 1980, of the 27,178 families with children living in CHA projects, only 2,982, or 11 percent, were husband-and-wife families. And 67 percent of the family households received AFDC.[27] But family dissolution and welfare dependency are not confined to public housing projects. Rather the projects simply magnify such problems, problems that permeate inner-city neighborhoods and to a lesser extent metropolitan areas generally.

The increase in the number of families headed by women was dramatic during the 1970s. Whereas the total number of families grew by 12 percent from 1970 to 1979, the number headed by women increased by 51 percent. Moreover, the number of female-headed families with one or more of their children present in the home increased by 81 percent. If the change in family composition was notable for all families in the 1970s, it was close to phenomenal for black and Hispanic families. Whereas families headed by white women increased in number by 42.1 percent, families headed by black and Hispanic women increased in number by 72.9 and 76.5 percent respectively.[28]

In 1965, Moynihan expressed great concern that one quarter of all black families were headed by women. That figure had increased to 28 percent in 1969, to 37 percent in 1976, to 39 percent in 1977, and finally to a staggering 42 percent in 1980. By contrast, only 12 percent of white families and 22 percent of Hispanic families were maintained by women in 1980 even though each group recorded a significant increase in female-headed families during the 1970s.[29]

It is important to point out that in 1979, 73 percent of all female householders lived in metropolitan areas, with 41 percent living in central cities and 32 percent in the adjacent suburbs; moreover, of those who were black and Hispanic, 80 and 90 percent respectively resided in metropolitan areas, with 64 percent of each group living in the central city.[30] It is also significant to note that the women are younger than in previous years. For example, from 1970 to 1979, the number of female heads of families 45 years or older increased by 525,000 (17 percent), while those under 45 years of age increased by 2.3 million (96 percent), resulting in a decrease in the median age from 48.2 years in 1970 to 42.0 years in 1979. This represented a change in median age from 50.2 to 43.7 for white women maintaining families, from 41.3 to 37.9 for black women, and from 40.2 to 36.1 for Hispanic women.[31]

Even if a female householder is employed full time, her earnings are usually significantly less than a male worker's and are not likely to be supplemented with income from a second full-time employed person in the household. The economic situation of women heads of families who are not employed, including those who have never been employed or have dropped out of the labor force to become full-time mothers or are employed only part time, is often desperate.[32] In 1980, the median income of female-headed families ($10,408) was only 45 percent of the median income of married-couple families ($23,141).[33] And the median income of families headed by black women ($7,425) was only 40 percent of the median income of married-couple black families ($18,592).[34] In 1978, roughly 3.2 million families received incomes of less than $4,000 and more than half (54 percent) of these families were headed by women.[35]

The association between level of family income and family composition is even more pronounced among black families. As shown in Table 3, whereas 80.3 percent of all black families who had incomes under $4,000 were headed by women in 1978, only 7.7 percent who had incomes of $25,000 or more were maintained by women; in metropolitan areas, the difference was even greater: 85.1 versus 7.6 percent. As shown in Table 3, the relationship between level of income and type of family is much stronger for blacks than for whites.

Economic hardship has become an even greater problem for black female-headed families: only 30 percent of all *poor* black families were headed by women in 1959, but by 1978 the proportion reached 74 percent (though it dipped to 71 percent in 1980). By contrast, 38 percent of all poor white families and 48 percent of all poor Hispanic families were headed by women.[36]

The proportion of black children in husband-wife families consequently dropped significantly, from 64 percent in 1970 to 56 percent in 1974 to 48.5 percent in 1978. Moreover, 41.2 percent of black children under 18 years of age and 42.5 of all those under six years of age were living in families whose incomes were below the poverty level in 1978 (Table 4). Even more astonishing, 32.1 percent of all black children under 18 years of age and 33.6 percent of those under six years of age were living in poor, female-headed families in 1978.[37]

The rise of female-headed families among blacks corresponds closely with the increase in the rate of out-of-wedlock births. Only 15 percent of all births to black women in 1959 were out of wedlock; roughly 25 percent in 1965 were; and more than half (53 percent) in 1978 were out of wedlock, six times greater than the white ratio of 8.7.[38] Indeed, despite the great difference in total population, the number of out-of-wedlock black births (293,400) actually exceeded

TABLE 3. Proportion of Families by Race, Income Level, Female Head, and Metropolitan Residence 1978

Subject	All Families (%)	Female Heads (%)	Families in Metropolitan Areas (%)	Metropolitan Families with Female Heads (%)
Black				
Under $4,000	15.9	80.3	71.1	85.1
$4,000 to $6,999	16.2	63.8	74.7	71.2
$7,000 to $10,999	18.3	46.2	74.8	50.7
$11,000 to $15,999	16.7	28.9	76.3	31.8
$16,000 to $24,999	19.2	15.3	82.7	15.4
$25,000 and over	13.4	7.7	88.5	7.6
White				
Under $4,000	4.3	42.1	53.3	50.2
$4,000 to $6,999	4.7	27.6	56.2	33.7
$7,000 to $10,999	12.7	19.5	57.7	21.8
$11,000 to $15,999	16.9	13.4	59.9	16.7
$16,000 to $24,999	28.8	7.2	66.0	8.5
$25,000 and over	29.5	2.9	75.4	3.1

SOURCE: U.S. Bureau of the Census, *Current Population Reports*, Consumer Income, Series P-60, No. 123 (Washington, D.C.: Government Printing Office, 1980).

TABLE 4. Percentage of All Related Children in Families Below the Poverty Level by Race and Family Type

	White Families			Black Families		
SUBJECT	MALE HEADED (%)	FEMALE HEADED (%)	TOTAL (%)	MALE HEADED (%)	FEMALE HEADED (%)	TOTAL (%)
Related Children Under 18	5.9	5.1	11.0	9.1	32.1	41.2
Related Children Under 6	6.8	5.6	12.4	8.9	33.6	42.5

SOURCE: U.S. Bureau of the Census, *Current Population Reports*, Consumer Income, Series P-60, No. 124 (Washington, D.C.: Government Printing Office, 1980).

the number of out-of-wedlock white births (233,600) in 1978. Although the proportion of black births that are out of wedlock is, in part, a function of the general decline in marital fertility among blacks (a point which is further discussed below), it is also a reflection of the growing prevalence of births among black teenagers outside of marriage. In 1978, 83 percent of the births to black teenagers (and 29 percent of the births to white teenagers) were out of wedlock. Teenagers accounted for almost half (45.8 percent) of out-of-wedlock births in 1978.[39]

Again we may focus on Chicago to see the dimensions of this problem in a large, northern urban area. In 1978 almost 42 percent of the births in Chicago were out of wedlock, more than twice the percentage of 1968; 76 percent of the 12,008 babies born to Chicago teenagers in 1978 were outside of marriage. Just as in other cities across the country, out-of-wedlock births in Chicago are closely related to race. In 1978, 67 percent of the black births in Chicago were outside of marriage (in contrast to 17 percent of the white births); more than 80 percent of Chicago's total out-of-wedlock births were to black women.[40]

These developments have, to repeat, significant implications for the problems of dependency. In 1977 the proportion of families receiving AFDC who were black (43 percent) slightly exceeded the proportion who were white other than Spanish (42.5 percent) despite the far greater white population.[41] It is estimated that about 60 percent of the children who are born outside of marriage and are alive and not adopted receive welfare.[42] A 1979 unpublished study by the Department of City Planning in New York found that 75 percent of all the children born out of wedlock in that city during the previous 18 years are AFDC recipients.[43] And a study by the Urban Institute reported that "more than half of all AFDC assistance in 1975 was paid to women who were or had been teenage mothers."[44]

I focus on female-headed families and out-of-wedlock births because they have become inextricably connected with poverty and dependency. The sharp rise in these and other forms of social dislocation in the inner city (including joblessness and violent crime) presents a difficult challenge to liberal policymakers. Because there has been so little recent systematic research on and a paucity of thoughtful explanations of these problems, racial stereotypes of life and behavior in the urban ghetto have not been sufficiently rebutted. The physical and social isolation of residents in the inner city is thereby reinforced. The fundamental question remains: why have the social conditions of the urban underclass deteriorated so rapidly since the mid-1960s?

TOWARD A COMPREHENSIVE EXPLANATION OF URBAN SOCIAL DISLOCATIONS

There is no single explanation for the racial or ethnic variations in the rates of social problems I have described. But I would like to suggest several interrelated explanations that range from those fairly obvious to students of social science to ones that most observers overlook altogether. In the process, I hope to be able to show that these problems are not intractable, as some people have suggested, and that their solution calls for imaginative and comprehensive programs of economic and social reform that are in sharp contrast to the current approaches to social policy in America based on short-term political considerations.

THE EFFECTS OF HISTORIC AND CONTEMPORARY DISCRIMINATION

Discrimination is the most frequently invoked explanation of social dislocations in the inner city. However, proponents of the discrimination thesis often fail to make a distinction between the effects of historic discrimination, that is, discrimination prior to the mid-twentieth century, and the effects of contemporary discrimination, that is, discrimination after the mid-twentieth century. They therefore find it difficult to explain why the economic position of the black underclass actually deteriorated during the very period in which the most sweeping antidiscrimination legislation and programs were enacted and implemented.[45] And their emphasis on discrimination becomes even more vulnerable in light of the economic progress of the black middle class during the same period.

There is no doubt that contemporary discrimination has contributed to or aggravated the social and economic problems of poor blacks. But is discrimination greater today than in 1948 when, as shown in Table 5, black unemployment was less than half (5.9 per-

TABLE 5. Unemployment Rates by Race for Persons Sixteen Years and Over, 1948–1980

Unemployment Rate

YEAR	BLACK AND OTHER RACES*	WHITE	RATIO OF BLACK AND OTHER RACES TO WHITE
1948	5.9%	3.5%	1.7
1949	8.9	5.6	1.6
1950	9.0	4.9	1.8
1951	5.3	3.1	1.7
1952	5.4	2.8	1.9
1953	4.5	2.7	1.7
1954	9.9	5.0	2.0
1955	8.7	3.9	2.2
1956	8.3	3.6	2.3
1957	7.9	3.8	2.1
1958	12.6	6.1	2.1
1959	10.7	4.8	2.3
1960	10.2	4.9	2.1
1961	12.4	6.0	2.1
1962	10.9	4.9	2.2
1963	10.8	5.0	2.2
1964	9.6	4.6	2.1
1965	8.1	4.1	2.0
1966	7.3	3.3	2.2
1967	7.4	3.4	2.2
1968	6.7	3.2	2.1
1969	6.4	3.1	2.1
1970	8.2	4.5	1.8
1971	9.9	5.4	1.8
1972	10.0	5.0	2.0
1973	8.9	4.3	2.1
1974	9.9	5.0	2.0
1975	13.9	7.8	1.8
1976	13.1	7.0	1.9
1977	13.1	6.2	2.1
1978	11.9	5.2	2.3
1979	11.3	5.1	2.2
1980	12.3	5.9	2.1

SOURCES: U.S. Bureau of the Census, "The Social and Economic Status of the Black Population in the United States, 1974," *Current Population Reports*, Series P-23, No. 48 (Washington, D.C.: Government Printing Office, 1975); and U.S. Bureau of the Census, *Statistical Abstract of the United States: 1980*, (101 ed.), (Washington, D.C.: Government Printing Office, 1980).

NOTE: The unemployment rate is the percentage of the civilian labor force that is unemployed. The black/white employment ratio is the percentage of blacks who are unemployed divided by the percentage of whites who are unemployed.

*"Black and other races" is a U.S. Census Bureau designation and is used in those cases where data are not available solely for blacks. However, because about 90% of the population designated by "Black and other races" is black, statistics reported for this category generally reflect the condition of the black population.

cent) of the rate of 1980 (12.3 percent), and the black/white unemployment ratio (1.7) was almost a quarter less than the ratio of 1980 (2.1)? Although labor economists have noted the shortcomings of the official unemployment rates as an indicator of the economic well-being of groups, nonetheless these rates have generally been accepted as one significant measure of relative disadvantage.[46] It is, therefore, important to point out that it was not until 1954 that the two-to-one unemployment ratio between blacks and whites was reached, and that since 1954, despite shifts from good to bad economic years, the ratio between black and white unemployment has shown very little change. There are obviously many reasons for the higher levels of black joblessness since the mid-1950s, but to suggest contemporary discrimination as the main factor is to obscure the impact of demographic and economic changes and to leave unanswered the question of why black unemployment was lower not after but prior to 1950 (see Table 5).

The question has also been raised about the relationship of contemporary discrimination within the criminal justice system to the disproportionate rates of black crime. An answer was provided by Alfred Blumstein's important study of the racial disproportionality of America's state prison populations.[47] Blumstein found that 80 percent of the disproportionate black incarceration rates throughout the decade of the 1970s could be attributed to the disproportionate number of blacks as arrestees; and that the more serious the offense, the stronger the association between arrest rates and incarceration rates (for example, 97.2 percent, 84.6 percent, and 94.8 percent of the disproportionate black incarceration rates for homicide, aggravated assault, and robbery could be accounted for by the differential black arrest rates). He points out, therefore, that discrimination very likely plays a more important role in the black incarceration rates for the less serious crimes. He also notes that, "Even if the relatively large racial differences in handling these offenses were totally eliminated, however, that would not result in a major shift in the racial mix of prison populations."[48]

However, is the racial disproportionality in United States prisons largely the consequence of black bias in arrest? Recent research demonstrates consistent relationships between the distribution of crimes by race as reported in the arrest statistics of the *Uniform Crime*

Reports and the distribution based on reports by victims of assault, robbery, and rape (where contact with the offender was direct).[49] "While these results are certainly short of definitive evidence that there is not bias in arrests," states Blumstein, "they do strongly suggest that the arrest process, whose demographics we can observe, is reasonably representative of the crime process for at least these serious crime types."[50]

It should also be pointed out that, contrary to prevailing opinion, the black family showed signs of deterioration not before but after the mid-twentieth century. Until the publication of Herbert Gutman's impressive historical study on the black family, it had been widely assumed that the contemporary problems of the black family could be traced back to slavery.[51] "Stimulated by the bitter public and academic controversy" surrounding the Moynihan Report,[52] Gutman produced data that convincingly demonstrated that the black family was neither particularly disorganized during slavery nor during the early years of their first migration to the urban North, thereby suggesting that the present problems of black family disorganization are a product of more recent forces.

But are these problems mainly a consequence of contemporary discrimination or are they related to other factors that may have little or nothing to do with race? If contemporary discrimination is the main culprit, why has it produced the most severe problems of urban social dislocation, including joblessness, during the 1970s, a decade which followed an unprecedented period of antidiscrimination legislation and which ushered in the affirmative action programs? The problem, as I see it, is unraveling the effects of contemporary discrimination, on the one hand, and historic discrimination, on the other.

The argument I would like to advance is that historic discrimination is far more important than contemporary discrimination in understanding the plight of the urban underclass, but that a full appreciation of the legacy of historic discrimination is impossible without taking into account other historical and contemporary forces that have also shaped the experiences and behavior of impoverished urban minorities.

One of the major effects of historic discrimination is the presence of the large black underclass in central cities. Whereas blacks were 23 percent of the population of central cities in 1977, they constituted 46 percent of the poor in these cities.[53] In accounting for the historical developments that contributed to this concentration of urban black poverty, I would like to draw briefly upon Stanley Lieberson's recent and original study, *A Piece of the Pie: Black and White Immigrants since 1880.*[54] On the basis of a systematic analysis of early U.S. censuses and other sources of data, Lieberson concluded that in many areas of life, including the labor market, blacks were discriminated against far more severely in the early twentieth century than were the new white immigrants from southern, central, and eastern Europe. Disadvantages of skin color, in the sense that the dominant white population preferred whites over nonwhites, is one that blacks shared with Chinese, Japanese, American Indians, and other non-white groups. But skin color per se "was not an insurmountable obstacle."[55] Changes in immigration policy cut off Asian migration to America in the late nineteenth and earlier twentieth century, and the Japanese and Chinese populations, in sharp contrast to blacks, did not reach large numbers and, therefore, did not pose as great a threat to the white population. Lieberson was aware that the "response of whites to Chinese and Japanese was of the same violent and savage character in areas where they were concentrated," but he noted that "the threat was quickly stopped through changes in immigration policy."[56] Furthermore, the discontinuation of large-scale immigration from China and Japan enabled those already here to solidify networks of ethnic contact and to occupy particular occupational niches.

THE IMPORTANCE OF THE FLOW OF MIGRANTS

If differences in the size of the population account for a good deal of the difference in the economic success of blacks and Asians, it also helped to determine the dissimilar rates of progress of urban blacks and the new Europeans. The dynamic factor behind these differences, and perhaps the most important single contributor to the varying rates of urban racial and ethnic progress in the twentieth century, is the flow of migrants. Changes in immigration policy first halted Asian immigration to America and then curtailed the new European immigration. However, black migration to the urban North continued in substantial numbers several decades after the new European immigration ceased. Accordingly, there "are many more blacks who are recent migrants to the North whereas the immigrant component of the new Europeans drops off over time."[57]

The sizable and continuous migration of blacks from the South to the North coupled with the cessation of immigration from eastern, central, and southern Europe created a situation in which other whites muffled their negative disposition toward the new Europeans and focused antagonisms toward blacks; "the presence of blacks made it harder to discriminate against the new Europeans because the alternative was viewed less favorably."[58]

The flow of migrants also made it much more difficult for blacks to follow the path of both Asian Americans and the new Europeans in overcoming the negative effects of discrimination through special occupational niches. Only a small percentage of a group's total work force can be absorbed in such specialities when the group's population increases rapidly or is a sizable proportion of the total population. Furthermore, the continuing flow of migrants has had a harmful effect on the earlier-arriving or longer-standing black residents of the North. Lieberson insightfully points out that:

> Sizable numbers of newcomers raise the level of ethnic and/or racial consciousness on the part of others in the city; moreover, if these newcomers are less able to compete for more desirable positions than are the longer-standing residents, they will tend to undercut the position of other members of the group. This is because the older residents and those of higher socioeconomic status cannot totally avoid the newcomers, although they work at it through subgroup residential isolation. Hence, there is some deterioration in the quality of residential areas, schools, and the like for those earlier residents who might otherwise enjoy more fully the rewards of their mobility. Beyond this, from the point of view of the dominant outsiders, the newcomers may reinforce stereotypes and negative dispositions that affect all members of the group.[59]

In sum, because substantial black migration to the cities continued several decades after the new European and Asian migration ceased, urban blacks, having their ranks constantly replenished with poor migrants, found it much more difficult to follow the path of both the new Europeans and the Asian immigrants in overcoming the effects of discrimination.[60] The pattern of rural black migration to industrial centers has in recent years been strong in the South. In

Houston and Atlanta, to illustrate, the continuous influx of rural southern blacks, due in large measure to the increasing mechanization of agriculture, has resulted in the creation of large urban ghettos that closely resemble those in the North. The net result in both the North and South is that as the nation entered the last quarter of this century, its large urban areas continued to have a disproportionate concentration of poor blacks who have been especially vulnerable to recent structural changes in the economy.

A cause for optimism is that black migration to urban areas has been minimal in recent years. Indeed, between 1970 and 1977, there was actually a net outmigration of 653,000 from the central cities.[61] In most large cities the number of blacks increased only moderately and in some, in fact, declined. As the demographer Philip Hauser pointed out, increases in the urban black population during the 1970s "were mainly due to births."[62] This would indicate that for the first time in the twentieth century, the ranks of blacks in central cities are no longer being replenished by poor migrants. This strongly suggests that, other things being equal, the average socioeconomic status of urban blacks will show a steady improvement, including a decrease in joblessness, and with this a decrease in crime, out-of-wedlock births, single-parent homes, and welfare dependency. In other words, just as the Asian and new European immigrants benefited from a cessation of migration, so too is there reason to expect that the cessation of black migration will help to improve the socioeconomic status of urban blacks. There are other factors that affect the differential rate of ethnic progress at different periods of time, such as structural changes in the economy, size of the population, and discrimination. But I am saying that one of the major obstacles to urban black advancement—the constant flow of migrants—has been removed.[63]

Hispanics, on the other hand, appear to be migrating to urban centers in increasing numbers. The comparative status of Hispanics as an ethnic group is not entirely clear because there are no comparable figures on their types of residence in 1970. But data collected since 1974 indicate that their numbers in central cities are increasing rapidly, as a consequence of both immigration and births. Indeed, in several large cities, including New York, Los Angeles, San Francisco, San Diego, Phoenix, and Denver "they apparently outnumber American blacks."[64] Although the Hispanic population is diverse in terms of nationalities and socioeconomic status—for example, in 1979, the median income of Puerto Ricans ($8,822) was significantly less than that of Mexicans ($12,825) and Cubans ($15,326)—they are often identified collectively as a distinct ethnic community because of their common Spanish-speaking origins.[65] Accordingly, the rapid growth of the Hispanic population in urban areas, accompanied by the opposite trend for black Americans, could contribute significantly to different outcomes for these two groups in the last two decades of the twentieth century. More specifically, whereas blacks could very well record a decrease in their rates of joblessness, crime, out-of-wedlock births, single-parent homes, and welfare dependency, Hispanics could show a steady increase in each. Moreover, whereas blacks could experience a decrease in the ethnic hostility directed toward them, Hispanics, with their increasing visibility, could be victims of increasing ethnic antagonisms.

However, Hispanics are not the only ethnic group in urban America experiencing a rapid growth in population. According to the Census Bureau, Asians, who make up less than two percent of the nation's population, were the fastest-growing American ethnic group in the 1970s. Following the liberalization of immigration policies, the large influx of immigrants from Southeast Asia and, to a lesser degree, from China and South Korea has been associated with reports of increasing problems including anti-Asian sentiments, joblessness, and violent crime.[66] There are reports that the nation's economic woes have exacerbated the situation, as the newcomers compete with black, white, and Hispanic urban workers for jobs.[67] Moreover, the steady inpouring of immigrants from Taiwan, Hong Kong, and China has upset the social organization of "Chinatowns." Once homogeneous and stable, Chinatowns are now suffering from problems that have plagued inner-city black neighborhoods, such as joblessness, violent street crimes, gang warfare, school dropouts, and overcrowding.[68]

THE RELEVANCE OF CHANGES IN THE AGE STRUCTURE

If the flow of migrants is associated with the concentration of urban ethnic poverty and its social ramifications, it also has implications for the average age of an ethnic group. The higher the median age of a group, the greater its representation in higher income and professional categories. It is, therefore, not surprising that ethnic groups, such as blacks and Hispanics, who average younger than whites, also tend to have high unemployment and crime rates.[69] As revealed in Table 6, ethnic groups differed significantly in median age in 1980, ranging from 23.2 years for blacks and Hispanics to 31.3 years for whites. Moreover, only 21.3 percent of American whites are under age 15 as compared with 28.7 percent of blacks and 32 percent of Hispanics.

In the nation's central cities in 1977, the median age for whites was 30.3, for blacks 23.9, and for Hispanics 21.8. One cannot overemphasize the importance of the sudden increase of young minorities in the central cities. More specifically, the number of central-city black youths aged 16 to 19 increased by almost 75 percent from 1960 to 1969, compared with an increase of only 14 percent for white teenagers of the same age. Furthermore, young black adults in the central city (aged 20 to 24) increased in number by two thirds during the same period, three times the increase for comparable whites.[70] From 1970 to 1977 the increase in the number of young blacks slackened off somewhat but it was still substantial. For example, the number of young blacks, age 14 to 24, in the central cities of metropolitan areas of more than 1,000,000 increased by 22 percent from 1970 to 1977, and the number of Hispanics by 26 percent, while whites of this age group decreased by 7 percent.[71]

On the basis of these demographic changes alone we would expect blacks and Hispanics to contribute disproportionately to the increasing social problems of the central city such as crime. Indeed, in 1980, 55 percent of all those arrested for violent and property crimes in American cities were under 21 years of age.[72]

TABLE 6. Age Structure of Racial and Ethnic Groups, 1980

	Under Age 15	65 and Over	Median Age
United States	22.6%	11.3%	30.0%
White	21.3	12.2	31.3
Black	28.7	7.9	23.2
Spanish Origin	32.0	4.9	23.2

SOURCE: Philip M. Hauser, "The Census of 1980," *Scientific American* 245 (November 1981), p. 61.

Age is not only a factor in crime, it is also related to out-of-wedlock births, female-headed homes, and welfare dependency. Teenagers accounted for almost half of all out-of-wedlock births in 1978; moreover, 80 percent of all out-of-wedlock black births in 1978 were to teenage and young adult (20 to 24) women;[73] furthermore, the median age of female householders has decreased significantly in recent years. In 1970, black female householders, age 14 to 24, were 30.9 percent of all black women householders with children under 18, and by 1979 their proportion had increased to 37.2 percent; there were increases from 22.4 to 27.9 percent for comparable white families and from 29.9 to 38.3 for Hispanics.[74] And finally, the explosion of teenage births has contributed significantly to the increase in the number of children on AFDC from 35 per 1,000 children under 18 in 1960 to 113 per 1,000 in 1979.[75]

In short, the increases in crime, out-of-wedlock births, female-headed homes, and welfare dependency is, in part, related to the sheer explosion of young people, especially young minorities. However, as James Q. Wilson has pointed out in his analysis of the proliferation of social problems in the 1960s, a decade of general economic prosperity, "changes in the age structure of the population cannot alone account for the social dislocations" of that decade.[76] He argues, for example, that from 1960 to 1970 the rate of serious crime in the District of Columbia increased by over 400 percent, and unemployment rates by 100 percent, yet the number of young persons between 16 and 21 years of age increased by only 32 percent. Also, the number of murders in Detroit rose from 100 in 1960 to 500 in 1971, "yet the number of young persons did not quintuple."[77]

Wilson notes that the "increase in the murder rate during the 1960s was more than ten times greater than what one would have expected from the changing age structure of the population alone" and that "only 13.4 percent of the increase in arrests for robbery between 1950 and 1965 could be accounted for by the increase in the numbers of persons between the ages of ten and twenty-four."[78] Speculating on this problem, Wilson advances the hypothesis that the abrupt increase in the number of young persons has an "exponential effect on the rate of certain social problems."[79] In other words, there may be a "critical mass" of young persons such that when that mass is reached or is increased suddenly and substantially, "a self-sustaining chain reaction is set off that creates an explosive increase in the amount of crime, addiction, and welfare dependency."[80]

This hypothesis seems to be especially relevant to densely populated ghetto neighborhoods, and even more especially to those with large public housing projects. Opposition from organized community groups to the building of public housing in their neighborhoods has "led to massive, segregated housing projects, which become ghettos for minorities and the economically disadvantaged."[81] As Robert Taylor Homes and Cabrini-Green in Chicago suggest, when poor large families were placed in high-density low- and high-rise housing projects in the inner city, both family and neighborhood life suffered. Family deterioration, high crime rates, and vandalism flourished in these projects. In St. Louis, for another example, the Pruit-Igoe project, which included about 10,000 children and adults, developed serious problems five years after it opened "and it became so unlivable that it was destroyed in 1976, 22 years after it was built."[82]

Wilson's critical mass theory would seem to be demonstrated convincingly in densely populated poor neighborhoods with a heavy concentration of teenagers and young adults. As Oscar Newman has shown, the population concentration in these projects, the types of housing, and the surrounding population have interactive effects on the occurrence and types of crimes.[83] In other words, the crime problem, generally high in poor minority neighborhoods, is exacerbated by the conditions in the housing projects. Additionally, as Lee Rainwater has suggested, the character of family life in the federal housing projects "shares much with the family life of lower-class Negroes" in other parts of the city.[84] The population explosion of young minorities in the already densely settled ghetto neighborhoods during the past two decades created a situation whereby life throughout ghetto neighborhoods came close to approximating life in the housing projects.

In both the housing projects and other densely settled ghetto neighborhoods, residents have difficulty recognizing their neighbors. They are, therefore, less likely to be concerned for them or to engage in reciprocal guardian behavior. The more densely a neighborhood or block is populated, the less contact and interaction among neighbors and the less likely that potential offenders can be detected or distinguished. Events in one part of the neighborhood or block tend to be of little concern to those residing in other parts.[85] And it hardly needs further emphasizing that these conditions of social disorganization are as acute as they are because of the unprecedented increase in the number of younger blacks in these neighborhoods, many of whom are not enrolled in school, are jobless, and are a source of delinquency, crime, and unrest.

The cessation of black in-migration to the central cities and the steady out-migration to the suburbs[86] will help to relieve the population pressures in the inner city. Perhaps even more significant is the fact that there were 6 percent fewer blacks in the age cohort 13 and under in 1977 than in 1970; in metropolitan areas there were 6 percent fewer blacks in that cohort and in the central cities 13 percent fewer. White children in this age category also decreased from 1970 to 1977 by even larger percentages: 14 percent overall, 17 percent in metropolitan areas, and 24 percent in the central cities. By contrast, Hispanic children, age 13 and under, *increased* during this same period by 18 percent overall, by 16 percent in metropolitan areas, and by 12 percent in the central cities. Thus, just as the change in migration flow could affect the differential rates of ethnic involvement in certain types of social problems, so too could changes in the age structure. In short, whereas whites and blacks—all other things being equal—are likely to experience a decrease in problems such as joblessness, crime, out-of-wedlock births, family dissolution, and welfare dependency in the near future, the growing Hispanic population, due to the rapid increases in births and migration, is more likely to show increasing rates of social dislocation.

THE IMPACT OF BASIC ECONOMIC CHANGES

If historic and contemporary discrimination, the flow of migrants, and demographic changes have accounted in significant ways for the social dislocations of the urban underclass, its problems have also been profoundly exacerbated by recent structural changes in the economy. The population explosion of young minorities in recent years has occurred at a time when changes in the economy pose serious problems for unskilled workers, both in and out of the labor force.

Urban minorities are particularly ·vulnerable to structural economic changes, such as the shift from goods-producing to service-producing industries, the increasing separation of the labor market into low-wage and high-wage sectors, technological innovations, and the relocation of manufacturing industries out of the central cities. These economic shifts serve to remind us that nearly all of our large and densely populated urban centers experienced their most rapid development during an earlier industrial and transportation era. Today these metropolises are undergoing an irreversible "structural transformation from centers of production and distribution of material goods to centers of administration, information exchange and service provision."[87] The character of the central city labor market has been profoundly altered in the process. As John D. Kasarda has put it: "The central cities have become increasingly specialized in jobs that have high educational prerequisites just at the time that their resident populations are increasingly composed of those with poor educational backgrounds. As a result, inner-city unemployment rates are more than twice the national average and even higher among inner-city residents who have traditionally found employment in blue-collar industries that have migrated to suburban locations."[88]

The extent to which white-collar jobs are replacing blue-collar positions in the central cities is illustrated by the data in five selected occupational categories in 18 older northern cities (Table 7). Whereas the professional, technical, and clerical employment increased by 291,055 positions from 1960 to 1970, blue-collar employment—craftsmen, operatives, and laborers—decreased by 749,774. And the overwhelming majority of the jobs lost were the higher paying blue-collar positions (craftsmen and operatives). There is also some indication that the blue-collar jobs decline in large northern cities has accelerated. During the decade of the 1970s Chicago lost more than 200,000 jobs, mostly in manufacturing. New York City lost 600,000 during the 1970s, despite the fact that the number of white-collar, professional, managerial, and clerical jobs increased in Manhattan.[89]

Roughly 60 percent of the unemployed blacks in the United States reside in central cities, mostly within the cities' low-income areas. There is much more dispersion among unemployed whites, as approximately 40 percent live in suburban areas and an additional 30

TABLE 7. Number of Jobs in Five Occupational Categories in
Eighteen Northern Cities, 1960–1970

Occupation	1960	1970	Change
Professional and technical	1,018,663	1,222,650	203,987
Clerical	1,833,483	1,920,551	87,068
Craftsmen	1,099,584	904,231	− 195,353
Operatives	1,673,811	1,188,200	− 485,611
Laborers	320,074	251,264	− 68,810

SOURCE: Adapted from John D. Kasarda, "Urbanization, Community, and the
Metropolitan Problem," in *Handbook of Contemporary Urban Life,* ed. David
Street (San Francisco: Jossey-Bass, 1978).
NOTE: "Figures are for eighteen SMSA central cities in the Northeast and North
Central regions that had populations of at least 50,000 each before 1900 and did
not annex more than 5% of their population between 1960 and 1970. The data
were computed from metropolitan place-of-work reports from the 1960 and 1970
censuses" (Kasarda, "Urbanization, Community, and the Metropolitan Problem").

percent reside in nonmetropolitan areas. Furthermore, the proportion of black men employed as laborers and service workers is twice
that of white workers. The lack of economic opportunity for lower-
class blacks means that they are forced to remain in economically
depressed ghettos and their children are forced to attend inferior
ghetto schools. This leads into a vicious cycle, as ghetto isolation and
inferior opportunities in education reinforce their disadvantaged position in the labor market and contribute to problems of crime, family
dissolution, and welfare dependency.

Indeed, the problems of joblessness among blacks, especially
poor blacks, are more acute than those of any other large ethnic
group in America. Heavily concentrated in inner cities, they have
experienced a worsening of their economic position on the basis of
nearly all the major labor-market indicators. Four of these indicators
are presented in Tables 8 through 11, and they indicate the percentage
of persons *in the labor force* who are without a job (Table 8); the
proportion who are in the labor force (Table 9); the fraction who are
employed *including those not in the labor force* (Table 10); and the
percentage who have work experience (Table 11).

More black workers are unemployed. As set out in Table 8, the
unemployment rates for both black men and black women from 1955

TABLE 8. Unemployment Rates by Race, Sex, and Age, Selected Years, 1955–1978 (%)

Race, sex, and age	1955	1965	1973	1983*
White men				
16–19	11.3	12.9	12.3	18.7
16–17	12.2	14.7	15.1	22.6
18–19	10.4	11.4	10.0	16.4
20–24	7.0	5.9	6.5	10.9
25 and over	3.0	2.5	2.4	6.4
White women				
16–19	9.1	14.0	13.0	13.6
16–17	11.6	15.0	15.7	15.9
18–19	7.7	13.4	10.9	12.1
20–24	5.1	6.3	7.0	7.6
25 and over	3.7	3.6	3.7	5.5
Black and other men				
16–19	13.4	23.3	26.9	41.5
16–17	14.8	27.1	34.4	49.2
18–19	12.9	20.2	22.1	38.2
20–24	12.4	9.3	12.6	26.9
25 and over	8.0	5.5	4.2	13.1
Black and other women				
16–19	19.2	31.7	34.5	43.9
16–17	15.4	37.8	36.5	46.5
18–19	21.4	27.8	33.3	42.9
20–24	13.0	13.7	17.6	26.1
25 and over	6.9	6.4	6.1	13.1

SOURCES: U.S. Department of Labor, *Monthly Labor Review* (Washington, D.C.: Government Printing Office, October 1979), and U.S. Department of Labor, Bureau of Labor Statistics, *Employment and Earnings* (Washington, D.C.: Government Printing Office, January 1984).
*December 1983.

to December 1983 have evidenced a far greater increase at all age levels than those of whites, with black teenage unemployment showing the sharpest increase (from 13.4 percent in 1955 to 41.5 percent in 1983 for men, and from 19.2 percent in 1955 to 43.9 percent in 1983 for women). The unemployment rates of blacks aged 20 to 24 also reached very high proportions in 1983 (26.9 percent for men and 26.1 percent for women), extending a trend of increasing joblessness that began in the mid-1960s. The significant rise in unemployment for younger blacks contrasts with the change in the rate of unemployment for blacks aged 25 years and over. Older blacks did not experience a sharp increase in unemployment until after 1973. Nonetheless, since 1955 their rates have been substantially higher than those of comparable whites.

Blacks, especially young males, are dropping out of the labor force entirely. The severe problems of joblessness for black teenagers and young adults are also seen in the data on changes in the male civilian labor-force participation rates (Table 9). The percentage of blacks who were in the labor force fell from 45.6 in 1960 to 21.1 in December 1983 for those age 16 and 17, from 71.2 to 50.3 for those age 18 and 19, and from 90.4 to 74.0 for those age 20 to 24. Even blacks age 25 to 34 experienced a decline in labor-force participation; however, the drop was not nearly as steep as that recorded by younger blacks (from 96.2 percent to 88.0 percent). Whereas black males began dropping out of the labor force in significant numbers as early as 1975, white males either maintained or increased their rate of participation until 1977, followed by sharp declines in all the age categories, except 24 to 34, from 1977 to December 1983—a period marked by a deep recession.

But even these figures do not reveal the real depth of jobless-

TABLE 9. Male Civilian Labor-Force Participation Rates for Persons 16 and Over by Race and Age for Selected Years

Age	1960	1965	1968	1970	1973	1983*
White males						
16–17	46.0	44.6	47.7	48.9	52.7	39.0
18–19	69.0	65.8	65.8	67.4	72.3	65.4
20–24	87.8	85.3	82.4	83.3	85.8	82.9
25–34	97.7	97.4	97.2	96.7	96.3	94.2
Black males and other males						
16–17	45.6	39.3	37.9	34.8	33.4	21.1
18–19	71.2	66.7	63.3	61.8	61.4	50.3
20–24	90.4	89.8	85.0	83.5	81.8	74.0
25–34	96.2	95.7	95.0	93.7	91.7	88.0

SOURCES: U.S. Department of Labor, *Employment and Training Report of the President* (Washington, D.C.: Government Printing Office, 1978), and U.S. Department of Labor, Bureau of Labor Statistics, *Employment and Earnings* (Washington, D.C.: Government Printing Office, January 1984).
*December 1983.

TABLE 10. Employment-Population Ratios of Civilian Black and White Males for Selected Years

Age	1955	1965	1973	1983*
Black males				
16–19	55.7	39.4	33.9	20.9
16–17	41.7	28.8	22.0	10.7
18–19	66.0	53.4	27.9	31.1
20–24	78.6	81.6	71.4	54.1
White males				
16–19	52.0	47.1	54.4	45.5
16–17	42.0	38.0	44.8	33.2
18–19	64.2	58.3	65.1	57.3
20–24	80.4	80.2	80.2	75.3

SOURCES: U.S. Department of Labor, *Monthly Labor Review* (Washington, D.C.: Government Printing Office, October 1979), and U.S. Department of Labor, Bureau of Labor Statistics, *Employment and Earnings* (Washington, D.C.: Government Printing Office, January 1984).
*December 1983.

ness among younger blacks. *Only a minority of out-of-prison black youths are employed.* As shown in Table 10, the ratio of the employed civilian population to the total civilian noninstitutional population among young black males has shown a steep and steady decline since 1955, whereas among white males it has increased slightly for teenagers and virtually not at all for ages 20 to 24 until 1978. However, the years of recession after 1978 took their toll on white workers, as seen in the noticeable increase in joblessness for all the age categories by December 1983. The fact that fewer than 21 percent of all black male teenagers were employed in December 1983 and only 54 percent of all black young adult males (age 20 to 24) reveals a problem of joblessness for young black men that has reached catastrophic proportions.

Finally, the bleak employment picture for young blacks is further demonstrated by the data on work experience (Table 11). *Fewer black youths are obtaining any work experience at all.* Whereas the proportion of white male teenagers and young adults with work experience has changed very little from 1966 to 1977, and the proportion of white female teenagers and young adults with work experiences has increased, the proportion of blacks with work experience has decreased from 67.3 to 47.2 percent for male teenag-

TABLE 11. Percent of the Population 16 to 24 Years of Age with Work Experience During the Year by Race and Sex, 1966–1977

	White				Black			
	MEN		WOMEN		MEN		WOMEN	
	age 16–19	age 20–24	age 16–19	age 20–24	age 16–19	age 20–24	age 16–19	age 20–24
1966	75.9	93.8	59.8	69.8	67.3	90.1	48.9	67.2
1967	76.0	90.5	61.3	71.2	69.3	88.2	49.8	69.2
1968	77.2	91.5	59.9	73.1	65.2	87.4	51.6	69.2
1969	75.5	90.2	61.3	74.1	67.3	87.2	40.0	69.7
1970	72.7	90.1	60.1	73.9	58.3	80.8	44.6	67.0
1971	70.5	89.6	57.8	72.4	54.7	81.1	39.6	63.2
1972	72.1	91.8	58.8	75.0	50.2	83.5	37.8	63.7
1973	75.1	93.0	64.1	76.2	57.6	85.5	41.8	62.8
1974	75.0	92.7	64.0	77.0	56.0	82.0	41.8	65.1
1975	70.1	90.5	62.0	75.7	47.2	77.9	36.9	61.5
1976	72.4	92.8	63.6	78.5	46.1	79.8	34.1	60.3
1977	73.8	93.2	64.8	79.0	47.2	76.7	37.5	63.6

SOURCE: U.S. Department of Labor, *Monthly Labor Review* (Washington, D.C.: Government Printing Office, October 1979).

ers, from 90.1 to 76.7 percent for male young adults, from 48.9 to 37.5 percent for female teenagers, and from 67.2 to 63.6 for female young adults.

Thus, the combined indicators of unemployment, labor-force participation, employment-population ratios, and work experience reveal a disturbing picture of black joblessness, especially among younger blacks. If the evidence presented in recent longitudinal research is correct, then joblessness during youth will have a long-term harmful effect on later chances in the labor market.[90]

The changes brought about by the cessation of migration to the central city and the sharp drop in the number of black children under age 13 may increase the likelihood that the economic situation of blacks as a group will improve in the near future. However, the present problems of black joblessness are so overwhelming that it is just as likely that only a major program of economic reform will be sufficient to prevent a significant segment of the urban underclass from being permanently locked out of the mainstream of the American occupational system.

THE ROLE OF ETHNIC CULTURE

In focusing on different explanations of the social dislocations of the urban underclass, I have yet to say anything about the role of ethnic culture. Even after considering the matter of discrimination, flow of migrants, changes in ethnic demography, structural changes in the economy, and the problem of joblessness which is related to all of these factors, some would still maintain that ethnic differences in culture account in large measure for ethnic variations in certain social problems. But any cultural explanation of group differences in behavior would have to consider, among other things, the often considerable variation within groups on several aspects of behavior. For example, as earlier pointed out, whereas only 7 percent of urban black families with incomes of $25,000 and more in 1978 were headed by women, 85 percent of those with incomes below $4,000 were headed by women. The higher the economic position of black families, the greater the percentage of two-parent households. Moreover, the proportion of black children born out of wedlock is partly a function of the sharp decrease in fertility among married blacks (i.e., husband and wife families), who have on the average a higher economic status in the black community. By treating blacks and other ethnics as monolithic groups, we lose sight of the fact that high-income blacks, Hispanics, and Indians have even *fewer* children than their counterparts in the general population.[91]

But in the face of some puzzling facts concerning rates of welfare and crime in the 1960s, the cultural explanation seems to have some validity to some observers. For example, from the Great Depression to 1960, unemployment accounted in large measure for dependency. Indeed, the correlation between the nonwhite male unemployment and the rate of new AFDC cases was very nearly perfect during this period.[92] As the nonwhite male unemployment rate increased, the rate of new AFDC cases increased; as the former decreased, the latter correspondingly decreased. Commenting on this relationship, Moynihan stated: "The correlation was among the strongest known to social science. It could not be established that the men who lost their jobs were the ones who left their families, but the mathematical relationship of the two statistical series—unemployment rates and new AFDC cases—was astonishingly close."[93] Suddenly, however, the relationship began to weaken at the beginning of the 1960s, had vanished by 1963, and had completely reversed itself during the remainder of that decade, which saw a steady decline in the rate of nonwhite male unemployment and a steady increase in the number of new AFDC cases.[94]

Some observers quickly seized on these figures to suggest that welfare dependency had become a cultural trait because, they argued, even during periods of an economic upswing welfare rates among minorities were increasing. However, upon closer inspection we see that even though nonwhite male unemployment did drop during the 1960s, the percentage of nonwhite males who dropped out of the labor force increased steadily throughout the 1960s (see Table 8), thereby maintaining the association between economic dislocation and welfare dependency. A similar argument concerning crime was advanced in a recent empirical study that demonstrated that labor-force participation rates, not unemployment rates, explain the increase in crime among youth during the last half of the 1960s.[95]

A well-founded sociological assumption is that different ethnic behavior and outcomes are largely reflections of different opportunities for and external obstacles against advancement, ones determined by different historical and material circumstances, including different times of arrival and patterns of settlement in the United States.[96] Moreover, even if we were able to show that different behavior is related to differences in ethnic group values, mobility, and success, this hardly constitutes an adequate explanation. By revealing cultural differences we reach only the first step in a proper sociological investigation. The analysis of their social and historical basis represents the succeeding and, indeed, more fundamental steps.[97]

In short, cultural values do not *determine* behavior or success. Rather, cultural values grow out of specific circumstances and life changes and reflect one's position in the class structure. Thus, if lower-class blacks have low aspirations or do not plan for the future, it is not ultimately the result of a different cultural norm but because they are responding to restricted opportunities, a bleak future, and feelings of resignation originating in bitter personal experiences. Accordingly, behavior described as social pathological and associated with lower-class ethnics should not be analyzed as a cultural aberration but as a symptom of class inequality. If impoverished conditions produced exceedingly high rates of crime among first-generation Irish, Italians, and Jews, what would have been the outcome of these groups had they been mired in poverty for five to ten generations, as have been so many black families in the United States?[98]

Responses to recurrent situations to which people have to adapt take the form of behavior patterns, norms, and aspirations. As economic and social opportunities change, new behavioral solutions originate, become patternized, and are later upheld and complemented by norms. If new conditions emerge, both the behavior patterns and the norms eventually undergo change. As Herbert Gans has put it: "Some behavioral norms are more persistent than others, but over the long run, all of the norms and aspirations by which people live are nonpersistent: they rise and fall with changes in situations."[99]

CONCLUSION

To hold, as I do, that changes in social and economic situations will bring about changes in behavior patterns and norms raises the issue of what public policy can deal effectively with the social dislocations that have plagued the urban underclass for the past several decades. Any significant reduction of problems of joblessness and related problems of crime, out-of-wedlock births, single-parent homes, and welfare dependency will call for a far more comprehensive program of economic and social reform than Americans have usually regarded as appropriate or desirable. In short, it will require a radicalism that neither Democratic nor Republican parties have been as yet realistic enough to propose.

A shift away from the convenient focus on "racism" would probably result in a greater appreciation and understanding of the complex factors that account for the recent increases in the rates of social dislocation among the urban underclass. Although current discrimination undoubtedly contributes to their persistent social problems, in the last 20 years these problems have been more profoundly affected by shifts in the American economy from goods-manufacturing to service-producing industries that have produced incredible joblessness in the inner city and that have exacerbated conditions generated by the historic flow of migrants to the large metropolises; and by changes in the urban minority age structure and consequent population changes in the central city.

For all these reasons, the urban underclass has not significantly benefited from race-specific policy programs such as affirmative action, which have helped in the advancement of trained and educated blacks. Their economic and social plights call for public policies that benefit all the poor, not just the minority poor. These will need to be policies that address the broader problems of generating full employment, of achieving effective welfare reform, and of developing sustained and balanced urban economic growth. Unless such problems are seriously addressed, we should hold little hope for the effectiveness of other policies, including race-specific ones, in significantly reducing social dislocations among the urban underclass.

I am reminded, in this connection, of Bayard Rustin's plea in the early 1960s that blacks ought to recognize the importance of *fundamental* economic reform and the need for a broad-based coalition to achieve it. It is more evident now than at any time in this last half of the twentieth century that blacks and other minorities will need allies to generate a reform program that could improve the conditions of the underclass. And since an effective political coalition will depend in part upon how the issues are defined, it is essential that the political message underscore the need for economic and social reform that benefits all groups in society, not just poor minorities. Politicians and civil rights organizations, as two important examples, ought to shift or expand their definition of racial problems in America and broaden the scope of suggested policy programs to address them. They would, of course, continue to stress the immediate goal of eliminating racial discrimination, but they will also have to recognize that poor minorities are profoundly affected by problems in America that go beyond racial considerations and that the dislocations which

follow have made and, if left alone, will continue to make an underclass an American reality.

NOTES

1. Kenneth B. Clark, *Dark Ghetto: Dilemmas of Social Power* (New York:
   Harper & Row, 1965); Lee Rainwater, "Crucible of Identity: The
   Negro Lower Class Family," *Daedalus* 95 (1966): 176–216; Daniel P.
   Moynihan, *The Negro Family: The Case for National Action* (Washington, D.C.: Office of Policy Planning and Research, U.S. Department of
   Labor, 1965); and "Employment, Income and the Ordeal of the Negro
   Family," in *The Negro American*, ed. Talcott Parsons and Kenneth B.
   Clark (Boston: Beacon Press, 1965), pp. 134–159.
2. Clark, *Dark Ghetto*, p. 27.
3. Rainwater, "Crucible of Identity," p. 10.
4. Clark, *Dark Ghetto*, p. 81.
5. For an excellent discussion of the "Moynihan Report" and the controversy surrounding it, see Lee Rainwater and William L. Yancey, *The
   Moynihan Report and the Politics of Controversy* (Cambridge, Mass.:
   M.I.T. Press, 1967).
6. *Ibid.*
7. E. Franklin Frazier, *The Negro Family in the United States* (Chicago:
   University of Chicago Press, 1939); Kenneth B. Clark, "Youth in the
   Ghetto: A Study of the Consequences of Powerlessness and a Blueprint
   for Change" (1964), Harlem Youth Opportunities (HARYOU) Report;
   and Bayard Rustin, "From Protest to Politics: The Future of the Civil
   Rights Movement," *Commentary* 39 (1965): 25–31.
8. Moynihan, *The Negro Family*, pp. 5–6.
9. *Ibid.*, p. 48.
10. It is interesting to point out that President Lyndon Johnson's widely
    heralded Howard University commencement speech on human rights,
    which was partly drafted by Moynihan, drew heavily from the "Moyni-
    han Report" when it was still an in-house document. The speech was
    uniformly praised by black civil rights leaders.
11. See, for example, Joyce Ladner, ed., *The Death of White Sociology* (New
    York: Random House, 1973); Robert B. Hill, *The Strength of Black
    Families* (New York: Emerson Hall, 1972); Nathan Hare, "The Chal-
    lenge of a Black Scholar," *Black Scholar* 1 (1969): 58–63; Abd-al Hakim
    Ibn Alkalimat (Gerald McWorter), "The Ideology of Black Social Sci-
    ence," *Black Scholar* 1 (1969): 28–35; and Robert Staples, "The Myth
    of the Black Matriarchy," *Black Scholar* 2 (1970): 9–16.
12. Orlando Patterson, *Ethnic Chauvinism: The Reactionary Response* (New
    York: Stein and Day, 1977), p. 155.
13. U.S. Department of Justice, *Uniform Crime Reports for the United States,
    1980* (Washington, D.C.: Government Printing Office, 1981).

14. Norval Morris and Michael Tonry, "Blacks, Crime Rates and Prisons —A Profound Challenge," *Chicago Tribune,* August 18, 1980, p. 2.

15. U.S. Department of Justice, *Uniform Crime Reports.*

16. Morris and Tonry, "Blacks, Crime Rates and Prisons."

17. My discussion of violent crime in Chicago is indebted to Rick Greenberg, "Murder Victims: Most Blacks, Latinos Now Surpassing Whites," *Chicago Reporter: A Monthly Information Service on Racial Issues in Metropolitan Chicago* 10, no. 1 (January 1981): 1 and 4–7.

18. As pointed out in the *Chicago Reporter,* "In its yearly murder analysis, the Chicago Police Department defines the killer of an individual as someone who has been arrested for the crime or is a prime suspect. Because there are a number of unsolved murders each year, calculations of 'who killed whom' are based only on the number of murders in which the police knew or suspected whom the offender was, not on the total number of homicide victims in any racial or ethnic group." Greenberg, "Murder Victims," p. 7.

19. *Ibid.,* p. 6.

20. *Ibid.*

21. Nathaniel Sheppard, Jr., "Chicago Project Dwellers Live Under Siege," *New York Times,* August 6, 1980, p. A14.

22. Chicago Housing Authority, *Statistical Report, 1980* (Chicago Housing Authority Executive Office, 1981).

23. Sheppard, "Chicago Project Dwellers."

24. *Ibid.,* p. A14.

25. Chicago Housing Authority, *Statistical Report, 1980.*

26. Paul Galloway, "Nine Weeks, Ten Murders," *Chicago Sun-Times,* March 22, 1981, pp. 66–67.

27. Chicago Housing Authority, *Statistical Report, 1980.*

28. U.S. Bureau of the Census, "Families Maintained by Female Households, 1970–79," *Current Population Reports,* Series P-23, No. 107 (Washington, D.C.: Government Printing Office, 1980).

29. Based on calculations from *ibid.;* U.S. Bureau of the Census, "Money Income and Poverty Status of Families and Persons in the United States, 1978," *Current Population Reports,* Series P-60, No. 120 (Washington, D.C.: Government Printing Office, 1979); U.S. Bureau of the Census, "Money Income and Poverty Status of Persons in the United States, 1977," *Current Population Reports,* Series P-60, No. 116 (Washington, D.C.: Government Printing Office, 1978); U.S. Bureau of the Census, "The Social and Economic Status of the Black Population in the United States, 1970," *Current Population Reports,* Series P-23, No. 38 (Washington, D.C.: Government Printing Office, 1971); and U.S. Bureau of the Census, "Money Income and Poverty Status of Families and Persons in the United States, 1980," *Current Population Reports,* Series P-60, No. 127 (Washington, D.C.: Government Printing Office, 1981).

30. U.S. Bureau of the Census, "Families Maintained by Female Households, 1970–79."
31. *Ibid.*
32. U.S. Bureau of the Census, "Money Income and Poverty Status of Families, 1980."
33. *Ibid.*
34. *Ibid.*
35. U.S. Bureau of the Census, "Families Maintained by Female Households, 1970–79."
36. Based on calculations from U.S. Bureau of the Census, "Families Maintained by Female Households, 1970–79."
37. Based on calculations from U.S. Bureau of the Census, "Characteristics of the Population of the Poverty Level, 1978," *Current Population Reports,* Series P-60, No. 124 (Washington, D.C.: Government Printing Office, 1978) and U.S. Bureau of the Census, "Families Maintained by Female Households, 1970–79."
38. National Center for Health Statistics, "Final Natality Statistics, 1979," *Monthly Vital Statistics Report,* U.S. Department of Health and Human Services (Washington, D.C.: Government Printing Office, 1981).
39. *Ibid.*
40. Nancy Fisher Schlute, "Illegitimacy Soars, Begets Legacy of Health, Social Hardships," *Chicago Reporter: A Monthly Information Service on Racial Issues in Metropolitan Chicago* 9, no. 6 (June 1980): 1 and 4–6.
41. U. S. Department of Health and Human Services, "Aid to Families with Dependent Children, 1977," *Recipient Characteristics Study,* Social Security Administration Office of Policy (Washington, D.C.: Government Printing Office, 1980).
42. Kristin Moore and Steven B. Cardwell, *Out-of-Wedlock Pregnancy and Childbearing* (Washington, D.C.: Urban Institute, 1976).
43. Reported in Ken Auletta, *The Underclass* (New York: Random House, 1982).
44. Moore and Cardwell, *Out-of-Wedlock Pregnancy.*
45. William Julius Wilson, *The Declining Significance of Race: Blacks and Changing American Institutions,* 2nd ed. (Chicago: University of Chicago Press, 1980), and "The Black Community in the 1980s: Questions of Race, Class and Public Policy," *Annals of the American Academy of Politics and Social Science* 454 (1981): 26–41.
46. Charles C. Killingsworth, Jr., *Jobs and Income for Negroes* (Ann Arbor: University of Michigan Press, 1963).
47. Alfred Blumstein, "On the Racial Disproportionality of United States' Prison Population," *Journal of Criminal Law and Criminology* 73, no. 3 (1983): 1259–1281.
48. *Ibid.,* p. 1281.
49. Michael Hindelang, "Race and Involvement in Common Law Personal Crimes," *American Sociological Review* 43, 1 (February 1978): 93–109,

and *Criminal Victimization in Eight American Cities: A Descriptive Analysis of Common Theft and Assault* (Cambridge, Mass.: Ballinger, 1976).

50. Blumstein, "Racial Disproportionality," p. 1278.
51. Herbert Gutman, *The Black Family in Slavery and Freedom, 1750–1925* (New York: Pantheon Books, 1976).
52. *Ibid.*, p. xvii.
53. U.S. Bureau of the Census, "Social and Economic Characteristics of the Metropolitan and Nonmetropolitan Population, 1977 and 1970," *Current Population Reports*, Series P-23, No. 75 (Washington, D.C.: Government Printing Office, 1978).
54. Stanley Lieberson, *A Piece of the Pie: Black and White Immigrants since 1880* (Berkeley: University of California Press, 1981).
55. *Ibid.*, p. 369.
56. *Ibid.*, p. 368.
57. *Ibid.*, p. 381.
58. *Ibid.*, p. 377.
59. *Ibid.*, p. 380.
60. Some social scientists have attempted to explain the deterioration of the position of urban blacks as their numbers increased with the argument that there was a shift in the "quality" of the migrants. But as Lieberson points out, "there is evidence to indicate that southern black migrants to the North in recent years have done relatively well when compared with northern-born blacks in terms of welfare, employment rates, earnings after background factors are taken into account and so on." *Ibid.*, p. 374.
61. U.S. Bureau of the Census, "Social and Economic Characteristics."
62. Philip M. Hauser, "The Census of 1980," *Scientific American* 245, no. 5 (1981): 61.
63. As Hauser has noted: "Data from the census indicate that blacks who migrate from nonmetropolitan areas are now going to the metropolitan centers of the South and West rather than to those of the urban North as they had in earlier decades." *Ibid.*, p. 61.
64. John Herbers, "Census Finds Blacks Gaining Majorities in Big Cities," *New York Times*, April 16, 1981, p. 1.
65. For a good discussion of socioeconomic differences among Hispanics, see Joseph P. Fitzpatrick and Lourdes Traviesco Parker, "Hispanic-Americans in the Eastern United States," *Annals of the American Academy of Political and Social Sciences* 454 (1981): 98–124.
66. Ralph Blumenthal, "Gunmen Firing Wildly Kill Three in Chinatown Bar," *New York Times*, December 24, 1982, pp. 1, 13; Richard Bernstein, "Tension and Gangs Mar the Chinatown Image," *New York Times*, December 24, 1982, p. 13; and Robert Lindsey, "Asian Americans See Growing Bias," *New York Times*, September 10, 1983, pp. 1, 9.
67. Lindsey, "Asian Americans."

68. Bernstein, "Tension and Gangs," and Blumenthal, "Gunmen Firing Wildly."
69. Thomas Sowell, *Ethnic America: A History* (New York: Basic Books, 1981).
70. U.S. Department of Labor, *Manpower Report to the President* (Washington, D.C.: Government Printing Office, 1972).
71. U.S. Bureau of the Census, "Social and Economic Characteristics."
72. U.S. Department of Justice, *Uniform Crime Reports.*
73. National Center for Health Statistics, "Final Natality Statistics, 1979."
74. U.S. Bureau of the Census, "Families Maintained by Female Households, 1970–79."
75. U.S. Bureau of the Census, *Statistical Abstract of the United States, 1980,* 101st ed. (Washington, D.C.: Government Printing Office, 1980).
76. James Q. Wilson, *Thinking About Crime* (New York: Basic Books, 1975), p. 16.
77. *Ibid.,* p. 17.
78. *Ibid.* Also see Arnold Barnett, David J. Kleitman, and Richard C. Larson, "On Urban Homicide," working paper WP-04-74, Operations Research Center, Massachusetts Institute of Technology, 1974; and Theodore Ferdinand, "Reported Index Crime Increases between 1950 and 1965 Due to Urbanization and Changes in the Age Structure of the Population Alone," in *Crimes of Violence,* ed. Donald J. Mulvihaill and Melvin Tumin, Staff Report to the National Commission on the Causes and Prevention of Violence, vol. 2 (Washington, D.C.: Government Printing Office, 1969).
79. Wilson, *Thinking About Crime,* p. 17.
80. *Ibid.,* p. 18.
81. Dennis Roncek, Ralph Bell, and Jeffrey M.A. Francik, "Housing Projects and Crime: Testing a Proximity Hypothesis," *Social Problems* 29 (1981): 151.
82. *Ibid,* p. 152. See also Rainwater, *Behind Ghetto Walls.*
83. Oscar Newman, *Defensible Space: Crime Prevention Through Urban Design* (New York: Collier Books, 1973); and *Community of Interest* (New York: Anchor Books, 1980); Roncek et al., "Housing Projects and Crime"; and Dennis Roncek, "Dangerous Places: Crime and Residential Environment," *Social Forces* 60 (1981): 74–96. Research by Roncek et al., although showing that crime is high in the housing projects, reveals that neighborhood proximity to the housing projects has a statistically significant effect only for violent crimes in adjacent poor neighborhoods.
84. Rainwater, *Behind Ghetto Walls,* p. 1.
85. Roncek, "Dangerous Places," and Newman, *Defensible Space and Community of Interest.*
86. As reported in a recent report of the U.S. Bureau of the Census, "During the 1970s blacks have accounted for an increasing large proportion

of the net increase in suburban population attributable to migration. Between 1975 and 1977, for example, black movement to suburbs accounted for 14 percent of the net increase in suburban population attributable to migration, compared with only 7 percent in the 1970–75 period. Blacks who moved to suburbs between 1976 and 1977 comprised 16 percent of the total black population living in the suburbs in 1977." U.S. Bureau of the Census, "Social and Economic Characteristics," p. 4.

87. John D. Kasarda, "Deindustrialization and the Future of American Cities" (paper delivered at the University of Chicago Symposium Honoring Morris Janowitz, Chicago, Illinois, May, 1982), p. 2.

88. John D. Kasarda, "Urbanization, Community, and the Metropolitan Problems," in *Handbook of Contemporary Urban Life*, ed. David Street (San Francisco: Jossey Bass, 1978), pp. 27–57.

89. John D. Kasarda, "The Implications of Contemporary Redistribution Trends for National Policy," *Social Science Quarterly* 61 (1980): 373–400.

90. Brian Becker and Stephen Hills, "Today's Teenage Unemployed—Tomorrow's Working Poor?" *Monthly Labor Review* (January, 1979): 67–71.

91. Sowell, *Ethnic America*, p. 7.

92. Daniel P. Moynihan, *The Politics of a Guaranteed Income* (New York: Random House, 1973).

93. *Ibid.*, p. 82.

94. *Ibid.*, pp. 82–83; and Wilson, *Thinking About Crime*, p. 9.

95. Llad Phillips, Harold L. Vatey, Jr., and Darold Maxwell, "Crime, Youth, and the Labor Market," *Journal of Political Economy* 80 (1972): 491–504.

96. Stephen Steinberg, *The Ethnic Myth: Race, Ethnicity and Class in America* (New York: Atheneum Press, 1981).

97. *Ibid.*, p. 7.

98. *Ibid.*

99. Herbert Gans, "Culture and Class in the Study of Poverty: An Approach to Anti-Poverty Research," in *Understanding Poverty: Perspectives for the Social Sciences*, ed. Daniel P. Moynihan (New York: Basic Books, 1968), pp. 201–228.

EQUAL PROTECTION, UNEQUAL JUSTICE

DIANA R. GORDON

On August 10, 1983, Miami Police Chief William Darden was indicted by a federal grand jury for racketeering. At the same time Johnny Jones, Superintendent of Schools for Dade County, was appealing his conviction for planning to put school funds to his private use. And Judge Alcee Hastings of the Federal District Court in Florida had just been acquitted of charges that he took bribes.[1] This concentration of prosecutorial vigilance in south Florida would have been noteworthy under any circumstances, but it warranted particular attention because all three defendants—community leaders by any standard—were black.

Some may have found in this pattern confirmation of their belief that blacks are predisposed to steal. Many others, on the other hand, may have suspected that the prosecutions evinced selective treatment of black people of influence. The devices of crime control have repeatedly been used in this country to coerce black deference to white power or to strip other minorities of what whites coveted—land from the Indians, jobs from the Chinese.[2] So whether or not the conclusion is correct, it is not surprising that a local observer said of the investigations in Florida, "I think clearly there is a case to be made concerning black males—especially those who attain some position of power and influence—almost always being sought out."

Equal treatment has been an ideal for the administration of justice for many centuries. John Locke argued for "one rule for rich and poor [alike], for the favorite at court and the countryman at plough."[3] Since the Magna Carta, formal ideals of Anglo-American justice have included the principle that each member of society should be protected equally from harm intentionally inflicted. A corollary principle would protect individuals equally and with fundamental fairness from the excessive exercise of state authority in investigating criminal acts and punishing offenders. This suggests two relevant (and related) historical standards of public security: the duty to defend all individuals and groups from social harm; and the long-standing principle, embodied in the Fourteenth Amendment, of equal protection under the laws.

And yet evenhanded justice has been an elusive goal for minorities in the United States. In the almost 250 years between the arrival of the first blacks in Virginia and the passage of the initial Civil Rights Act in 1866, law enforcement served as a legalized instrument of racial oppression. It contributed in no small way to the creation of Negroes as an outcast group in the minds of most white Americans. Then, after the Civil War, for the hundred years until the civil rights movement of the 1960s, local custom and federal passivity supported flagrant and brutal bias in police and court practices.

In the last 20 years, the criminal justice process has moved toward equal treatment of blacks and other minorities. The widespread application of notions of equal protection, embodied in the Fourteenth Amendment, in areas like education and voting rights spread, in the 1960s, to criminal justice policy and practice. As a society, we began to acknowledge more explicitly the great coercive power of criminal justice and the need to temper that power when it impinges on civil rights. In the 1980s we are closer than at any other time in our history to formulating and applying similar standards for the distribution of criminal sanctions to people of different colors and ethnic backgrounds.

To recognize progress is not to find it sufficient. *Equal protection under law cannot be equated with equal justice.* Relief from blatant racism may mask current inequities that have equally insidious, if less ubiquitous consequences for the achievement of full equality of both opportunity and outcome for minority groups in American society. The Constitution promised to "insure domestic tranquility," but the performance of law enforcement especially falls far short of that objective for blacks and Hispanics. And differential treatment in criminal justice has not vanished, particularly with regard to the imposition of the death penalty and the use of force by police.

Finally, and perhaps most intractably, class issues pervade the administration of justice and shape the experiences of minority groups with police, prosecution, and prison. Law enforcement is still designed to protect individual personal safety and property first and broader public interests—industrial safety and officeholder integrity, for example—second. The lesser economic and political power of many minority groups has shaped the ways we define criminality so that the crimes of minorities are more susceptible to prosecution and punishment than are the offenses of others who may have wrought equal or greater social harm. This inequality, executed though not conceived by the criminal justice system, feeds back upon our definitions and treatment of criminal behavior.

The philosopher John Rawls defines justice as "the way in which the major social institutions distribute fundamental rights and duties and determine the division of advantages from social cooperation." He notes that "the institutions of society favor certain starting places over others" and holds that the degree of justice in a society "depends essentially on how fundamental rights and duties are assigned and on the economic opportunities and social conditions in the various sectors of society."[4] This is obviously too broad a definition of justice to shape the functions and duties of law enforcement. But if social progress in criminal justice is to continue, current definitions may have to broaden. We are now up against the intersection of the principles of equal protection under the law and equal justice in the basic structure of society, and we have not found a way to bring them together.

Our declared democratic principles claim to make of justice an evenhanded dispenser of both protection and punishment, ensuring not only equal process but also equal effects. But we live with a pervasive tendency for official social control policies and mechanisms to reflect the underlying inequalities in our society, inequalities that go deeper than the status of individuals before the law. The resulting tension—between aspirations to equal protection and the persistent reality of unequal justice—is an obvious and fundamental challenge to American social progress in the 1980s.

In this essay I examine that tension, its origins, current patterns, and possible future resolutions. I trace the change in law enforcement against black people from an oppression that was systemic and official to one which, until the 1960s, was selective and unofficial (or at least local), but nonetheless brutal. With some historical detail, I show that slavery and the rapid industrial development that followed it have shaped today's uneasy resolution of the tension. I suggest that we now live with an apparently dispassionate criminal justice process that nonetheless generates outcomes that reflect and reinforce inequalities in the larger society. I conclude that as long as we limit our standards of justice primarily to the ideal of equal protection under the law, we have probably reached the limits of progress possible. While this society may be close to a reasonable standard of equal protection, we are far from equal justice. A truly fair and effective system of police, courts, and corrections depends on a more profound kind of social commitment that must primarily—but not solely—be realized outside the administration of justice.

THE ROOTS OF UNEQUAL JUSTICE

Scholars have uncovered experiences of unequal treatment of blacks in the administration of justice from a very early time. A Virginia court in 1640, imposing penalties on three runaway servants, assigned to the two whites four additional years of servitude, but ordered the Negro John Punch to serve his master for the rest of his life. Shortly thereafter six out of seven runaways were given longer terms of servitude, but the black among them was not, presumably because he was already a slave in permanent bondage.[5]

The criminal sanction in colonial America had a long reach. Common-law crimes were punished severely; in some places—both North and South—stealing by a black was a capital offense, and breaking into a store or home could be punished with whipping and cropping the ears. And some acts that simply suggested resistance to slave status (or white fear of it), such as associating with whites or acting insolent, were also treated as crimes.

Punishments were often imposed summarily and informally. Special "slave courts" in the South often supplemented ordinary courts, allowing slaveholders to order the runaway punished "either by dismembering [castration] or any other way [e.g., amputation of foot], not touching his life, as they in their discretion shall think fit. . . ."[6] New York law in the early eighteenth century provided that any slaves caught traveling 40 miles north of Albany—on their way to freedom in Canada, it was assumed—could be executed on the spot on the testimony of two witnesses.[7]

Laws protecting slaves were rare and rarely enforced. Historians of the colonial and later periods cite countless examples of cruel overseers, masters, and mistresses who beat, burned, and otherwise abused their slaves with impunity.[8] Seventeenth-century Massachusetts seems to have been something of an exception—perhaps because slavery was a less entrenched and fundamental institution there—but even there special restrictions on blacks were imposed and sanctioned by the 1680s.[9] Slaves often could not redress grievances provided for under what protective laws there were, as they were not allowed to give testimony or file a complaint.

In many jurisdictions the distinction between the sanctions imposed for mistreatment of blacks and whites was explicit. In seventeenth-century Virginia a white man could not legally be found guilty of murder if he killed a slave. Throughout most of the eighteenth century, murder of a slave was only a misdemeanor in South Carolina.[10] In general:

> A slave could not strike a white person, even in defense; but the killing of a slave, no matter how malicious the act, was rarely regarded as murder. The rape of a female slave was regarded as a crime, but only because it involved trespassing.[11]

The notion that rape was a trespass is an important clue to the underlying relation of slaves to criminal justice. They were chattel under the laws, like domestic animals, furniture, or real estate.[12] Ironically, while that status obviated rights, it did not preclude responsibilities. Because they were rational beings, it was argued, blacks were capable of committing crime, and were therefore to be punished.[13]

Law was sometimes harsher than practice, with increasing flexibility in the application of brutal penalties in the decades before the Civil War.[14] Criminal statutes, vigilante patrols, and courts in the seventeenth and eighteenth centuries had been important instrumentalities in the maintenance of the labor force needed to clear the land and develop the agricultural products demanded by a new world market. Some historians say that by the nineteenth century, however, the complex mutual obligations of a paternalistic system provided some informal protections to many slaves.[15]

The interaction of material imperatives and moral rationalizations is nowhere clearer than in white perspectives on black crime in the antebellum South. Immediate economic necessity and its service to the creation of an American class structure joined with nearly universal beliefs that black skin represented evil, that blacks were less than fully human, and that God meant the races to be separate in all activities of life. Together they constituted a powerful force for harsh and arbitrary law enforcement, particularly when it was apparent that some slaves did steal, commit arson, and occasionally murder their masters and each other. That these acts were largely manifestations of resistance to slavery did not excuse them or mitigate the impact of official and unofficial punishments.[16]

Before the Civil War, then, criminal justice policies were explicitly and unapologetically discriminatory at all levels. For the hundred years after the end of the war, however, the declaration of egalitarian principles in the Constitution and in federal legislation coexisted with blatantly differential treatment which was sometimes endorsed by the Supreme Court and was standard practice at state and local levels, particularly in the South. Although the principal force behind the drive for endorsement of the Fourteenth Amendment was the Republican aim of imposing national standards on the South, both supporters and opponents suspected that the evident social and political effect of the amendment would be the transformation of the status of the Negro in the United States. Testifying before the Joint Committee on Reconstruction of the 39th Congress, Alexander H. Stephens, who had been the Confederacy's vice-president, was asked what features of life in the southern states were most threatened by the prospect of Reconstruction. He summed up the common view (and the view of the administration of President Andrew Johnson as well) in his answer: "Principally the subordination of the African race, as it existed under their laws and institutions."[17]

Theoretical protection of blacks from governmental excesses in the administration of justice was part of Reconstruction. The Civil Rights Act of 1866 provided that all citizens (American Indians were excluded) "shall be subjected to like punishment, pains, and penalties," and the Fourteenth Amendment (1868), through its due process and equal protection clauses, proscribed any exercise of state authority which adversely affected blacks or other groups because of their racial status. Both measures were intended to make the Thirteenth Amendment, prohibiting slavery and involuntary servitude, effective in the southern states which had enacted codes and ordinances specifically to reduce blacks to slavelike status.[18] The equal protection clause, which has become the principal constitutional recourse for those protesting governmental discrimination on whatever basis, was originally intended only for the protection of former slaves.[19]

But these standards meant little as blacks experienced minimal protection and summary justice until the mid-twentieth century. For the hundred years after the Civil War, most white citizens assumed that it was legitimate to accord minimal attention to the public security of the black man and woman, that unusual surveillance and containment of dark people were justified because of their greater dangerousness, and that the use of violence in enforcing the law was a natural concomitant of encounters with people who, in the words of President Andrew Johnson, had shown "an instant tendency to relapse into barbarism."[20] Until the 1960s, in most parts of this country it was true that, as Gunnar Myrdal wrote in the 1940s in his study of the American race problem, "any white man can strike or beat a Negro, steal or destroy his property, cheat him in a transaction and even take his life without fear of legal reprisal."[21] More than 300 years after the first blacks came to the British colonies, the criminal sanction was still, for them, applied or withheld according to essentially political standards.

Racial oppression was not a discrete phenomenon, independent of larger political and economic tendencies. Law enforcement is always an instrument for creating and maintaining social and economic stratification. In a greedy young nation building law and custom on the ownership of property, crime control—both during the period of slavery and after—was part of the maintenance of that sacred foundation. This was, after all, the country of which Alexis de Tocqueville said in 1835, "I know of no country where the love of money has taken stronger hold on the affections of men and where a profounder contempt is expressed for the theory of permanent equality of property."[22]

The continuing use of law enforcement to control blacks was often as much an expression of conflicts of class as of race. Postbellum efforts to extend to blacks rights to full participation in American society collapsed—first in the South after Reconstruction and then in the North toward the end of the nineteenth century—partly as the result of growing industrialization, which created new competition between black and white workers.[23] The enforcement of Jim Crow laws, often supported by working-class whites whose economic interests were threatened, provided new vehicles for official and unofficial violence against blacks.

Law enforcement officials were not simply bystanders in this history; they shared and encouraged the lawlessness of others in the interests of suppressing minorities. After the Civil War, suffrage was center stage. Police participated in brutal attacks on black voters, and were rarely disciplined for their actions.[24] Disqualifications from voting included having had a conviction for petty larceny, a condition which applied to many blacks.[25] The federal government did not live up to its own declared standards; in 1876 the Supreme Court, in two separate cases, refused to order enforcement of the Fifteenth Amendment guarantee of the right to vote, and in 1878 Congress prohibited the use of federal troops to monitor elections.[26]

Race riots made clear to blacks and whites alike that law enforcement was not going to protect Negroes. Often police stood by while angry mobs lynched blacks. The lynchings continued well into the twentieth century, yet whites were virtually never convicted of murdering blacks.[27] Though the race riots of 1919 produced a few trials and an investigation mounted by the newly-formed NAACP, no official action was taken against interracial conflict.

Law enforcement officials played a similar role with respect to other minorities. As Indian lands were seized and tribes massacred, federal officials looked the other way or often participated themselves. When the Chinese were beaten and raped in California mining camps, prosecutions were rare because Chinese were not allowed by law to testify in court and whites were not willing to accuse each other.[28] If society defined minorities as inferior, the noble (though rarely enforced) federal principles of equal protection were virtually impotent to overcome such inequalities.

INCHING TOWARD EQUAL PROTECTION

By the 1960s, a tide of civil rights activism was pushing the criminal justice system toward delivery on constitutional and legislative promises of equal protection. The Supreme Court's support of voting rights for Negroes in 1944 and its rejection of segregated public education a decade later had set the stage for challenges to the pervasive inequalities between whites and minorities.

Spurred by the civil rights movement, the country has made substantial progress. As a society, we no longer use our criminal justice institutions solely to contain and control, rather than protect, various segments of our population, particularly minorities. In this section I examine the effects of criminal justice in the 1980s on minorities in the United States and assess the current likelihood of equal treatment.

The equal protection clause of the Fourteenth Amendment may have had more substantive effect on the areas of employment, education, and voting than on the administration of justice. While the law has developed the rights of indigent defendants to participation in the processes of justice—ensuring adequate appellate review and the right to counsel, for example—equal protection has not been held to require equal access to bail or sentences that are applied without regard to the financial circumstances of the defendant.[29]

But ideals of equality under law have gone far beyond the constitutional requirements as interpreted by the Supreme Court. The equal protection clause, as important as it is on its own terms, has found its greatest meaning as a framework for the pursuit—formal and informal—of human rights in all areas of state action. The claim of racial minorities on those rights continues to be a major item on the domestic policy agenda.

The population of the United States now includes 26 million blacks—a little less than 12 percent of the total population, a slightly lower proportion than at the time of Emancipation—half of whom are under the age of 25. People of Spanish origin—from Puerto Rico, Mexico and, increasingly, other Latin American countries—now number more than 14 million (or just over 6 percent of the population) and share with blacks many of the same living conditions and problems of status which make protection from crime and equitable treatment by the criminal justice system a similarly pressing issue.[30] The 800,000 American Indians counted by the census (students of Indian affairs say there are at least 200,000 more uncounted) have special problems with criminal justice because the federal government administers jurisdictional arrangements wherein tribal justice and the dominant western ethic come together in a complicated, and sometimes conflicting, mixture. Asian peoples—still fewer than two million but increasing very rapidly—face some of the same barriers to security from crime and discrimination as other groups, but to a lesser degree. The mechanisms of official social control have not been brought to bear against them with such systematic oppression, with two notable exceptions: the frontier injustices of the California mining towns, and the internment of the Japanese in western states during World War II.

How far have we come in the 1980s toward equal treatment of these minorities by the criminal justice system?

EQUAL DEFENSE FROM HARM?

We can begin to answer this question by looking at minorities' needs for protection from harm inflicted by others and by considering conditions in the lives of blacks and Hispanics which affect both their demand for law enforcement and their relations with the criminal justice system which is supposed to protect them.

Social scientists, politicians, and the popular press make much of the prevalence of street crime in many minority communities. They tend to focus on blacks and Hispanics—particularly young urban males—as offenders. But minorities are also more likely than whites to be victims of serious street crimes like robbery and aggravated assault, even when their incomes are similar.[31] In comparison with whites, blacks in 1980 were 22 percent more likely to be victims of rape and 125 percent more likely to be victims of robbery with serious assault. Victimization rates of blacks were 211 percent higher than those of whites for purse snatching, 106 percent higher for pocket picking.[32] For males that year blacks were more than two-and-a-half times as likely to be victims of robbery. And murder has become the leading cause of death among urban minority males ages 16–24. Black males are more than six times as likely to become victims of homicide as whites.[33]

These figures are aggregated for the country as a whole. If broken down to reflect the reality of crime in urban minority neighborhoods, they would be far more dramatic. And the pattern is not limited to inner-city areas. *Newsday*, Long Island's prize-winning newspaper, reports, as the consequence of a two-year study:

> While suburban black neighborhoods are still far safer than many urban neighborhoods—black or white—they are far less safe than white areas. In the seven Long Island communities where blacks represent a majority, residents had a four times greater chance of being robbed than residents of Nassau and Suffolk as a whole. . . .[34]

Hispanics, too, are disproportionately victimized, though not to the same degree as blacks. During the 1970s Hispanics had higher victimization rates than non-Hispanics for burglary, larceny, and motor vehicle theft.[35] In 1980 they were almost twice as likely to be victims of robbery as non-Hispanics, but victimization for other crimes did not differ significantly.[36]

Not surprisingly, public opinion polls show a far higher proportion of blacks than whites citing crime as one of the country's most serious problems. A 1979 Gallup poll reported that 57 percent of blacks surveyed were afraid to walk somewhere in their neighborhood at night, while 40 percent of whites felt similarly. Another poll found that while only 22 percent of whites now avoided places where they used to feel safe, 34 percent of blacks had changed their behavior.[37] A 1982 *Newsday* poll found that black families in Nassau and

Suffolk counties must earn $35,000 a year to feel the same degree of security in their neighborhoods as whites earning $15,000.[38]

If blacks and Hispanics are disproportionately victimized by street crime, it could be argued that their needs are appropriately met only by a corresponding concentration of our law enforcement energies and resources in minority communities. All minority groups (except American Indians on reservations) have their principal criminal justice contact with local police. It is the cop on the beat who is supposed to be the agent of prevention, the maintainer of order. Because history has so often given the lie to that objective, and because such a large percentage of blacks live in urban areas (81 percent as opposed to 72 percent of whites) where police activity is very visible, police performance is an important indicator of the quality and equality of the defense against harm which law enforcement should provide.

It is extremely difficult to compare police effectiveness at crime-fighting in white and minority communities. The percentage of serious street crimes for which an arrest is ever made is tiny in *any* urban area—probably considerably less than 10 percent—and there is no conclusive evidence on the question of whether well-justified arrests are made as often in minority communities as in others. But the ability of police to instill a belief in their effectiveness is an important part of law enforcement, and on that question data do exist.

The picture is interesting. On the one hand, minorities seem to have less faith in law enforcement, and on the other, they make more demands on it. A 1981 Harris poll indicated that blacks nationwide gave higher negative ratings to their local police than whites; 48 percent rated law enforcement in their community either "only fair" or "poor" as opposed to 34 percent of whites.[39] Despite this apparent lack of confidence, the latest victimization surveys show that blacks report most crimes to police with slightly greater frequency than do whites.[40]

It is virtually impossible, in assessing attitudes of blacks toward police, to separate opinions about performance of law enforcement tasks and feelings about the conduct of police toward the communities they are policing. The view persists among many black citizens that the police are primarily inquisitors in the community, rather than protectors, and data from the 1960s support that view. The National Advisory Commission on Civil Disorders found in 1969 that two to three times as many blacks as whites reported unjustified searches by police, the use of insulting language, or excessive use of force.[41] Those problems persist—probably in lesser degree—into the 1980s. The *Newsday* study found, for instance, that the police department of the white Long Island suburb of Garden City maintains a policy of stopping "suspicious" people who enter the community and that blacks are considered suspicious.[42] It also remains true that whites—including white police and witnesses—have more difficulty distinguishing among blacks than among whites, hampering accurate identification for crime control purposes. And complaints about the lack of Spanish-speaking officers in cities with high Hispanic populations are common.[43]

The continued use of excessive force by police is a major source of distrust by minorities. Incidents are still reported of trigger-happy cops in big cities where training and talent might be expected to have weeded out that kind of behavior. The police killing in Houston of a Chicano who was then thrown into a canal; the fatal clubbing that started the Miami riots of 1980; the payment in 1981 by the city of New Orleans of large sums in out-of-court settlements for cases charging police brutality; the 1983 Justice Department investigation of the slaying of four black men by Richmond, California, police—all are evidence that historic tensions between minority communities and largely white police forces are still strong.

But problems should not obscure progress. Southern law enforcement is no longer in the service of repressive policies forbidding blacks to vote or worship or get an education. Public sensitivity and higher professional standards probably would not now permit such blatant police violence as the FBI's shooting of Fred Hampton in 1969. Better officer training, higher educational requirements, and the necessity of accommodating greater citizen involvement with crime control have reduced tensions between minority communities and local law enforcement in many (but not all) cities. Patrick V. Murphy, former police commissioner of New York City and now director of the Police Foundation, testifies, "The police today are far more likely than a decade ago to rely on negotiation and patience rather than on snap decisions and arbitrary commands to establish and preserve order."[44] And recent efforts in many cities to define the situations in which police are justified in resorting to deadly force—limiting them to defense of life, for example—appear to be reducing the number of citizen complaints of excessive force.[45]

But the fundamental determinant of the level of trust between community and police is a sense of shared concerns which is difficult to achieve in a society where some are strong and some are powerless and everyone knows who is which. Lee Brown, the black police director of Houston—a progressive leader in a city which has had a reputation for tough treatment of its minority and low-income residents—has described this problem:

> In homogeneous communities where there exist similar cultures, values, class, race and social status, the police tend to function as part of the community with a minimum of conflict existing between the two groups. In such situations the actions of the police are supported by the life-styles of the community they are serving. In heterogeneous communities characterized by differences in race, values, cultures, social class and status, the police often are at odds with certain segments of the community. The problem in police-community relations occurs because the police tend to be responsive not to all segments of the community but to the prevailing power structure of the community. Thus blacks, for example, come to view the police not as their protectors but as the protectors of the status quo and representatives of those forces they view as the source of their frustrations.[46]

One recommendation made by professionals and observers for improving both the services and attitudes of law enforcement in minority communities has been to increase minority participation in the administration of justice. Two major commissions of the 1960s—the 1967 President's Commission on Law Enforcement and Administration of Justice and, the following year, the National Advisory Commission on Civil Disorders—concluded that the lack of black representation in police departments contributed to hostility toward law enforcement in communities with high proportions of black residents.

In the last decade substantial progress—though hardly uniform around the country—has been made in moving blacks into professional positions. Title VII of the Civil Rights Act of 1964 prohibits racial discrimination in employment practices. Resulting lawsuits and voluntary adoption of new personnel practices stimulated active recruitment of minority police in the 1970s. The cities of Newark, Houston, New York, Washington, Cleveland, Charleston, S.C., and Detroit all now have black chiefs; the director of public safety in Atlanta is black. About half the officers in Washington, D.C., and Atlanta and at least 30 percent in Detroit are black.

Employment of Hispanics in law enforcement has not kept pace; approximately 90 percent of minority police personnel are black. But some cities show progress. Miami has 344 Hispanic officers out of a uniformed force of 964 (as of August 1982), and Phoenix has a Mexican-American chief.[47]

It is not certain, of course, that appointing minority group members to jobs in criminal justice will render its daily administration more humane or equitable. Commentators on police behavior have noted that professional loyalties often supersede racial ones for minority officers.[48] But there are other potential gains, some more far-reaching than others. On the practical side, identifications of suspects are likely to be more reliable; less tangibly, black and Hispanic appointments in police departments may make it more difficult to disregard minority rights. James Q. Wilson's 1960s study of police behavior quotes a black man as saying that a police officer told him, "You know how this police department is run. Our motto is, let the niggers kill each other off."[49] Big-city departments with blacks in the upper ranks are unlikely to be dominated by such attitudes. And while that change may not mean that every black or Hispanic citizen has a better chance at humane treatment, it may help equalize the odds between white and minority communities.

FAIR AND EQUAL PUNISHMENT?

Mirroring the experience of minorities as crime victims is their overrepresentation as subjects of criminal justice—as arrestees, defendants, and prisoners. Are "like punishments, pains, and penalties" —from arrest through parole revocation—being applied to whites and to members of minority groups? We are making progress toward equal defense of minorities from criminal victimization; are we making comparable progress toward fair and equal punishment, toward equal protection of minority subjects of the criminal justice system from discrimination and victimization by that system itself?

By most standards, the answer is yes. We obviously no longer allow outrageously discriminatory legislation like the 1848 Virginia statute that specified the death penalty for blacks convicted of crimes for which whites might get a three-year sentence. State laws excluding blacks from jury service were invalidated after the Civil War as a violation of the due process and equal protection clauses of the Fourteenth Amendment, and *Norris* v. *Alabama* established a precedent in 1935 for the inclusion of blacks on juries in jurisdictions where blacks live.[50] Discriminatory practices not embodied in legislation have also been disallowed. Police are no longer allowed to book people for vagrancy because their race and dress and hairstyle make them look "suspicious" by the cultural standards which the officer grew up with.[51]

Law enforcement is not the only area of criminal justice where minority participation has increased substantially. While blacks and Hispanics have not entered prison administration in substantial numbers, the proportion of minority guards in urban prisons and jails is much greater than it was during the 1960s. In state prisons, for example, blacks now make up 34 percent of the employees in Alabama, 25 percent in New Jersey, 42 percent in South Carolina. In California 14 percent of correctional employees are Hispanic, and in New Mexico 55 percent.[52]

One of the most striking changes has been at the bench, where a decade of awareness has brought many racial minorities—and many women—to judgeships at all levels. Particularly striking is former President Carter's record of appointments to federal district and appeals courts. During 13 years of the Johnson, Nixon, and Ford administrations 20 minority judges were appointed to those courts, or only 4.4 percent of the total appointed. Carter used more than four-and-a-half times as high a proportion of his appointments for blacks and Hispanics: 53 judgeships out of 258 in four years. (Two Asians were also appointed, the same number as under President Ford.)[53]

But these very real accomplishments hide some glaring failures, predictably in areas where the very nature of the process requires subjective judgments. A recent study of jury selection procedures in eight southern states, for example, found that blacks were significantly underrepresented at several stages of the selection process, largely because that process permitted enough discretion so that the racial biases of prosecutors, judges, and jury commissioners prevailed.[54]

Subtler discrimination creeps into the process and its outcomes because of society's definitions of criminality. We measure social harm in ways that penalize the behavior of some groups but not others whose acts may be less visible and felt less immediately but are no less reprehensible. It is a reflection of our values in this area that the guard who discovered the Watergate break-in recently received a longer prison term for stealing a pair of sneakers than did most of those who tampered with the freedom of choice of the entire American electorate. Faced with obvious and frightening street crime disproportionately committed by the poor and black, we fail to confront the reality of the crimes the rest of us commit. We see as primary only our real and immediate need for social defense against street crime (usually through harsh remedies of questionable effectiveness).

In 1981 blacks accounted for almost half of all arrests for prostitution, rape, and murder, and 60 percent of arrests for robbery. In seven of the eight crime categories classified by the FBI as most serious—murder, rape, aggravated assault, robbery, burglary, larceny-theft, and auto theft—arrest rates for blacks were more than double the black proportion of the population.[55] Even more troubling is the picture of youth arrests; from half to two-thirds of arrestees under 18 for murder, rape, and robbery in 1981 were black.[56]

In the prisons the picture is similar; in 1981 46 percent of all inmates in state and federal institutions were black. The incarceration rate for blacks per 100,000 population is approximately eight times that for whites, a situation that has existed for a decade in every region of the country.[57] Prisons in many of the industrial and southern states—New Jersey, Illinois, Michigan, Georgia, Mississippi, Louisiana, North Carolina—are more than half full of blacks.[58] The black, Hispanic, and "other" population categories constituted 73 percent of New York State inmates at the end of 1982, a proportion almost 50 percent greater than 25 years ago.[59]

The impact of the prospect of arrest and confinement on black urban life can hardly be overstated. By the time a black male is 55, the odds are one in two that he has been arrested for a serious felony. (The odds for a white male are one in seven.)[60] On any given day in the United States three out of every 100 black men between the ages of 20 and 29 are in prison, 25 times the rate of the population in general.[61]

Contemporary criminologists are divided over whether the extreme disproportionality of minorities, particularly blacks, as defendants and prisoners indicates, at least to some extent, discriminatory processing at any or all stages. An alternative interpretation, of course, holds that the overrepresentation of blacks simply indicates that they commit more of the crimes that are regularly prosecuted by the system. In the latter case, the argument goes, the administration of justice is an essentially dispassionate process which merely reflects and reproduces the consequences of inequalities of condition suffered by offenders long before they run afoul of the law. A variant on this theme suggests that the inequalities of condition are not solely functions of class and poverty but also reflect the breakdown of a special black culture which arose out of the pain and humiliation of the American experience of African slaves. Charles Silberman, studying that culture, found one of its great achievements to be the transformation of rage into songs, tales, and "toasts." Now, he concluded, "the process no longer works; black adolescents and young men have begun to act out the violence and aggression that, in the past, had been contained and sublimated in fantasy and myth."[62]

Early examinations of the relationship between race and crime were misleadingly simple. In 1833 Beaumont and Tocqueville assumed that the high proportion of Negroes in American jails could be explained by higher rates of crime; 100 years later the Dutch Marxist criminologist William Bonger concluded the same thing without considering other possible explanations, such as selective arrest, conviction, or sentencing decisions.[63]

More sophisticated research in the 1960s inferred higher offense rates among blacks from arrest rates.[64] While discrimination in the apprehension process might account for some of the disproportionate arrests of blacks for street crime, victimization surveys, in which the perceived race of the offender is reported by victims, bear out the supposition that for some crimes—notably robbery—blacks are indeed committing offenses out of all proportion to their numbers in the population.[65]

Acknowledging that at least some of the overrepresentation of blacks in courts and prisons is attributable to high incidence of involvement in some crimes does not relieve us of the responsibility of looking at whether, where, and how discrimination exists in criminal justice decision-making. In recent years sentencing has been the focus of much research, with often puzzling results. A synthesis of 51 studies of racial disparities in sentencing begins by commenting that "the results of recent studies are provocative not only because they raise important issues of equality before the law but because they frequently appear to contradict one another."[66] Some studies have found that blacks get longer sentences than whites, even when convicted of similar crimes and having similar past records; others have not.[67] Even methodological differences in the studies cannot explain away the apparent ambiguities.

Studies of racial discrimination in arrest are far less common. That blacks are arrested at a higher rate than whites is indisputable; tracking the causes is more complex. One study has found that "nonwhites are more likely than whites to be arrested under circumstances that will not constitute sufficient grounds for prosecution."[68] And the decision to arrest is often influenced, it seems clear, by matters of demeanor—dress, attitude, race—as well as by perceptions of criminal behavior.[69] But the overall likelihood that anyone will be arrested for most crimes is so small—only two-tenths of one percent for drug sales, it has recently been estimated—that it is not surprising that criminologists find the research that exists inconclusive.[70]

Two recent efforts to confirm or deny discrimination, not just in sentencing or arrest but across the criminal justice process, are worth noting. One novel approach, developed from a concern with the startling overrepresentation of blacks in prison, is criminologist Alfred Blumstein's examination of the possibility that, once arrested, blacks are more likely than whites to end up in prison. He was able to predict, on the basis of arrest rates, 80 percent of the extent to which blacks were overrepresented in prison as compared with their representation in the general population.[71] While he was concerned that the remaining 20 percent represented a large number of people—10,500—he surmised that it might well reflect discretionary variables, like judges' consideration of circumstances of the crime that made it more serious. His conclusions seemed to minimize the likelihood of discrimination within the criminal justice system.

A two-year RAND study released in June 1983 came to quite different conclusions. Working with comprehensive statewide data on California offenders and a large RAND data base taken from 1400 self-reports of inmates in California, Michigan, and Texas, Joan Petersilia compared the experiences of white and minority offenders at each important decision point in the justice system. While she did not find "widespread and consistent" racial bias, she did conclude that, having been found guilty of a felony, minority offenders were given longer sentences than whites, controlling for other factors that might influence a judge, and that in two of the three states studied minority offenders did actually serve more time.[72]

The limitations of these studies suggest the complexity of the task of evaluating progress toward equal treatment of minorities. While the Petersilia study did test for the possibility that the probability of being arrested was greater for the nonwhite subjects of her study—and found no significant evidence of overarrest—it did not carry that concern about the effect of arrest one necessary step further. She did find blacks and Hispanics more likely than whites to be released after arrest, but she did not examine the likelihood that this was because arrests of minorities were based on weaker evidence.

The Blumstein research took arrests as a point of departure, making the questionable assumption that discrimination did not take place at that stage of the process. Other researchers have challenged his method of determining the degree of discrimination, asserting that refinements would substantially increase the effect of bias.[73] Blumstein's analysis is not broken down by state, which would certainly reveal discrimination in some jurisdictions and make the work more useful for local policymakers concerned with reducing it. And his analysis might have yielded different conclusions if he had based it on the number of prison admissions in a whole year, rather than on a one-day census. The overrepresentation of minorities in prison is generally greater among those who enter and leave prison within a year, so an admissions picture of the entire group incarcerated over time would have probably shown greater disproportionality.

Despite these limitations, both studies are useful. Taken together, they suggest a picture which is emerging in the synthesis of other research: of heavy involvement of blacks and Hispanics in street crime, particularly robbery; and of occasional, active discrimination at several points in the administration of justice, particularly with lesser offenses where judges have the greatest discretion. The picture suggests a primarily dispassionate process which nonetheless results in the use of criminal justice institutions to reproduce the inequalities outside it. While it is difficult to confirm prevailing suspicions of unfair and unequal punishment of minorities within the criminal justice system, it is equally difficult to set those suspicions aside.

THE PROBLEM OF UNEQUAL OUTCOMES

This is a bleak picture. Despite changes in the last quarter-century in its treatment of minorities, the American criminal justice system still impedes the pursuit of equal justice. It does not in theory classify minority people as more vulnerable than others to law enforcement, to be sure; and practices of police, courts, and corrections have significantly reduced bias. But *in terms of outcome*, the administration of criminal justice—dictated by the standards of the world beyond the station house or juvenile training school—continues to identify particular groups, blacks and Hispanics especially, as socially dangerous. In doing that, it increases the instability and insecurity of members of those groups, thereby creating some of the danger the image projects. The net effect, regardless of intent, is to stack the cards invidiously against the prospects of minorities in the United States.

Three separate examples of this persistence of unequal outcomes, though discrete and reflecting disparate causes, serve together to illustrate the complexity of the relationship between process and outcome.

1. Hispanics. Within the last few years, Hispanics have shown up in the crime data in significant disproportion to their numbers in the population. It is difficult to trace the course of this phenomenon because Hispanics were lumped together with whites in most surveys until very recently. There are some areas of reported crime where the disproportion is not extraordinary—the arrest rate for forcible rape, for example. But arrest rates of Hispanics for murder—particularly of those under 18—are very high, and aggravated assault and burglary arrests are disproportionately high.[74] Black arrests as a proportion of the total went down during the 1970s, a trend that suggests that Hispanic arrests may have increased as a share of the whole.[75] Hispanics were overrepresented as prisoners in many of the states with particularly high Spanish-origin populations, according to the 1970 census, and the 1980 census figures on persons in institutions are likely to show an increasing trend.[76] Data from New York State show that the Puerto Rican share of the prison population has risen from 14 percent in 1972 to 21 percent in 1982, an increase of 50 percent.[77]

Here is an ethnic group, perceived by many in the larger society as inferior because of limitations in education and language, which the administration of justice, even if performed without procedural discrimination, is further stigmatizing. Although Hispanics do not share the special history of blacks in this country, they seem to be inheriting the social and economic structure of life which produces the similar result of differential involvement in some kinds of crime. The criminal justice system, responding to society's mandate, records and condemns the pattern, contributing to the image of Spanish-origin groups as part of the "dangerous class."

2. *Structuring discretion.* In the past few years we have sought to increase rationality in criminal justice decisionmaking and remedy some of its inequities by reducing discretion.[78] It is almost tautological that where discretion is greatest, discrimination is most likely. That observation is presumably the basis for the notion of due process and the ideal of a "government of laws, not men." But commendable efforts to reduce discretion in order to reduce prejudice may, ironically, constrain prejudicial intent but further prejudicial outcome.

The current fashion of using a point system to guide many decisions on pretrial release, sentencing, and parole release is an example. This approach is one of a number of efforts to "structure" discretion, resulting in supposedly objective measures of the likelihood of future crime, the probability of appearance in court, and the identification of high-rate offenders. The factors considered, however, inevitably involve characteristics of the lives of poor blacks as indicators, so that a ghastly syllogism emerges: unemployment, family instability, prior institutionalization, and youthful idleness are associated with crime (at least the kind we punish); they are also associated with blackness; ergo crime equals blackness.

As we structure discretion and render decisionmaking more rational according to the currently accepted goals of criminal justice, we may simply be substituting the discretion of the larger societal group for the discretion of the individual. We call the results of these decisions "objective" because they conform to group values and do not include overt selectivity; but the group standards they reflect may still repress minorities and reinforce disadvantage.

The inequities of modern criminal justice are not always passive. Differential experience with police and prisons can be a major contributor to social and economic inequality. While the characterization of prisons and training schools as "colleges of crime" may be overstating the case, most of the literature on young offenders suggests that institutional treatment makes things worse.[79] And the association of "doing time" with tests of manhood in the ghetto creates a set of negative behaviors to add to the handicaps of poverty, poor education, and unemployment. If the structuring of sentencing, bail, and parole decisions reinforces the disproportionate exposure of minorities to the criminal justice system, it is, therefore, also likely to compound the problem of disproportionate crime rates among minorities. A destructive spiral has been set in motion, ironically by a genuine and informed concern for increased rationality and equity.

3. *The death penalty.*   Those who think we have arrived at the point where our "objective" system equally protects minorities must reckon with evidence on the application of the death penalty. What once seemed to be promising social progress in that area has been ambiguous at best, and may yield clues about why the increasing realization of equal protection of the laws cannot take us much further toward equal justice.

Until the Civil War, capital punishment statutes were often explicitly selective. In the early eighteenth century Pennsylvania's "Act for the Trial of Negroes" stipulated separate, harsher penalties for blacks; a hundred years later, a Virginia penal statute designated 70 capital offenses for blacks, five for whites. Emancipation probably did not substantially change the proclivities of white jurors, judges, or legislators. Raoul Berger argues that to assume that the framers of the Fourteenth Amendment meant to equalize murder penalties between whites and blacks "is to ignore the racism that ran deep in the North in 1866."[80]

The abolitionist movement which took form in the late eighteenth century and gathered force a century later did not eliminate discriminatory application of the death sentence where it prevailed. Eighty-nine percent of the 405 men executed for rape between 1930 and 1979 were black, a share that could not possibly be explained by disproportionate criminal involvement.[81] As one authority concludes about executions between 1864 and 1967:

> Particularly in the South, blacks have been executed for lesser offenses, at younger ages, and more often without appeals. And for rape, the death penalty has been reserved out of all proportion for blacks whose victims were white—a pattern implied by the antebellum Black Codes in the South.[82]

Although the 1972 Supreme Court rejection of capital punishment was seen as a victory for civil rights, *Furman* v. *Georgia* did not really repudiate discrimination in sentencing. Justice William O. Douglas was the only member of the majority in *Furman* who rested his opinion explicitly on the bias in death penalty laws.[83] He noted that they were applied primarily to "minorities whose members are few, who are outcasts of society, and who are unpopular, but whom society is willing to see suffer though it would not countenance general application of the same penalty across the board"; and he argued that the statutes before the Court were "pregnant with discrimination and discrimination is an ingredient not compatible with the ideal of equal protection of the laws that is implicit in the ban on 'cruel and unusual' punishments."[84] Justice Marshall, rejecting capital punishment as unconstitutional per se, took note of the substantial empirical evidence of discriminatory application provided during the case by arguing that if the public were fully informed of the implications and consequences of the death penalty, it would not support it. The issue of bias might have been a more determinative one if the justices had been more accustomed to relying on social science data to support arguments of unequal protection. As it was, the Court clearly did set a precedent for considering them, a precedent which Chief Justice Burger, in his dissent, deplored.

The precedent has not held. In 1976 the majority in *Gregg* v. *Georgia* and its companion cases ignored the accumulating empirical evidence on both discrimination in capital cases and the invalidity of the deterrence hypothesis with respect to capital punishment.[85] The decisions validated statutes in Georgia, Florida, and Texas which have since been shown to be just as likely as pre-*Furman* statutes to produce dispositions against blacks that are overwhelmingly biased.[86] During 1981, 44 percent of those sentenced to death were black, a share three-and-a-half times greater than their percentage in the general population.[87] A new study by David Baldus of 1,200 Georgia murder sentences imposed between 1973 and 1979 has found that a black who killed a white was 3.7 times as likely to be given the death penalty as a white who killed a white.[88]

The death penalty issue is a classic illustration of the limits of equal protection as a banner around which to rally minority efforts to obtain equal justice. Sociologist Hans Zeisel notes: "It is difficult to conceive that any [Supreme Court] Justice concerned with arbitrariness would knowingly tolerate a system of capital punishment in which race affects the decision who will live or die."[89] And yet most of these justices and others are reluctant to move beyond the common argument that, while a general pattern of discrimination may exist, the defendant must prove a case for particular bias against him. It seems that the judges are constrained by their individualistic approach to proof from relying on a general pattern in order to rule that equal protection has been denied. And yet that constraint, imposed by the traditions of our legal system, probably does not prevent them—however subconsciously—from being influenced in their individual judgments by the patterns which they perceive outside the courtroom of differential involvement by blacks in serious crimes. The social implications of this irony are vast and tragic.

CONCLUSION

In the previous section of this essay I have indicated the distinction between equal protection and equal justice by three examples of criminal justice outcomes which—although arrived at through an increasingly disinterested process—impede the societal objective of full equality for racial and ethnic minorities. I want now to examine why the pattern revealed in my examples is inevitable under current social practice, and to suggest some steps toward ensuring that movement toward equal protection in the administration of justice can also promote equal justice.

One explanation of the dilemma can be found in the traditions of our legal system. While the notion of equal protection has been the beacon for social progress for minorities in many areas over the last two decades, the equal protection clause of the Fourteenth Amendment was not intended to create equality. It was meant, rather, to preclude state authority from preventing equal treatment through prejudicial classifications. In being held, as it has been, to proscribe not only explicit public bias but also official acquiescence in private discrimination, the doctrine has probably already been extended beyond its original purpose. Justice Douglas once articulated the wish for a still broader interpretation of equal protection, in which the state could not endorse or even reflect biased private custom as expressed in "the unwritten commitment, stronger than ordinances, statutes, and regulations, by which men live and arrange their lives."[90] But that would put the Constitution in the position of being a document that requires outcomes like the redistribution of wealth and the equalizing of social conditions, something it clearly was not intended to do.

That fact suggests another partial explanation of the dilemma, perhaps one that is too obvious to linger over but should be mentioned. Inequality in this country—of class and gender as well as of race—is so deeply rooted as to be impervious to all but seismic jolts. Those jolts may occur—the civil rights movement, even with its limitations, was such a jolt—but they are far more likely to be triggered by the stresses of popular discontent than by the most considered reforms of, say, enlightened police chiefs, liberal judges, or competent criminologists. The Georgia prosecutors and juries whose discretion shaped the pattern of bias in capital sentences studied by Professor Baldus were acting in accordance with deeply ingrained assumptions about economic and social relations which millions of other Americans share and cannot be expected to abandon in short order.

Finally, a basic function guides the criminal justice system which may seem at times to contradict its duty to promote equal protection: the function of social protection from harm imposed by criminals. The social defense function is very dominant in most people's minds in the 1980s. Recent polls show that a large majority are now in favor of capital punishment and believe that the courts don't deal harshly enough with criminals.[91] Many see a tradeoff between a priority for social defense and a priority for equal justice.

Those pressing for increased police power, swifter conviction, and harsher sentences are by no means limited to white citizens in affluent neighborhoods. While the percentage of blacks in the poll cited above who wanted tougher treatment of criminals by the courts was smaller than the percentage of whites—77 percent as opposed to 84 percent—the increase in that sentiment among blacks over eight years from 1972 to 1980 was more than twice as high for blacks as for whites over the same period. A bare majority of blacks opposed the death penalty in 1980, as compared with 62 percent who had in 1972.[92]

So we are caught in the tension between the desire for equal justice and tougher criminal justice policies which many believe would better defend us from the criminals we most fear. If we yield to the tension in favor of the social defense function, we are unlikely to continue progressing toward equal protection under the law and will surely reinforce the persistence of unequal justice.

What can we do?

The longest-term answer is beyond the scope of criminal justice and seems very far off in 1984. It requires commitment to redressing the structural inequalities in American life through basic changes in the social and economic conditions that poor and minority young people encounter as they grow up. While the link between employment and crime is far from simple, there are some people and situations for whom connections can be seen. Common sense and some of the research tell us that we are hearing the truth from the 15-year-old dropout who told a crime researcher in a recent interview, "If the job pays good, I'll go to the job. If the street is good, I'll go to the street."[93]

But there are some middle-range measures that might be taken before we reach the millennium of full employment. We can shift our values about what constitutes social harm that we are prepared to label criminal. At present the deviance of the white and affluent counts for much less than the deviance of the dark and poor. To change that value will not be easy. While many recognize that a staggering amount of property loss and even personal injury is caused by white-collar crime, most people consider the mugger a far more serious criminal threat. Crime is generally thought of as something done by those not of our own race and class. Focusing popular attention on a broader range of social offenses and offenders will be a major task for social reformers. It will require both solid public information and a willingness to face our collective responsibility for crime.

The control of crime has become removed from the informal social controls of the American past and of some other societies even in modern times. The operations of courts and prisons are not easily affected by the daily dynamic of basic institutions like the family or the labor market, for example. We can do more to integrate criminal justice functions into community life, to create greater awareness on the part of both law enforcement professionals and citizens of how the administration of justice affects what John Rawls calls "the primary subject of justice . . . the way in which the major social institutions distribute fundamental rights and duties. . . ."[94]

The current interest in returning police to an older order-maintenance role—with service to the neighborhood as important a function as crime-fighting—is a step in this direction. So is the idea of giving to community groups or responsible individuals the custody of minor offenders who would otherwise have been jailed briefly or assigned to official probation supervision. Finally, we need a corrections policy that will actively encourage the involvement of social service volunteers, arts groups, colleges, and—perhaps most important—the civil rights organizations in addressing the needs of prisoners, particularly young and first offenders who still have a chance for a life not tainted by repeated contacts with law enforcement.

American society is not currently headed in these directions. We seem determined to separate criminal justice even further from the communities whose problems give rise to the need for it. The job of corrections officer is now among the 20 fastest-growing occupations in the country, according to the Bureau of Labor Statistics.[95] Lack of progress toward equal justice in the United States in the 1980s may have disastrous consequences for even the maintenance of our present standard of equal protection in the administration of justice. As long as individually justifiable outcomes like the essentially arbitrary death sentences which depend on defendants' color and class are possible, the subtler biases will prevail throughout criminal justice, hard to track because of the harm of the conduct being examined. Their prevalence will continue to oppress minorities, as well as those of us who are not black or Hispanic but who measure our degree of civilization at least partly by the evenhandedness with which our society restricts the liberties of its members.

NOTES

1. "Arrest of Black Police Chief Stirs Blacks' Fears in Florida," *New York Times,* August 17, 1983, p. A14.
2. See Frank Browning and John Gerassi, *The American Way of Crime* (New York: G.P. Putnam, 1980), especially Chapter 17, p. 263.
3. John Locke, *Second Treatise on Civil Government,* Chapter 11, #142.
4. John Rawls, *A Theory of Justice* (Cambridge, Mass.: Harvard University Press, 1971), p. 7.
5. Winthrop T. Jordan, "Modern Tensions and the Origins of American Slavery," in *Blacks in White America Before 1865,* ed. Robert V. Haynes (New York: David McKay Company, 1972), p. 109. See also A. Leon Higginbotham, Jr., *In the Matter of Color* (New York: Oxford University Press, 1978).
6. Quoted in J. Thorsten Sellin, *Slavery and the Penal System* (New York: Elsevier, 1976), p. 137.
7. John Hope Franklin, *From Slavery to Freedom: A History of Negro Americans* (New York: Alfred A. Knopf, 1974), p. 63.
8. *Ibid.,* page 157. See also Vincent Harding, *There Is a River* (Harcourt Brace Jovanovich, 1981), especially Chapters 3, 4, 5.
9. Robert C. Twombley and Robert H. Moore, "Black Puritan: The

Negro in Seventeenth-Century Massachusetts," in Haynes, *Blacks in White America*, pp. 117–133.

10. Eugene D. Genovese, *Roll, Jordan, Roll: The World the Slaves Made* (New York: Pantheon Books, 1974), pp. 37–38. See also Frank Tannenbaum, "Slave and Citizen," in Haynes, *Blacks in White America*, pp. 117–133.

11. Franklin, *From Slavery to Freedom*, p. 140.

12. Tannenbaum, "Slave and Citizen," p. 166. But this status did not preclude increasing white sensitivity to their own culpability for violence against slaves. See Genovese, *Roll, Jordan, Roll*, pp. 31–39 for a description of the developing paternalism toward blacks which increased penalties for whites shown to have murdered or mistreated slaves.

13. Carl N. Degler, "Slavery in Brazil and the United States: An Essay in Comparative History," in Haynes, *Blacks in White America*, p. 174.

14. Genovese, *Roll, Jordan, Roll*, pp. 31–32.

15. *Ibid*, pp. 3–7.

16. See Franklin, *From Slavery to Freedom*, pp. 155–163; and Genovese, *Roll, Jordan, Roll*, pp. 599–620.

17. David Montgomery, *Beyond Equality: Labor and the Radical Republicans, 1862–1872* (New York: Vintage Books, 1967), p. 55.

18. Paul A. Freund, Arthur E. Sutherland, Mark DeWolfe Howe, Ernest J. Brown, *Constitutional Law: Cases and Other Problems*, Volume II (Boston: Little, Brown, 1961), pp. 878–881.

19. Polyvios G. Polyviou, *The Equal Protection of the Laws* (London: Duckworth, 1980), p. 30.

20. Browning and Gerassi, *The American Way of Crime*, p. 206.

21. Gunnar Myrdal, *An American Dilemma* (New York: Harper & Row, 1944), p. 559.

22. *Democracy in America* (New York: Vintage Books, 1954), Part I, Chapter 3.

23. See William Julius Wilson, *The Declining Significance of Race* (Chicago: University of Chicago Press, 1980), pp. 52–61.

24. *Ibid.*, pp. 206–207.

25. Franklin, *From Slavery to Freedom*, p. 268.

26. *Ibid.*, pp. 266, 267. The federal cases are *United States* v. *Reese*, 92 U.S. 214 and *United States* v. *Cruinkshank*, 92 U.S. 542.

27. *Ibid.*, pp. 322–323; Browning and Gerassi, *The American Way of Crime*, p. 275.

28. Browning and Gerassi, *The American Way of Crime*, pp. 263–275.

29. See, for example, *Burns* v. *Ohio*, 360 U.S. 258 (1959); *Douglas* v. *California*, 372 U.S. 353 (1963); *Gideon* v. *Wainwright*, 372 U.S. 335 (1963); and *Miranda* v. *Arizona*, 384 U.S. 436 (1966).

30. Demographic information for this essay comes from U.S. Bureau of the Census tables found in that agency's *Statistical Abstract of the United States 1981*, nos. 31–63, 745, 748, 451, 452, 468.

31. Bureau of Justice Statistics, *Victimization in the United States* (Washington, D.C.: Government Printing Office, 1980), table 15, p. 29.
32. *Ibid.*, tables 6 and 7, p. 25.
33. U.S. National Center for Health Statistics, *Vital Statistics of the United States*, reprinted in Bureau of the Census, *Statistical Abstract of the United States* (Washington, D.C.: Government Printing Office, 1983), table 295, p. 178.
34. "Crime in Suburbia: The Fear and the Facts," *Newsday* reprint, May 15 to May 29, 1983, p. R49.
35. Bureau of Justice Statistics, *The Hispanic Victim: A National Crime Survey Report* (Washington, D.C.: Government Printing Office, 1981).
36. Bureau of Justice Statistics, *Victimization*, table 8, page 26.
37. Data on public attitudes in this and subsequent paragraphs, unless otherwise noted, are taken from Bureau of Justice Statistics *Sourcebook of Criminal Justice Statistics—1981* (Washington, D.C.: Government Printing Office, 1981), pp. 182–191.
38. "Crime in Suburbia," p. R49.
39. Louis Harris, *The Harris Survey* (New York: The Chicago Tribune–New York News Syndicate, February 26, 1981), pp. 3, 4, as adapted and reprinted in the *Sourcebook of Criminal Justice Statistics—1981* (U.S. Department of Justice, Bureau of Justice Statistics, 1982), p. 195.
40. Bureau of Justice Statistics, *Victimization*, tables 90 and 92, pp. 71–72.
41. See Albert J. Reiss, Jr., *The Police and the Public* (New Haven: Yale University Press, 1971), p. 142.
42. "Crime in Suburbia," p. R50.
43. See InterAmerica Research Associates, *A Report from the National Hispanic Conference on Law Enforcement and Criminal Justice* (Washington, D.C., 1981).
44. Patrick V. Murphy, "Preface" in Catherine H. Milton, Jeanne Wahl Halleck, James Lardner, and Gary L. Albrecht, *Police Use of Deadly Force* (Washington, D.C.: Police Foundation, 1977), p. iii.
45. "Changes in U.S. Spurring War on Police Methods," *New York Times*, Nov. 13, 1983, Section 1, p. 30.
46. Lee P. Brown, "New Directions in Law Enforcement," in *Crime and Its Impact on the Black Community*, ed. Lawrence E. Gary and Lee P. Brown (Washington, D.C.: Howard University Institute for Urban Affairs and Research, 1975), pp. 145–146.
47. Personal communication from Peggy Triplett, whose 1982 survey of twelve police departments is available in an unpublished paper from the Police Foundation, Washington, D.C. See also Police Executive Research Forum, *Survey of Police Operational and Administrative Practices 1977* (Washington, D.C.: Police Executive Research Forum, 1978).
48. See Scott H. Decker and Russell L. Smith, "Police Minority Recruitment: A Note on Its Effectiveness in Improving Black Evaluations of the Police," *Journal of Criminal Justice* 8 (1980): 387–393.

49. James Q. Wilson, *Varieties of Police Behavior*, (Cambridge, Mass.: Harvard University Press, 1968), p. 162.
50. *Norris* v. *Alabama*, 294 U.S. 587 (1935).
51. *Kalender* v. *Lawson*, No. 81-1320, decided May 2, 1983 by the Supreme Court.
52. Percentages derived from American Correctional Association, *1983 Juvenile and Adult Correctional Departments, Institutions, Agencies and Paroling Authorities Directory* (College Park, Md.: American Correctional Association, 1983), page xviii.
53. Calculations based on data in Bureau of Justice Statistics, *Sourcebook of Criminal Justice Statistics—1981*, tables 1.33 and 1.34, pp. 84–85.
54. Nijole Benokraitis, "Racial Exclusion in Juries," *Journal of Applied Behavioral Science* 18 (1982): 29.
55. *FBI Uniform Crime Reports 1981* (Washington, D.C.: Government Printing Office, 1981), table 36, p. 179.
56. *Ibid.*, p. 180.
57. Scott Christianson, "Our Black Prisons," *Crime and Delinquency* 27, no. 3 (1981): 364.
58. Bureau of Justice Statistics, "Prisoners 1925–81," (Washington, D.C.: Government Printing Office, 1982), p. 4; Bureau of Justice Statistics, *Prisoners in State and Federal Institutions* (Washington, D.C.: Government Printing Office, 1979), p. 16.
59. Unpublished table prepared by Scott Christianson from New York State data.
60. Alfred Blumstein and Elizabeth Graddy, "Prevalence and Recidivism in Index Arrests: A Feedback Model," *Law and Society Review* 16, no. 2 (1981–82): 280.
61. Alfred Blumstein, "On the Racial Disproportionality of United States Prison Populations," *Journal of Criminal Law and Criminology* 73, no. 3 (1982): 1259.
62. Charles E. Silberman, *Criminal Violence, Criminal Justice* (New York: Random House, 1978), pp. 132–165.
63. Gustave de Beaumont and Alexis de Tocqueville, *On the Penitentiary System in the United States and Its Application in France* (Carbondale: Southern Illinois University Press, 1979), p. 93. See also Willem Adriaan Bonger, *Race and Crime*, trans. Margaret Mathews Hordyk (Montclair, N.J.: Patterson, Smith, 1969).
64. Marvin Wolfgang and Bernard Cohen, *Crime and Race* (New York: Institute of Human Relations Press, 1970).
65. Bureau of Justice Statistics, *Victimization*, table 41, p. 48.
66. John Hagan and Kristin Bumiller, "Making Sense of Sentencing: A Review and Critique of Sentencing Research," *Research on Sentencing: The Search for Reform*, ed. Alfred Blumstein, Jacqueline Cohen, Susan E. Martin, and Michael H. Tonry (Washington, D.C.: National Academy Press, 1983), p. 1.

67. *Ibid.*, table A–1, pp. 36–46.
68. John R. Hepburn, "Race and the Decision to Arrest: An Analysis of Warrants Issued," *Journal of Research in Crime and Delinquency* 15, no. 1 (1978): 66.
69. Irving Piliavin and Scott Briar, "Police Encounters with Juveniles," *American Journal of Sociology* 70 (1964).
70. See Mark A. Peterson and Harriet B. Braiker, *Who Commits Crimes: A Survey of Prison Inmates* (Cambridge, Mass.: Oelgeschloger, Gunn & Hain, 1981).
71. Blumstein, "On Racial Disproportionality."
72. Joan Petersilia, *Racial Disparities in the Criminal Justice System* (Santa Monica, Calif.: Rand, 1983).
73. See Scott Christianson, "Disproportionate Imprisonment of Blacks in the United States: Policy, Practice, Impact and Change," unpublished paper prepared for the National Association of Blacks in Criminal Justice, 1982, pp. 52–59.
74. *FBI Uniform Crime Reports 1981*, table 37, pp. 182–183.
75. Christianson, "Disproportionate Imprisonment," table 31.
76. See table 2 in Bonnie J. Boudavelli and Bruno Boudavelli, "Spanish-Speaking People and the North American Criminal Justice System," *Race, Crime and Criminal Justice*, ed. R.L. McNeely and Carl E. Pope (Beverly Hills, Calif.: Sage Publications, 1981), p. 53.
77. Unpublished table by Scott Christianson from New York State data.
78. See Michael Gottfredson and Don M. Gottfredson, *Decision Making in Criminal Justice: Toward the Rational Exercise of Discretion* (Cambridge, Mass.: Bollinger, 1980).
79. See, for example, Donna Hamparian, Richard Schuster, Simon Dinitz and John Conrad, *The Violent Few: A Study of Dangerous Juvenile Offenders* (Lexington, Mass.: Lexington Books, 1978).
80. Raoul Berger, *Death Penalties* (New York: Oxford University Press, 1982), p. R57.
81. Bureau of Justice Statistics, "Capital Punishment 1979" (Washington, D.C.: Government Printing Office, 1980).
82. W.J. Bowers, *Executions in America* (Lexington, Mass.: D.C. Heath, 1974), p. 175.
83. *Furman* v. *Georgia*, 408 U.S. 238 (1972).
84. *Ibid.*, pp. 255–257.
85. *Gregg* v. *Georgia*, 428 U.S. 153 (1976); *Profitt* v. *Florida*, 428 U.S. 242 (1976); *Jurek* v. *Texas*, 428 U.S. 262 (1976). See Marvin E. Wolfgang, "The Death Penalty: Social Philosophy and Social Science Research," *Criminal Justice Law Bulletin* 14 (1978): 18.
86. W.J. Bowers and G.L. Pierce, "Arbitrariness and Discrimination under Post-*Furman* Capital Statutes," *Crime and Delinquency* 26 (1980): 563.
87. Bureau of Justice Statistics, "Capital Punishment 1981," p. 4–7.

88. Anthony Lewis, "Kill Him, Kill Him, Kill Him," *New York Times*, October 12, 1983.
89. Hans Zeisel, "Race Bias in the Administration of the Death Penalty: The Florida Experience," *Harvard Law Review* 95 (1981): 457.
90. *Adickes* v. *Kress*, 398 U.S. 144, 179 (1970).
91. See Roper polls in *Sourcebook of Criminal Justice Statistics—1981*, tables 2.33 and 2.36, pp. 204–211.
92. *Ibid.*
93. "Growing Out of Crime, Into Jobs," *New York Times*, June 20, 1983.
94. Rawls, *A Theory of Justice*, p. 7.
95. "Careers '84," *New York Times*, Oct. 16, 1983, Section 12, p. 52.

LAND

AND

NATURAL

RESOURCES

VINE DELORIA, JR.

Rural America is in the final days of a profound transformation. The people who formerly owned and worked the land are rapidly being displaced as large corporations purchase their lands. They are taking up jobs where they can find them in adjacent towns and large metropolitan areas. Many of these former landowners lack the social skills needed for life in the cities, are generally able to secure only jobs that require little training and experience, and frequently become welfare clients of the national government. Among these dispossessed, racial minorities and Appalachian whites bulk very large.

Although most people perceive racial minorities as distinct groups, they do not usually act like groups. Instead, like other people, each individual member makes decisions based on his best solutions to his own problems. When we look at a large number of individual decisions, it becomes apparent that personal choices in certain situations have been identical and have produced conditions that radically affect the fortunes of groups identifiable by a set of commonly distinguishable characteristics. But the decisions were made individually; consistent collective action is as strange to minorities as to Americans generally. What racial minorities in rural areas do share consistently is a common profile of poverty and deprivation which makes them particularly vulnerable to economic and social changes, and for two or three decades they have been reluctantly selling their lands and moving away.

Today rural minorities share a common fate, although they arrived at it through distinctive paths. At least a glimpse at historical background is necessary to understand the rural roots of these racial minorities and to be able to grasp the complexity of the situation in which they find themselves.* That common history may be summarized this way: *every one of the nation's principal racial minorities— blacks, Mexican Americans, Indians, Orientals—in the original conception of the American owning and employing classes was to work the land, by cultivation or by construction on it; they were all primarily agrarian at the start of their American experience and in other people's service; as the need for their labor on the land has rapidly declined and as the land they have worked has become valuable for nonagricultural reasons, they have been displaced by a combination of political and economic forces, and in the process have changed from rural to urban poor, with no likelihood of improved economic prospects.*

THE PROBLEMS OF PROPERTY

AMERICAN INDIANS: WATER AND MINERALS

American Indians, of course, were the original inhabitants of this country. Under federal pressures the tribes agreed to cede their lands, in advance of the wave of settlement that threatened to engulf them, and surrendered their occupancy of most of the continent, the majority of tribes retiring to remote western reservations by the late 1870s. In 1887 Congress passed the General Allotment Act,[1] which authorized the president to negotiate with the tribes for division of their reservations into farm-sized tracts to be distributed to tribal members. The remaining lands were declared surplus to Indian needs and purchased by the government for a fraction of their true value and

---

* With apologies, this chapter cannot discuss the rural situations of all minorities. Omitting Puerto Ricans on the island and Alaskan and Hawaiian natives is especially regrettable. My belief is, nevertheless, that despite many differences they would be found to be part of what below I call "the common lot."

opened to settlers for homesteading. In 1891 Congress amended the General Allotment Act to provide for the management of individual allotments by the secretary of the interior in those instances in which Indians did not use their lands,[2] generally the allotments of old people and children. This statute was the first of many laws that moved authority for managing property out of the hands of the Indians and into the grasp of the federal bureaucracy.

In 1907 the Bureau of Indian Affairs and the Bureau of Reclamation entered into an agreement to develop irrigation projects on Indian lands.[3] Under the *Winters*[4] case, reservations were thought to own priority water rights on waters arising on or flowing through their boundaries. Nearly a dozen projects were developed on Indian lands following this working agreement between the two federal agencies, but on the whole they were badly conceived and poorly operated. In 1924 Congress authorized the leasing of Indian lands for oil and gas exploration and extraction by the secretary of the interior, with the consent of the community council representing the residents of the reservation.[5] After a series of minor amendments and administrative rulings Congress approved a major revision of the laws governing the leasing of Indian mineral resources in 1938,[6] and with some minor modifications this statute today governs the use of mineral resources on Indian reservations.

Today Indians hold property in two ways. Tribal governments are the single largest landowner on most reservations. Tribes preserved some lands intact during allotment, and under the programs of the Indian Reorganization Act of 1934[7] have recovered other lands within the reservation through land purchase and consolidation programs. Individual Indians own family allotments which have been passed down from the original allottee. Most individual lands have fallen into heirship status (i.e., ownership by a number of individual heirs) since they were issued, and the management of these lands is a major problem in the use and development of Indian lands today. Farming allotments are usually leased to non-Indians who have the financial resources to purchase the equipment necessary to achieve success in today's agricultural enterprises. Grazing lands are generally placed in a large grazing unit which is leased to a big cattle operator who sometimes controls several townships of land, the individual Indian landowners receiving a pro rata share of the income from the leasing unit.

Tribal lands containing minerals are generally leased to oil, gas, and mining companies with the tribes retaining a royalty interest in the operation. With the expansion of social programs by the tribal governments in recent years, there has been an increasing pressure to lease tribal lands to secure an adequate income to keep these social programs functioning. Thus a considerable amount of Indian land is actually controlled and exploited by non-Indians to provide the tribal government with an income. The individual Indian does not generally receive much benefit from the expansion of tribal governments unless he has a particular problem that can be met by a tribal social program. Reservations have become simply locations that have a multitude of exploitable resources, rather than homes, to many Indians. Developmental questions regarding their land's natural resources have become in Indian life the principal issues, today and for its foreseeable future.

Not all tribes have mineral resources, however, and only 38 reservations have deposits sufficiently large for commercial exploitation—uranium for the Navajo and the Laguna Pueblo, oil and gas for Wind River, Fort Peck, Navajo, Southern Ute, Jicarilla Apache, and Fort Berthold; coal for the Navaho, Crow, and Northern Cheyenne. In eastern Oklahoma the lands of the Five Civilized Tribes are now almost completely allotted, many with oil or gas on them. As important as mineral resources in the western states is water, which is used agriculturally and in most mineral production activities as well. The struggle over Indian mineral resources thus includes reservations that do not have minerals but that do possess water in sufficient quantity to be wanted commercially.

Indian tribes do manage to receive an increasing income from the exploitation of minerals on their lands. In 1982 some 5.5 million acres of Indian land, representing 22,000 leases, produced income for Indians totalling more than $396 million. The figure represented an increase of 58 percent over the royalties received in 1981, indicating that Indians were starting to be much better businessmen than before. Petroleum income constituted the bulk of Indian mineral income, representing $368 million of the total. Coal production accounted only for $11.4 million and uranium brought in $9.5 million. Of the oil and gas income a substantial portion represented Indian allotments in Oklahoma located in older producing fields developed earlier in the century.[8]

Coal has been the most difficult resource to manage. Many tribes did not recognize the value of their deposits and consequently made very unfavorable leases in the early sixties which returned them royalties of only a few cents per ton. When the tribes learned that they had virtually given their resources away they attempted to cancel the leases. The Northern Cheyennes of Montana had the most difficult time renegotiating coal leases and eventually had to win a lawsuit against the secretary of the interior which allowed them to renegotiate terms. On the Navajo-Hopi lands in Arizona strip-mining by Peabody Coal has become a point of contention since Black Mesa, where the coal is primarily located, is in an area disputed by the two tribes. More important, strip-mining renders the land virtually useless for other activities and the Navajo and Hopi still have many members who earn their living as cattlemen and sheepherders, and grazing and mining are incompatible in western lands where water is scarce and essential to both activities. Tribes with mineral resources are angrily divided between those members who would exploit to bolster sagging tribal incomes and those who want to continue an agricultural and pastoral way of life.

BLACKS AND THE LEGACY OF KING COTTON

Blacks were brought to this continent as slaves for southern plantations which raised labor-intensive cash crops such as cotton, tobacco, and later sugar cane. In 1865 at the end of the Civil War, Congress established the Bureau of Refugees, Freedmen, and Abandoned Lands[9] with the intent of confiscating the lands and property of the rebels and distributing them to the former slaves. But President Andrew Johnson declared a general amnesty and the plan was never carried out. Two years later Representative Thaddeus Stevens of Pennsylvania introduced legislation that would have provided 40 acres and $50 to former slaves who were heads of households.[10] But this belated gesture was defeated, leaving the freed blacks no alternative but to reach some kind of economic accommodation with their former masters.

The white southerners were determined to keep blacks at the bottom of the social and economic ladder and sharecropping was devised as a means of maintaining large cash-crop agriculture, continuing to use blacks as field workers. Under sharecropping the worker was allocated a tract of land, provided with seed, tools, fuel, work animals, and housing of a sort. The landowner would closely supervise the planting and harvesting of the crop, keep records, weigh the produce, and market it, taking half the proceeds as rent. His often dubious integrity was all the sharecropper had to rely on for an honest accounting of the proceeds of his labors and he was encouraged to borrow from the landowner, which ensured that he would remain perpetually in debt and therefore subject to the control of the landowner. Sharecropping had all the disadvantages of slavery, plus the dreadful reality of old age, when the sharecropper was no longer able to work and the landowner felt no responsibility to provide for him.

Many blacks successfully purchased their own lands after the Civil War, but this was a hazardous venture, a social as well as an economic act resented by southern whites fearing the blacks' independent assertion of their legal rights. Individuals often had to appear unusually subservient in order to get a white man to sell land to them. Even then, blacks were often charged exorbitant rates of interest or sold property that had been exhausted by single-crop farming or which was in remote areas away from the roads, making it tough to market their crops profitably. Nevertheless, the desire to own land was intense and by 1910 blacks owned some 15 million acres of land in the southern states, representing 218,000 farms. Blacks made up 16.5 percent of all southern landowners. Black tenant farmers operated an additional 670,000 farms.[11]

Southern agriculture as a whole suffered substantially during the First World War. Transatlantic trading virtually ceased with the outbreak of hostilities and the bottom dropped out of the cotton market. Southern banking circles met the crisis by extending credit to cotton farmers to allow them to store their surpluses in state warehouses, thus enabling many white farmers to survive. No credit was given to black farmers, however, and many of them could not meet their mortgage payments and had to sell their lands for a fraction of true value.[12] At the same time, the invasion of the boll weevil reduced the cotton crop by as much as one half in some areas. The Black Belt of Alabama, where the majority of farmers were black, was particularly hard hit; many were compelled to sell their farms and return to sharecropping again. Between 1920 and 1930, 37,596 black farmers lost their lands and losses totaled 2,749,619 acres, an area twice the size of Delaware.[13] During the boll weevil crisis many white farmers again obtained credit and diversified their activities, enabling them to survive and hold their land. But such broad credit was not available to blacks; cotton was the only crop against which storekeepers would give them temporary credit for living expenses. This enforced single-crop agriculture badly depleted the productivity of black farmers' lands.

Cotton never did truly recover from these crises. In 1932 the price was only five cents a pound. Congress in 1933 attempted in the Agricultural Adjustment Act[14] to bolster the cotton market by withdrawing planted acreage and compensating farmers for their reduced operations. Between 25 and 50 percent of each producer's acreage was taken out of production, and the AAA instructed landlords to divide the subsidy benefits with tenants in proportion to their share of the reduced acreage. But most landlords collected back debts before sharing with tenants, thus effectively reducing any cash benefits that tenants or sharecroppers might have received from this program. Large landowners could afford to enter the program because they had hundreds or even thousands of acres and reducing planted acreage was not difficult. Small farmers, however, could not realistically reduce their planting when they owned fewer than 100 acres; any reduction would force them to bankruptcy.

Enforcement of the AAA was the job of the Extension Service County Farm Demonstration agents and agricultural conservation committees. These agents and committees largely represented the big landowners, and blacks and small white farmers had little voice in the selection of these people or in the direction of the program. Agents determined the allotment of cotton acreage and benefit payments and particularly in the South their goodwill and honesty was critical to participation in the federal program. Most southern agents systematically excluded blacks from the program, when they considered them at all. As black farmers fell from landowners to tenant farmers to sharecroppers or even seasonal wage laborers, their New Deal benefits fell accordingly.

Postwar agriculture in the South quickly became mechanized as technological and chemical advances made during the war placed new machines and poisons at the disposal of the farmer. Tractors capable of pulling immense plows, mechanical harvesters (some even AAA-financed), and new chemical weed controls resulted in the loss of a significant number of sharecropping jobs. "Between 1945 and 1959 the number of black tenant farmers declined by 70 percent."[15] Local credit restrictions continued to hamper the expansion of black agriculture into new, more profitable crops. "As of 1959, 56 percent of the nonwhite-operated commercial-size farms in the South concentrated on cotton, 26 percent were in tobacco, 6 percent were in general farms (usually a combination of either cotton, tobacco, and peanuts), and 3 percent were in other field crops, usually peanuts. This crop distribution contrasted with that of white-operated farms, of which only 18 percent were concentrated in cotton, 19 percent in tobacco, and 62 percent in other crops."[16]

Beginning in the 1960s agriculture assumed a predominantly corporate form. Automation in new confinement technology for raising chickens and hogs meant that agricultural jobs in traditional stock-raising activities fell sharply. Labor-saving technology and tax relief came together. "A high income investor in a hog factory using a combination of tax credits and deductions can recover one-half of his initial (personal) investment in the facility in the first year; over the life of the facility, depending on the circumstances, he can recover from 80 to 100 percent of that investment in the form of reduced taxes."[17] In many instances, depending upon other more profitable investments, a large farmer can actually make money by operating his farm at a loss until he reaches a year when there is a good market and he can sell his goods. In the meantime he can use a variety of credit devices to maintain himself, all of them deductible on his tax forms. Agribusiness is therefore not really farming as much as it is the proper manipulation of figures within a balance sheet and on the income tax forms.

Small black farmers in the South simply could not compete with mechanized farms. If the markets fell dramatically, they could not absorb the loss of income that reduced prices entailed. Lacking capital for investment and relying on labor-intensive methods for planting and harvesting meant that black farmers were falling behind significantly every year they remained in business. It was not long before many decided to quit. Beginning in 1960 and continuing until the present, black agriculture has suffered overwhelming, perhaps fatal losses. Between 1959 and 1969, "the number of black cotton farmers fell from 87,074 to 3,191 and tobacco farmers declined from 40,670 to 9,083,"[18] losses of catastrophic proportions that are continuing today.

Black lands were easily purchased by people with capital at tax sales, through mortgage foreclosures, and during estate settlements. When farms were lost families often moved in with friends and relatives, transforming a small subsistence farm into a residence for a number of families or a large extended family, generally on some form of welfare subsistence. Young blacks could see no future in farming and began to seek other employment in nearby towns, or left for the northern industrial areas, or some few accepted life as a marginal farmer or rural odd-job worker. Often those people who remained in the rural areas, lacking any employable skills and unable to farm profitably, simply turned to welfare and food stamps.

MEXICAN AMERICANS: LAND AND LABOR

Mexican Americans have a unique history as a rural people. When Mexican and Spanish immigrants established a baronial society in Texas, New Mexico, and California, a poorer class of people were brought from Mexico to help develop the large tracts of land which court favorites had obtained from the Spanish king. They intermarried with the Indians of the area creating a large mixed-blood population. Spanish culture was resilient and the children of these marriages looked not to the cultural heritage of their Indian mothers, but adopted the customs, traditions, and values of their Spanish and Mexican fathers.

Following the Texan revolt against Mexico and the Mexican War, Mexican holders of land grants found themselves dispossessed. The land grants were always vague in their descriptions of metes and bounds and the new American courts, accustomed to the rectangular survey used by the federal government, often refused to recognize their validity.[19] Although this displacement was unjust, it did not affect most of the Mexicans who lived within the area that had been ceded to the United States. They simply had worked for the large landowners and actually owned little themselves.[20] Only in New Mexico, where several towns had land grants, did the change in political status affect the country Mexicans. In that state a large part of the communal lands in the north were lost after the areas came under American jurisdiction, because of unclear or erroneous boundary descriptions or because the people did not understand how they could protect themselves against the acquisitive Anglos who sought the best farming and grazing lands and preempted the use of water.

The Mexican population of the United States remained remarkably stable in the Southwest until the 1880s. By that time, the disparity in living conditions between Mexico and the United States was considerable and people began to cross the border to do seasonal work, accumulate a little nest egg, and return to their homes south of the border. The Chinese Exclusion Act of 1882 and the troubles with the Japanese at the turn of the century created a vacuum in the available labor supply in California and insured continuing opportunities for Mexicans who wanted to work briefly in the United States. Trained during the construction of the railroad from the central plateau of Mexico to the American border, by 1910 Mexicans had built nearly 1,500 miles of track. They became in demand for railway work in the United States itself, and by 1929, they constituted almost 60 percent of the common labor force for nine western railroads—almost 23,000 strong.[21]

The Mexican Revolution in 1911 profoundly disrupted Mexican life and thousands of people sought refuge in the United States from the brutal and indiscriminate violence. The Mexican economy took a dramatic turn downward, the cost of living escalated almost beyond the ability of the people to maintain themselves, and Mexican immigration to the north climbed rapidly. Fortunately, the opening of new lands in the Southwest through federally financed irrigation projects created a demand for additional field workers, so that Mexicans were welcomed into the United States at precisely the time when many were seeking to leave their homeland.

Because Mexican workers would do the back-breaking labor that other Americans rejected, it was not long before other American businesses were seeking to employ them. "The Bethlehem Steel

Company, in need of immediate labor in 1923, recruited approximately one thousand Mexican nationals from San Antonio, Texas, for its plant in Bethlehem, Pennsylvania."[22] But once located in the North, they began searching for other jobs which they preferred to steel work and by 1930 only 46 of the original thousand were still employed at Bethlehem. By 1929 there were colonies of Mexican nationals in many of the northern cities where they had been encouraged to move by nonagricultural industries. As children were born to these families while living in the United States, the Mexican population in the United States rapidly expanded. The census and immigration offices found it impossible to determine separately the number of immigrant and native Mexicans in the United States because the federal officials did not speak Spanish, knew little of the history of Mexican Americans in this country, and had no inclination to learn.

The presence of so many Mexicans in the United States finally attracted attention and people began to agitate for a closing of the border. The *Saturday Evening Post* ran a series of articles in 1928 which demanded that Mexican immigration be severely restricted because it foreshadowed a future race problem in the Southwest.[23] Lobbyists for agricultural interests who exploited Mexican workers struck back with a barrage of letters during Senate hearings on "Restriction of Western Hemisphere Immigration" in the winter of 1928, and the agricultural forces easily won the battle over restrictions. One argument particularly dear to the hearts of the growers was that Mexicans, because they were immigrants, could easily be deported and would not form a permanent part of American society.

Following the stock market crash in 1929 serious agitation began to remove aliens. Whites had never been eager to do the back-breaking work harvesting the fruits and vegetables of southern California; but now with jobs becoming increasingly scarce and families starting to migrate from the Midwest's Dust Bowl to the Pacific coast, people began to feel that agricultural jobs should be given to American citizens. Secretary of Labor James Doaks announced in December 1930 that over 400,000 illegal aliens were living and working in the United States.[24] He argued that rounding up and deporting these people would significantly ease the unemployment problem in the United States, making at least 100,000 jobs immediately available to

Americans. Of this number, an estimated 4,000 people lived in the Los Angeles area, and were of Mexican descent. Some Mexicans had previously sought repatriation, and the secretary of labor was convinced they would all go willingly.

Although repatriation of Mexican nationals had begun as a voluntary program in 1929, in February 1931 the Immigration Service began wholesale deportation. The federal government eventually deported over 450,000 Mexicans between 1929 and 1938,[25] including many who were American citizens but could not prove it. The County of Los Angeles was so eager to see them deported that it sponsored special trains to Mexico to move them out more quickly. Speculation regarding the degree of welfare relief which the county would experience when the Mexicans were removed caught the popular imagination. Repatriation declined as America began its climb out of its economic depression and by 1938 the program for deporting Mexicans had died, even in southern California.

Following the Second World War western agriculture expanded significantly. New irrigation techniques made large-scale farming feasible on previously arid lands and the major crops raised were ones that had to be picked by hand, raising the strong seasonal demand for migratory labor. Mexicans filled this bill admirably and American recruiters went into Mexico to enlist workers. Through the *bracero* program (1942–47, 1951–64), the national government gave its strong support, thus showing again its cyclical fluctuations of policy and almost schizoid behavior toward a minority. With the standard of living high in the United States and comparatively low in Mexico, recruitment was not difficult, even with the dreadful conditions which persisted in the work camps. Migrational patterns soon developed that extended to Washington and Oregon for fruit and vegetable picking, to Michigan and New York for apples, and to Florida for citrus crops.

Smuggling workers across the border became a way of life for many Americans who sought to fill the labor quotas of large farming enterprises any way they could. These "coyotes" often abandoned their workers to their fate after they had delivered them. Even legal migrants faced low wages, but those without permit cards had virtually no protection against exploitation and rarely sought redress against those who exploited them.

By the early sixties it had become apparent that unless the migratory workers organized and negotiated contracts with the growers, they would not be able to improve the conditions under which they worked. The United Farm Workers under the leadership of Cesar Chavez began a series of strikes and boycotts of certain products such as lettuce and grapes in an effort to bring the big farmers to the negotiating table. The Teamsters organized a rival drive that competed for the right to represent the migrant workers. Eventually a good deal of the seasonal farm work in the fields and canneries of California was placed under some form of union contract. There was some success elsewhere, too, although Texas remained a difficult place to organize. As the disparity between the standard of living in the United States and Mexico continued to grow, the stream of illegals increased dramatically. Today no one knows exactly how many Mexicans are living in the United States but Mexican Americans are regarded as the fastest-growing racial minority in the country and both political parties are courting them. Without any appreciable land base of their own, Mexican Americans have become one of our heavily urbanized populations. Even its one large rural element—the seasonal farm workers—are in large numbers urban dwellers in the off-season.

APPALACHIAN WHITES: LIVING IN THE MARGINS

Appalachian whites are not usually considered a *racial* minority, but in rural areas they are comparable in many respects to American Indians, blacks, and Mexican Americans. In early colonial days, when the plantations were not able to import enough black slaves to harvest their tobacco crops, some brought orphans and indentured servants over from England. Freed of ordinary restraints by the lure of the wilderness, many of these people promptly ran away from the plantations on the coast and took refuge in the Appalachian mountains to the west. Living like Indians, they soon mastered life in the eastern mountains, perhaps became more efficient than Indians in living off the land, and occupied the remote areas of this chain of mountains beginning in southern New York and continuing south into Georgia. Some later moved west into the Missouri and Arkansas Ozarks.

These people occupied a marginal economic niche, doing subsistence farming in the mountains and hollows, supplementing their food supply with hunting and fishing, and occasionally cutting and selling the hardwood trees that covered the region. As some families achieved more prosperity they might purchase slaves to help with their farming, and two distinct economic classes began to emerge.

In the 1880s representatives from eastern investment companies invaded the Appalachian hills in search of timber and quickly obtained very favorable purchases of standing timber on the lands of the mountain people. They also discovered that a good deal of land had not been properly surveyed and recorded and learned that title could be had from the state governments for a small fee and a willingness to do accurate surveys. Thus a good many families who did not have proper title found themselves defrauded of their ancestral homes. The timber companies had hardly finished purchasing timber before coal companies sent representatives into the hills to obtain the rights to minerals lying beneath the surface. Coal mining technology had not radically changed for centuries and the people could not believe that selling the coal lying deep beneath their farms could possibly harm them. Some mountaineers, Harry Caudill explained, even thought they had gotten the better of the city slickers.[26]

Around the time of the First World War the coal mining companies arrived in Appalachia in force to claim their dues. Several companies had built railroads into the southern counties of Kentucky as early as 1912 and started construction of company towns.[27] Special comfortable houses were built for supervisory personnel as well as some rather flimsy row houses in which the companies insisted that everyone working in the mines live. They also required their employees to purchase their food and household goods at the company stores, and send their children to schools which the companies had built and leased to the state. The coal companies easily recouped investments through these devices and subsequently removed millions of tons of coal at virtually no cost to themselves, the return on their town operations paying a substantial portion of their expenses. Local politics quickly came under corporate influence and control and as a result the property tax structure of Appalachia was purposely designed so that coal companies paid only a token amount of taxes on the valuable resources they controlled.

The Great Depression hit the coal industry very hard, and even

a few years before the stock market crash. Orders for coal had significantly declined by the late 1920s and by the early 1930s Appalachia
was in desperate straits.[28] New Deal relief programs helped to ease
the suffering of people but only the increase in coal production
brought about by the Second World War made a return to prosperity
possible. Following the war there was again a period of relative
affluence as coal production soared. But the companies recognized
that oil and natural gas were being increasingly used instead of coal
in many important industries, and made arrangements to sell their
holdings in the company towns before they reduced their mining
operations. They encouraged the miners to purchase the houses they
had formerly rented, and then they reduced or terminated operations, often leaving the miners with newly purchased homes and no
jobs.[29]

When new methods of production, strip-mining and auguring,
made it possible for coal to be mined more easily from the surface,
the industry shifted its operations accordingly. The large companies
could now simply lease coal reserves to small operators and still make
a good profit through royalties. The large companies such as Peabody, Consolidation, Island Creek, Pittson, and the captive inte-
grated mining of U.S. Steel and Bethlehem still continued to
dominate the field. But by subcontracting to small operators, many
companies no longer had to deal with the United Mine Workers
Union, which had become very powerful under John L. Lewis, nor
did they have to bother about the superficial and flimsy federal regulations then governing the coal industry.

Throughout the 1950s and 1960s, Appalachia suffered periods of
boom and bust. The new coal operators, generally former miners
who had purchased equipment and become independent contractors,
were suddenly hit by large income tax payments. They had not
known anything about filing tax returns, withholding from the
wages of their workers, or other simple business tasks which a small
business must perform for the government. As a result many miners
who had become coal operators were sold out by the Internal Reve-
nue Service and were unable to secure further employment, losing
everything they had.[30]

Appalachia became a gigantic welfare region as methods of coal
production became more sophisticated. Many miners, middle-aged

and with no skills other than underground mining, sought to be certified as invalids in order to collect disability payments. In 1962 the United Mine Workers closed its hospitals in Appalachia[31] because of high costs and declining union membership, as an increasing number of miners worked for nonunion producers. Farming became difficult if not impossible wherever the new mining methods, which were very destructive of the land, prevailed. Topsoil overlay that had been removed in order to free the coal for loading was piled in great heaps by the giant strip-mining bulldozers. As rain and snow loosened its tenuous hold on the hillsides, it slowly made its way down the mountains, invading fields and polluting domestic water supplies.

Harry Caudill, in *Night Comes to the Cumberlands*, described the plight of these mountain people now living among the refuse of modern mining. Caudill suggested that new industries be found which would make a more constructive use of the land. One alternative he suggested was the development of the Appalachian region as a recreation and resort area.[32] Unfortunately for the local people, others were already thinking along these lines. Since the late sixties, land developers have purchased many untouched areas of Appalachia in order to create second-home and recreational projects there. The rapid escalation of land values has made it easier for the mountain people to sell their lands, and the increased valuation of their lands brought about by the proximity of recreational developments has made it more difficult for them to pay their property taxes. The Appalachian people are now being ruthlessly crushed between economic forces beyond their control. An increasing number are selling their ancestral lands and living in small towns on welfare, unable to maintain any semblance of farming on the land that remains to them. Most cities of the North have an Appalachian section where former mountain people live.

THE COMMON LOT

Today, these American minorities find themselves isolated in enclaves that are desperately poor. Energy developments, corporate farming, and recreational projects hem those who remain outside cities into rural ghettos, making it impossible to maintain any separate and identifiable culture. The different groups share common social characteristics: a rising number of single-head households, a substantial portion of the people on welfare or other subsistence programs, a land base that is rapidly declining, and a decided lack of vocational and employment skills that would enable members to succeed in another setting.

Institutional and cultural barriers make proposing a program of ready assistance for these rural groups exceedingly difficult. Recent efforts to rehabilitate the rural areas assume that all people respond to the same motivations and stimuli. It is important to note that these particular rural groups have long been isolated or distant from the values and institutions of mainstream America. Therefore solutions that treat them as if they had the same value system as other Americans usually come to naught. Nevertheless, there are within the present organization of rural America definite miscarriages of justice which, if corrected, would ease the tensions under which these groups now live. Changes in law, administration of programs, and conceptions of community can add a great deal to the substance of their lives without conflicting with other developments in American society.

INSTITUTIONAL BARRIERS

The case of Appalachian whites emphasizes for us that rural poverty is not simply a function of race. True, Appalachians by special qualities of culture and history have made of themselves a somewhat distinct people. But small farmers, tenant farmers, and farm workers throughout America—and the rural economies of which they were the center—have declined, in numbers and influence. What is important to note about racial minorities is that they led that downward descent and that very few of them have not been part of it: there are, in other words, an insignificant number of well-to-do minority people in rural America.

Although American society grew diffusely as people settled the land, today almost everything is organized from the top down. The social programs of the New Deal and Great Society answered a demand for immediate government action in areas of human need and produced an army of clients for federal and state governments. Agencies created to answer these needs have long since established their own clientele and now systematically exclude those people who do not fit into the categories of aid they provide. The agencies charged with helping impoverished Americans now can be institutional barriers to assistance.

Tax laws are another formidable barrier to the progress of rural minorities. Both federal and state laws work together to provide many benefits for those people already possessing wealth; accordingly they also dispossess those people who live in marginal economic circumstances. Subsidies in the form of tax benefits are not considered as such by most Americans because they are hidden within the rhetoric of individualism and capitalism. Yet they act more profoundly to change the nature of the distribution of income and the accumulation of capital than do the admired virtues of hard work, thrift, and honesty in business dealings. A public recognition of the role that the tax laws play in keeping permanent an American underclass, at tremendous expense to the national treasury, might help to bring about some basic reforms in the manner in which the governments, state and federal, look at wealth and come to grips with it.

American society is now a credit society; with the proper connections or credentials, one need not actually own property. Credit has replaced capital for many people who use money rather than accumulate it. Transactions are increasingly speculative, and the participants don't earn money directly from production so much as from the fact that the money has passed through their hands as it makes its way through society. Rural people have never been recipients of large amounts of credit and the rural poor have had little if any credit at any time in their lives. The federal government, on the other hand, has recognized the need for credit in rural areas and has sponsored programs that provide grants and long-term loans for development in rural areas. Rural electrification, for example, was not possible for most areas without low-interest federal loans; most agricultural programs give credit for a variety of farming activities under a number of guises. The situation in rural areas today is such that credit must be replaced by outright grants, and renewable ones at that, to the very poor, since there is no longer any way whereby capital can be quickly generated to meet the credit obligations of the poor landowners and small farmers. Grants in many instances may be the least expensive way of rehabilitating rural areas that suffer chronic poverty. They may be no more expensive than the welfare payments that are the likely alternative, and unlike those might help restore families to self-sufficiency.

Inheritance laws seek to allocate the property of the deceased among immediate relatives in a fair and impartial manner. Inheritance laws presume a family unit which often no longer exists as an emotional entity. The mechanical operation of these laws often allocates interests in property to remote blood relatives who have no real connection with the immediate survivors of the deceased and who simply intrude upon them, motivated by the desire to gain from their remote relationship. New categories of property holding should be devised that can prevent the dissipation of property, so that small property owners can benefit from their inheritance.

Social welfare programs are devised as temporary and expedient measures to assist people who have suddenly suffered misfortune. The underlying assumption of most welfare programs is that people will quickly use government assistance to better themselves and disappear from the list of clients. Our experience tells us that this goal is rarely achieved and that chronic misfortune is the lot of many Americans, making it impossible for them to catapult from their desperate economic situation. Sensible transformation of welfare programs involves a recognition that machines and other aspects of technology have made employment a privilege and not a realistic possibility for many people, and in rural America, which is so thoroughly mechanized, that means "most" people. Labor-saving devices have not enabled us to use properly the labor that we have saved. If we wish to make welfare programs efficient then we must buy the labor of people whose skills have become technologically obsolete and put it to a constructive use.

A major problem in erasing institutional barriers today is the Protestant mythology that has undergirded capitalism from its inception. Much of our present difficulty in formulating national domestic policy results from our stubborn insistence that people must act in a certain way to become morally worthy of social assistance. Pragmatism would inform us that whether poor people are morally worthy or not, they nevertheless constitute an important part of the body politic and their problems must be confronted and resolved if we are to preserve the remainder of society.

LOOKING FOR SOLUTIONS

FEDERAL PROGRAMS

Two basic kinds of federal programs relate to and affect the rural poor. The first is the regional development corporation, which seeks to rehabilitate specific areas of the country and bring modern technology and institutions to serve the inhabitants, thereby bringing them up to the standard of living enjoyed by the rest of the country. The second includes a variety of agricultural subsidy and assistance programs designed to support and enhance the people in their economic and social activities. These programs are supposed to bolster the economic strength of individuals, making it possible for them to contribute to the strength of the national economy. By and large, minority peoples have been excluded from their operations.

The Tennessee Valley Authority[33] was America's first large-scale experiment in rehabilitating a region. Subject to periodic floods and economically depressed, the Tennessee valley was long a huge isolated pocket of rural poverty until TVA was organized. Dams were built for flood control and hydroelectric generation. Cheap electricity was made available to homes and businesses and encouraged new roads and industries; new activities in recreation and farming resulted from the new configuration of the valley. The TVA became the great success story of the partnership between federal power and local initiative. During the later years of the Depression a series of dams was built on the Columbia River in Washington state with the hope that the TVA success could be duplicated there and in the 1960s the Appalachian Regional Commission and the Four Corners Development Authority were established with similar hopes.

A closer look at regional development shows, however, that displacement occurs alongside development. The lives of local communities are disrupted as more efficient means of using resources are adopted. The TVA once generated power only through its dams; today it is one of the largest purchasers of strip-mined coal, contributing substantially to the problems of Appalachia to its north. The goal of continuing to provide cheap energy for industry has become more important than service to the region. Once industry was drawn to the Tennessee valley, more was needed or attracted, requiring additional supplies of energy, and it was only natural that the TVA would move from a regionally important authority to a national presence feeding on lesser regions to maintain itself.

Depressed regions require massive infusions of capital but the government never sees its role as that of primary provider; it rather encourages private capital to exploit an area. Both the Appalachian Regional Commission and the Four Corners Development Commission saw as their task the attraction of new industry. Bringing new technology involves the importation of technicians and experts who can operate the technology. A region is invaded by new people who are subservient to the industry that has brought them into the area or fiercely devoted to its basic operating tenets. The experience of southern blacks, Appalachian whites, western Indians, and Mexican Americans has been the same: local people rarely get either new jobs or the training that would enable them to benefit from the expansion of economic activities in their region. Service jobs at low wages are usually the only benefits that accrue to them.

Land prices generally rise significantly as industries look for favorable locations for their plants; farm lands soon become suburban tracts. Local land taxes generally rise considerably faster than do tax revenues from the increased economic activity. Since property tax is the basic local tax, the cost of new facilities is borne disproportionately by local property owners. Most industries will demand and receive tax concessions as part of their agreement to relocate.

Subsidiary businesses often arrive in the wake of industrial relocation. Chain stores and food franchises are able to supplant local "mom and pop" stores because they are able to provide services for the area as part of a national corporate network. Many newcomers arrive with considerable capital derived from their previous activities. They are able to compete with existing businesses and dominate local activities easily because they are linked to national credit and banking circles. Housing, entertainment, cultural programs, and recreational facilities are soon priced out of reach of local residents, making it difficult for them to participate in the activities of their own neighborhoods.

Federal agricultural programs designed to assist individual farmers have been in existence in one form or another for most of this century. The AAA was a major New Deal overture in this respect. Subsequent amendments and expansion of the basic AAA thrust have only added frills to the basic idea of taking land out of production, thereby raising the market price of food commodities. The government contributes a percentage of the farmer's income and in exchange he promises not to expand his production beyond a certain point. Obviously this philosophy conceives of farmers as capable of overproduction in the aggregate, and is designed to assist those farms, individual and corporate, that are capable of producing surpluses. Small, marginal farmers and subsistence family farms are excluded from these programs even though they appear to be the philosophical reference that justifies them to Congress.

Rural electrification, rural housing, rural home improvement, and conservation programs have basically the same flaw inherent in them. One must already have a certain amount of property in order for the program to be of assistance. Consequently the rural poor, including the "landed" poor, are rarely included.[34] Congress in 1978 did pass a "deep subsidy" home loan program designed for low-income rural people, but it has never appropriated funds for it. Most federal programs are planned in their administrative structure to serve political as well as economic purposes. Thus state and local subdivisions are used to determine areas of operation, and selection of personnel for these jobs is often the province of local or state politicians. The same power structure that has already precluded the rural poor is thus allowed to determine how federal programs will be administered in their areas. These people determine eligibility for programs and it is not uncommon to find that local people who do not qualify under any reasonable reading of the federal rules and their intent often do receive benefits from rural programs.

Another federal activity is the land grant college, but it has meant little to minority people. In 1862 Congress passed the Morrill Act,[35] the purpose of which was to establish, with land or the cash equivalent, colleges which could take the lead in agricultural research. Some 69 institutions were founded under the act and its later amendments. Over the years land grant colleges have served the large farmer considerably more than they have served the small subsistence farmer. They have, in fact, *changed* American agriculture by emphasizing efficiency and technology, thus narrowing their services to a select clientele which today is led by agribusiness interests. Institutions for blacks were later included in the land grant program,[36] but no federal funds were designated for agricultural research until 1969[37] when the secretary of agriculture took small amounts of money from his discretionary funds to provide them with some research monies. Until that time, the colleges were generally run by the states as "separate but equal" institutions, using state funds. Beginning in 1972,[38] black land grant colleges finally began to receive annual funding for assistance to small rural farmers. Appalachian whites and Mexican Americans had no public institutions specially devoted to assisting them and if they have received any help from the regular land grant colleges over the course of the past century it has been minimal. American Indians recently received funding for a number of community colleges[39] on the reservations, but these provide only vocational training and do no research into economic problems of the reservations.

TAX PROVISIONS

The Supreme Court has warned us that the power to tax is the power to destroy; unfortunately the refusal to tax is the power to create, when it allows income to be diverted from the treasury through artificial depreciations and deductions from the tax bill. American Indians do not have the problem with tax policies that other rural minorities do. Indian lands and the income from lands held in trust by the federal government are not subject to taxation. Neither are the incomes of businesses conducted on the reservations, including trading posts operated by Indians, cigarette stores, and bingo games. State attorneys general are continually seeking ways to levy state income and sales taxes on reservations but to date they have not been successful because of the doctrine of tribal sovereignty and federal preemption of Indian matters by the commerce clause.

Indian tribes, according to the Supreme Court in *Merrion* v. *Jicarilla Apache Tribe*,[40] have the power to levy severance taxes on the removal of minerals from lands on their reservations. This power, which is being eroded by the Bureau of Indian Affairs' insistence on issuing rules and regulations for the promulgation of tribal tax codes, places Indian tribes in a unique position, in which they can generate income for social welfare purposes in addition to the income they receive as landowners for leasing their lands to developers. Obviously this power, if given to local organizations of blacks, Mexican Americans, or Appalachian whites, would go a considerable distance toward equalizing the present tax situation. But there is no present vehicle for allocating such a taxing power to local nongovernmental organizations.

The other groups suffer from a variety of problems that revolve about state and federal tax codes. Property taxes are the most prevalent tax that farmers face. In many states farmlands are taxed at a lower level than other lands, such as residences and businesses. But small farms nevertheless pay disproportionate taxes compared to corporate lands held for farming or mineral exploitation purposes. In February 1981 the Appalachian Land Ownership Task Force released a study entitled "Land Ownership Patterns and Their Direct Impacts on Appalachian Communities."[41] In this report, which surveyed 80 mountain counties in seven southern states, a significant pattern of property taxes emerged which indicated a glaring discrepancy in the manner in which they were levied. "Not only do absentee owners pay less than local owners," the report stated, "but another related pattern is also found: larger owners tend to pay less per acre than do smaller owners."[42]

Development of a region substantially increases the value of lands, which backfires in the form of increased property taxes. During the Depression and more recently in some parts of the South, blacks lost a considerable amount of farmland because they were unable to pay the increased taxes; the continuing pressure for tax sales of black lands even today makes this an ongoing problem. Paul Kutsche points out that increased valuation of lands also plagues the Mexican Americans in northern New Mexico and is one of the major causes of their land loss. "In Canones, on the Chama, water land which 20 years ago was worth $100 an acre in the local market, and unwanted by anyone but local people, is suddenly worth several thousand dollars per acre and outsiders want it for summer homes. An heir occasionally found himself unable to pay inheritance taxes unless he sold the very source of the wealth that raised his estate above the minimum."[43] Much of the remaining minority-owned land in the South went out of cultivation years ago and has now reforested itself, to the point where, ironically, it and its timber have become attractive tax shelters, and investment houses such as Merrill Lynch and E. F. Hutton are actively buying and selling. These complicated arrangements—and their tax implications—all require special knowledge.[44]

The rural minority landowner is in a more precarious position when compared with outside purchasers of land than most people are willing to admit or believe. The chances are that he has inherited his land from his father or grandfather and has held it most of his life. Newcomers can purchase land for speculation and gain an immediate depreciation benefit from the tax laws, even though not putting the land into production. The small landowner, on the other hand, receives no depreciation benefit on his land; and his capital gain tax will likely be very large if he sells his land. His inheritance tax, because of the great appreciation in value of the land, is also likely to be large. His annual property tax increases every year without any corresponding benefits in the tax code which would allow him to maintain himself as a landowner. The tax laws militate against the family that holds and uses its land in favor of the speculator who only, in effect, brokers the value of the land.

Tax benefits for speculation are perhaps the sins of legislative omission. By design, federal tax laws, like federal agricultural programs, are to benefit people who already hold substantial property and are part of the "miracle" of American agricultural production. Large farmers wishing to invest in new machinery gain the benefit of tax credits and can thus afford to modernize their operations, increasing their income. But a farmer must already be well on the way to affluence in order to benefit. The small farmer who continues to use labor-intensive methods of farming or stock raising cannot spare funds to invest in machinery and many times does not have the income to make a deduction of this kind profitable. The rule of thumb is that the more capital a person has invested in farming activities, the better his chances of escaping a tax bill and the more efficient he can become by improving his farm. Small farmers pay tax directly on income that has few shelters, and thus bear an inordinate tax burden in comparison with their more affluent neighbors.

One way to equalize the tax burden now being carried primarily by the average citizen in the rural areas is to eliminate investment credits and tax directly income produced, and to eliminate the property tax in favor of income and sales taxes wherever land is being used for agricultural purposes. Land being held for speculative purposes should be taxed according to its true value and lands where minerals are being exploited should be taxed according to the value of the minerals and not as if it were simply farmland. The Appalachian Land Ownership Task Force report noted that energy companies were paying minuscule taxes on resources worth literally billions of dollars. The figures will seem startling for people living outside Appalachia who are accustomed to paying high property taxes on their homes:

> More than three-fourths of the owners of minerals in the 80 counties paid less than 25 cents an acre in property taxes. In the 12 counties of eastern Kentucky—including some of Appalachia's major coal producers—the average tax per acre of minerals is one-fifth of a cent. The *total* tax on minerals collected by these Kentucky counties is just $1,500.[45]

Further, the report calculated that "in 22 major coal counties, with more than a billion tons of coal reserves, the owners paid an average of one-fiftieth of a cent for each ton. A ton of coal reserves is currently valued at $30 to $40."[46] Obviously the tax burden should be substantially altered in Appalachia to reflect the true value of property. The average homeowner in New York or Boston pays more in property taxes to his county than do the energy companies of the Appalachian plateau.

CREDIT AVAILABILITY

Private credit sources virtually exclude rural minorities in their lending policies. Insurance companies generally make loans only for sums much higher than small farmers want or could qualify for. Local commercial banks do lend money to farmers but they usually require collateral considerably in excess of the loan amount, and then provide loans for only a short term, usually five years, which is hardly sufficient for a small farmer to secure himself from financial trouble. Most commercial banks will not give loans for property or activity of any kind on an Indian reservation. Federal law prohibits foreclosure on trust property, and the banks argue that they cannot protect themselves in case of default.

The loans that are made by private sources to the rural poor are often simply devices to gain control of their lands. The Civil Rights Commission and the Black Economic Research Center both point out the practice of local banks requiring the entire property owned by a poor farmer as collateral for a debt that may often represent only a small fraction of the value of the land. When the farmer is unable to meet his loan payments he is foreclosed and the land is purchased for a pittance to satisfy the debt. Minority farmers who happen to own good property are often and widely the targets of this practice. Unfortunately, local county agents in the Farmers Home Administration also use this device to assist white landowners in expanding their holdings and the Civil Rights Commission heard many complaints about the use of federal loan programs to divest the poor of their land.[47]

The Department of Agriculture is charged by law with administering a variety of loan programs. The most active agency within the department is the Farmers Home Administration, originally established as the Resettlement Administration[48] during the New Deal specifically to deal with rural poverty. The agency evolved into the Farm Security Administration[49] in the later years of the New Deal and in 1946 Congress reorganized it in the Farmers Home Administration Act, combining the FSA and the Emergency Crop and Feed Loan Program,[50] giving the FHA authority to insure loans made by banks, other agencies, and private individuals in addition to making direct federal loans itself.

A series of amendments passed since this basic act has made the FHA the chief source of federally guaranteed credit for rural Americans. In addition it can support rural home ownership, home repairs, construction of rental housing in rural areas, self-help housing, farm labor housing, water and waste disposal system construction, community facilities for both business and industry, and some forms of regional development. In 1978 an amendment to the Consolidated Farm and Rural Development Act[51] made private corporations eligible for FHA loans if they were controlled by families. Supporters argued that this change only recognized the fact that many farmers today use the corporate form of landholding. But small farmers are unlikely to use the corporate form of business activity. It seems clear to critics that agribusiness now threatens to supplant small farmers as clients of the FHA.

The FHA administers eight basic loan programs. The *Farm Ownership Loan Program* is designed to help borrowers who cannot obtain credit elsewhere to improve or purchase farms, refinance debts, finance nonfarm enterprises, and make additions to farms. The *Farm Operating Loan Program* may be used to purchase farm equipment, livestock supplies, home needs, and to reduce pollution. The *Emergency Disaster Loan Program* makes loans in designated disaster areas. *Economic Emergency Loans* are available to resolve tight credit situations brought about by national or areawide economic stresses. The *Soil and Water Loan Program* provides loans for land and water development use and conservation. *Limited Resource Loans* are designed for low-income farmers to assist them in increasing their income. The *Pilot Project for Small Farm Enterprises* program was a one-year project that attempted to serve farms grossing less than $3,000 a year in income. It was initiated in June 1980 and discontinued in December 1981. The *Small Farm Assistance Program* used the funds of the Community Services Administration and ACTION volunteers to try to motivate small farmers to improve their farming practices. Unfortunately the small farmers needed money, not motivation, and the program withered and died shortly after it was established.

The U.S. Civil Rights Commission and virtually all outside observers have found discrimination against minorities in these programs. Moreover, black participation, low as it had been, declined noticeably with the beginning of the Reagan administration. The commission has also found several instances in which relatively affluent white farmers received loans from these funds even though it was obvious that they had access to other credit sources. Additionally, the commission discovered that blacks, when they did receive the services of the FHA, were almost routinely given loans at higher rates of interest and were pushed to sell their lands when it was apparent they could not make loan payments. Had it been a national policy to dispossess rural minorities from their lands the government could not have chosen a more efficient agency to accomplish the task than the FHA, as actually empowered and administered, despite its nominal and by now sullied charge.

It seems apparent that loan programs will not work in helping the rural poor, who still lack sufficient property or other resources and who are discriminated against in every step of the loan guarantee programs from the initial application for funds to the final foreclosure or payment of their debts. It would be much simpler and probably less expensive simply to grant subsistence funds to farm families having less than $5,000 annual income from farming who own, lease, or sharecrop lands. They could then invest a continuing flow of capital into their operations, and gradually build their farms into economically viable units. Loans require that an applicant have a reasonable prospect of using the money to increase his income substantially, pay back what he has borrowed, and maintain a firm economic footing so that he does not have to borrow again. Rural minorities are so poor that only a steady infusion of grant money could bring about this ideal situation. Since many loans, even if they are made, will undoubtedly be defaulted, there is no good reason why grants cannot supplant loans and the business of assisting the rural poor be placed on a firm foundation.

HEIRSHIP LANDS

Rural minorities do share one distinctive and perplexing problem whether they live in the South, Appalachia, the Southwest, or on an Indian reservation. A substantial percentage of their lands are held by older people who have rarely, over the years, made wills. When the original owner dies intestate, any land he or she owned falls into heirship status and is divided among his or her heirs. Heirship has become one of the most bothersome problems in land ownership and management facing minorities. On Indian reservations, because there is a prohibition against selling heirship lands, the tract is usually kept intact; heirs share in whatever income the tract produces according to the fractional interest they hold.

Heirship lands can be sold or partitioned at the request of the heirs—even on an Indian reservation—and generally when such a tract is sold, no single heir is capable of purchasing the whole property. Many families agree that one of the heirs will live on the land, perhaps even farm it, and the others will defer to his use or receive a share of the annual income it produces. Hence heirship lands can be used to measure the degree of family solidarity still alive; relatives having a greater concern for each other will maintain the land in a common ownership, quarrelsome relatives will insist on selling or partitioning.

Rising land prices are the death knell for heirship lands in most instances. The family is usually poor and has few resources except the property. As the value of the land increases, tensions over whether or not to sell rise accordingly, and soon one of the heirs, usually someone who has moved away and sees no possibility of returning, demands a sale, often seeing his share of the proceeds as an unexpected bonanza that can temporarily ease his financial situation. Today in northern New Mexico, Appalachia, the Black Belt of the Deep South, and on small Indian reservations there is great pressure to sell the land while the present generation of owners is alive and can enjoy the money. Since all of these decisions are really individual decisions, heirship lands constitute a direct and continuing source of trouble for those rural minorities who want to keep their lands.

Most Indian tribes have land consolidation programs where there are numerous tracts of heirship lands. The tribe acts as a purchaser of last resort and also exercises the privilege of meeting the high bid when the land is sold. Some tribes, the Rosebud Sioux for example, have established programs whereby they can accept heirship land in tribal title and issue land certificates bearing interest in exchange; heirs can consolidate their holdings through accumulating certificates and then be issued a new title to lands owned by the tribe and contiguous to land they already own or wish to purchase from the tribe. In January 1983, Congress passed the Tribal Land Consolidation Act, which declared an escheat on heirship interests below a certain value, with the interests reverting to the tribal government. This provision has questionable constitutional roots but has not yet been challenged by anyone whose interests have been forfeited to the tribe.

Blacks, Mexican Americans, and Appalachians do not enjoy similar benefits of federal land trust, nor can they get Congress to pass acts that protect their heirship lands and keep them in the families.

Escheat provisions for heirship lands owned by members of these groups would require some available entity to receive the fractional interests until they could be consolidated; but how then could they be disposed? Cooperatives have tried various ways of ameliorating the heirship land problem but the complications involved are great.

American Indians have the benefit of living in concentrated areas, and fairly accurate genealogies are usually available to aid consolidation of interests. These records by and large do not exist in the other groups, making the resolution of heirship almost impossible. Kutsche suggests that a form of federal trust be imposed on these lands to prevent their loss. Certainly the solution to this problem, if there is one, is the imposition from above of a new legal status for this kind of property. This solution, however, would be hotly contested by everyone, including most strenuously the present people who own heirship interests. Consequently the making of wills and the education of landowners seems to be the only feasible solution to heirship. Unfortunately such a task must be spread over several generations for it to become a habit. By that time, there may well be no heirship lands—and probably scant land held by minorities in rural areas.

WELFARE PROGRAMS

Today a wide variety of welfare programs provides the rural poor with their primary source of income. Such is the waking of the Jeffersonian dream. Unemployment insurance, Aid to Families with Dependent Children, disability payments, and old-age benefits are the most common forms. In Appalachia some miners have small pensions from the United Mine Workers and on some Indian reservations the tribal government issues per capita payments from the timber or oil income received each year. But these sources of income are so small as to be unimportant in the larger picture of providing income to the rural poor. There is no question that were welfare payments reduced, significantly widespread suffering would result.

In the sixties, the "War on Poverty" brought a number of training programs into depressed areas, with payrolls that attracted a number of local people. In the 1970s CETA became the main source of income for many unemployed rural people. Such efforts have been substantially reduced, or terminated in some areas, leaving local people in a precarious position. Training programs have not been successful as such, though if seen simply as "welfare" they sustained people badly in need. People were trained for jobs that do not exist in most rural areas and migration to the cities does not resolve this problem; newcomers in cities have difficulty getting and holding jobs for which they have received so-called training. The basic rural problem is simply a lack of capital, and programs that attempt to substitute labor-intensive industries or new skills in place of capital simply cannot make a significant dent.

The only reasonable alternative to social welfare programs would seem to be the assumption of the responsibility by the federal government to become employer of last resort. Actual work in conservation, construction of public facilities, or public service of some kind could be undertaken. Educational programs that considered classroom training and on-the-job experience as compensable work could also be initiated. The cost of either alternative should not be significantly higher than present welfare programs. Instead of doling out insufficient funds to welfare clients, the government could be paying a living wage to these same people, enabling them to become purchasers and taxpayers. Caudill described in eloquent terms how miners in Appalachia simply gave up when the familiar employment vanished and sought to be declared disabled so they could receive welfare checks from the state. The same resigned lethargy exists in varying degrees among rural blacks, Indians, and Mexican Americans. No amount of enthusiastic reports about the American way of life or the virtues of hard work can raise such people, who feel themselves discarded, from their depression. Helplessness erodes human dignity and without dignity it is impossible for people to want to pick themselves up to accomplish anything.

American welfare programs have a curious theoretical framework undergirding them. The ideal American is hard-working, affluent or comfortable, independent, and usually a male head of a family. Welfare programs reimburse clients for each characteristic they possess that varies from this idealized figure; therefore, they inevitably and intentionally stigmatize. Old-age assistance compensates people for loss of youth; AFDC compensates mothers and children for the loss of the father and husband; disability payments compensate for physical handicaps; and so forth. Unemployment compensation adopts the fiction that unemployment is unnatural, temporary, and implies that the recipient is hard at work trying to secure other employment. The ideology of welfare programs is thus grounded in the old Protestant ethic, and demands a pretense by the government and the client that need is abnormal.

CULTURAL BARRIERS

Cultural barriers are of two kinds: the cultural perceptions of the majority and those of the minorities themselves. The cultural viewpoint of the majority largely determines aid programs. When the majority has a pejorative view of rural minorities, it excludes them from consideration in its plans and they remain beyond the social pale. The cultural view of the minorities is equally important. Clannish folk people generally tend to gather with their own kind to the exclusion of others, an attitude which creates undue suspicions of those outside the group, preventing the free and easy interchange of views. The minority may have excellent reasons for its restricted view of things and its suspicions of the majority. It must, nevertheless, be prepared to look beyond the immediate hurt and see the future course of events, eventually discovering an accommodation with the majority that preserves its identity. Accommodation need not mean assimilation; failure to make unavoidable accommodations with the majority can mean simply assimilation into the bottom of the social pyramid, not cultural, political, or economic freedom for the minority group.

THE VIEW OF THE MAJORITY

The collective stereotype of any group built over generations of interactions is usually hazy and full of conflicting messages. Contemporary stereotypes of American minorities range from the extremely romantic images of happy carefree people to brutal derogatory views of hopeless burdens on society, supported only by welfare programs that cost the taxpayer unending sums.

The Indian is the chief beneficiary of the romantic stereotypes —the child of nature, our first and most perfect ecologist, the noble savage. Appalachians share this romantic image, because of the popularity of television series dealing with hillbillies and the spread of country-western music into middle-American homes. Rural blacks are still often depicted as happy, childlike people and Mexican Americans pictured as pleasant "banditos" continually engaged in fiestas.

Some members of the majority may hold onto their romantic images because their own communal lives are devoid of the closeness and spontaneity that rural people seem to represent. There is a popular image often circulated which suggests that minorities live the way the majority would like to live and this style of life is then credited with intangible values which the majority has surrendered in order to act "responsibly." If one accepts this image, it becomes easier to bear one's tensions content in the belief that the choice was correct and reflected adult values consonant with the modern world. Minorities live in pristine beauty, simple and innocent, and would no doubt welcome the rest of the world if they chose to run away from their duties. Without this rustic fantasy the majority might be left without an escape, unable to convince itself that its material benefits have been worth the sacrifice.

The degrading images of minorities also serve the majority in its need to find scapegoats for the imbalance in modern society. The federal budget is perceived as out of kilter primarily because there are so many minority people on welfare. The fact that we have military weapons stacked all over the world and are paying outrageously high subsidies to a variety of businesses is cast aside.

Middle-class Americans never seem to get upset when wealthier people receive benefits from the government; perhaps they believe they will one day come to merit these privileges. When someone below them on the social and economic ladder receives benefits, however, they seem often to lose all sense of proportion, as if providing the less fortunate with some basic protections cancels all the hard work that they themselves have done to improve themselves. The poor—and particularly the conspicuous minority poor—are not felt to be morally worthy of government or private largess. Eligibility for programs is in many ways a secular statement regarding moral worth, not a rigorous definition of need or qualifications. Administrators spend an inordinate amount of time and energy checking eligibility. Discrimination is a factor. The U.S. Civil Rights Commission, in investigating the Farmers Home Administration, came across instances where people obviously capable of fending for themselves were beneficiaries of its programs, while a disproportionate number of minorities were rejected for the same benefits. The majority has come to believe that federal and state programs that benefit them are their "right," while ones designed to assist those people less fortunate are merely "privileges" which can and should be revoked for misconduct and cheating. Where, in majority opinion, subsidies end and rights begin cannot be easily determined. The clarification of this point would contribute substantially to the resolution of the perception of the minorities, and might include them within the circle of government largess.

THE VIEW OF THE MINORITIES

Like the majority, minorities we have been discussing have certain cultural viewpoints which handicap them in solving their conflicts with the rest of the world. Generally they are rural folk who place great emphasis on personal honor, family, clan, or circle of acquaintances, and are as inclined as anyone else to take the incidents of their lives personally. Some Appalachian mountain people, for example, continued the Civil War for another generation because of real or imagined personal insults. American Indians have widely refused, from a multitude of personal attitudes, to cooperate with federal officials in important programs that might have helped them. Rural blacks and Mexican Americans exhibit their own emotional responses to life which are markedly different from those of their urban counterparts.

Drawing one's living directly from one's land often gives people a certain independence, a feeling reflected in the tendency to remain aloof from highly organized community activities. Spontaneous celebrations and events will draw people from hundreds of miles, while more formally ordered events tend to create dissension and may not even draw a handful of people. The elevation of a neighbor to a position of local responsibility often causes resentment; minorities frequently see their immediate neighbors as more a threat to their own existence than are corporate manipulations and the impersonal oppressions of the middle class. Neighbors are an immediate presence, while the middle class is generally encountered in a social or business context in which their superiority is acknowledged, and the intrusions of corporations are never apparent until the bulldozer arrives at the gate.

Minorities often resist change even when the change may be to their own benefit. Adoption of new farming techniques or new forms of social organization, and the substitution of new beliefs for old ones are often rejected because they go against conventional wisdom passed down through many years. The urge to hold onto folk beliefs and remedies even in the face of more modern, technological medical treatment is strong. Rural folk often refuse to use banks, mistrusting institutions as a whole. Minorities often still seek personal revenge instead of taking legal action against those with whom they have a quarrel. Some educational programs never take off because they make little or no attempt to incorporate the existing knowledge or habits of the community in the proposed new programs.

Rejecting these "advances" or "advantages" often entails a hidden moral code in the community, one not articulated but studiously followed; thus some Indians and Mexican Americans refuse to open bank accounts because doing so might make them "like whites." Resistance to change is very closely linked to local group identity, which has a higher value than individual progress or enrichment.

Rural minorities are frequently fearful as well as distrustful of outside authority, however, and may be afraid to challenge what is told them by outsiders—leaving them in a very vulnerable position. They may respect people vested with a symbol of authority, even though common sense (and personal conviction) tells them to reject their advice. In criminal law, this attitude has prompted both voluntary confessions of wrongdoing and the inordinately severe sentences that the rural poor tend to receive from the courts. Seeing such disasters and misfortunes, they tend to blame only themselves, not considering it possible to look beyond the immediate circumstances that led to their troubles and question the institutions themselves. It is easy for the majority to perpetuate the feelings of helplessness and inevitability in minority communities which keep them at the bottom of the social and economic pyramid.

There is much discussion at all levels today about the plight of rural people and their relationship to the land. Despite the professed respect of urban peoples for the value and steadfastness of the rural tradition, the rush to secure national energy independence and the affluent majority's lust for recreational health seem destined to obliterate the rural minorities' security in the next two decades. Only a change of philosophical orientation by the majority can prevent this, or temper the brutal effects of such a drive. Without that, governmental action to preserve the lives of rural minorities could only establish a "reservation" mentality of paternalism or formalize already existing patterns of welfare statism which have been detrimental to any long-term solutions.

Is there any way to change these views, apart from removing the people from their environment and allowing several generations of urban experience to wash away all traces of rural heritage? To avoid that, resolution of their problems will have to come through the positive actions of a compassionate national administration willing to sweep away institutional barriers to minority progress, and to allow people to transform themselves gradually over several generations. An equitable tax code and just enforcement of existing laws may be the first and most vital steps we can take.

NOTES

1. 24 Stat. 388.
2. 26 Stat. 794.
3. Hearings, Senate Subcommittee on Indian Affairs, *Survey of Conditions of the Indians in the United States,* 71st Cong. 2d. sess. pt. 6, *Engle Report,* January 21, 1930, p. 2259.
4. 207 U.S. 564 (1908).
5. 43 Stat. 244.
6. 52 Stat. 347.
7. 48 Stat. 984.
8. *Camp Crier,* August 5, 1983, p. 7.
9. Act of March 3, 1865, 13 Stat. 507.
10. U.S. Civil Rights Commission, *The Decline of Black Farming* (Washington, D.C.: Government Printing Office, 1973), p. 15.
11. The Black Economic Research Center, *Only Six Million Acres* (New York, 1973), p. 19.
12. *The Decline of Black Farming,* pp. 23–24.
13. U.S. Bureau of the Census, *The Negro Farmer in the United States,* (Fifteenth Census of the United States: 1930 Census of Agriculture), p. 7.
14. Act of May 12, 1933, 48 Stat. 31.
15. *The Decline of Black Farming,* p. 38.
16. *Ibid.* pp. 39–40.

17. Center for Rural Affairs, "Take Hogs, for Example: The Transformation of Hog Farming in America," January 1981, p. 19.
18. *The Decline of Black Farming*, p. 40.
19. See "Mexican Land Claims in California," in Wayne Moquin and Charles Van Doren, *A Documentary History of the Mexican Americans* (New York: Bantam Books, 1971), pp. 263–271.
20. See "A Sante Fe Trader Looks at New Mexico," in *A Documentary History of the Mexican Americans*, pp. 234–240.
21. Abraham Hoffman, *Unwanted Mexican Americans in the Great Depression* (Tucson: University of Arizona Press, 1974), p. 7.
22. *Ibid.*, 11.
23. *Ibid.*, p. 28.
24. *Ibid.*, pp. 39–40.
25. *Ibid.*, pp. 174–175, Appendix D Charts.
26. Harry Caudill, *Night Comes to the Cumberlands* (Boston: Atlantic–Little, Brown, 1962), p. 63.
27. *Ibid.*, p. 93.
28. *Ibid.*, pp. 169–172.
29. *Ibid.*, pp. 263–265.
30. *Ibid.*, p. 237.
31. *Ibid.*, p. 393.
32. *Ibid.*, p. 376.
33. Act of May 18, 1934.
34. *The Decline of Black Farming* deals primarily with difficulties blacks have experienced with the Farm Home Administration.
35. Act of July 2, 1862.
36. Act of August 30, 1890, 26 Stat. 417.
37. *The Decline of Black Farming*, p. 54.
38. Authorized under P.L. 89–106.
39. Tribally Controlled Community College Assistance Act—92 Stat. 1325.
40. 102 S. Ct. 894 (1980).
41. The study consists of seven volumes—one regional overview and one volume for each of the six states studied: Alabama, Kentucky, North Carolina, Tennessee, Virginia, and West Virginia.
42. *Land Ownership Patterns and Their Impacts on Appalachian Communities*, 1981, p. 72.
43. Paul Kutsche, "Spanish and Mexican Land Grants Need a Separate Legal Status," a paper delivered at the Western Social Science Association meetings, Albuquerque, New Mexico, April 1983, p. 3.
44. Tom Hatley, "Forestry and Equity," *Southern Changes*, vol. 5, No. 4, July/August 1983.
45. John Gaventa and Bill Horton, "Land and Life in the Mountains," *Southern Exposure* 10, no. 1 (January–February 1982).
46. *Ibid.*
47. *Only Six Million Acres*, p. B-5.

48. The Resettlement Administration was established as an independent agency in 1935 and was assigned to the Department of Agriculture in 1937.
49. Bankhead-Jones Farm Tenant Act, 50 Stat. 522 (1937).
50. Farmers Home Administration Act of 1946, 60 Stat. 1062.
51. Agricultural Credit Act of 1978, 92 Stat. 420.

GOVERNMENT
FOR ALL
THE PEOPLE

LESLIE W. DUNBAR

The management of minorities is one of the oldest functions of governments. Writers about politics, even down to our day, have tended to see minorities as subgroups of the "poor"; governments have had to be more perceptive. It is hard to think of more than a very few modern governments not somehow bedeviled by their "minority question."

It is distasteful to speak of the "management" of minorities issues, just as it is jarring when one hears of "managing" the arms race. That is, nevertheless, what it has been, through the centuries, and nearly always with the assumption that the minority somehow is inferior. For long years, the American politic system has managed and controlled the minorities living here, with various policies and intensities. Special policies for Jews have been virtually extinguished, for blacks have been revolutionized, for Indians have gone through repeated transformations. The years between the world wars were the approximate watershed when this ceased to be a society in which it was tacitly understood that persons of northern European stock, in particular British and Dutch, had claims for preferment. Since then, there has been a great movement of new peoples into the field of those who "count," who are in fact as well as in legal fiction part of the "consent of the governed."

With some, the Italians for instance, that progress has been comparatively easy. With others—blacks, of course, most of all—it has been enormously hard, and is far from completed. John Jay thanked Providence that we were "one united people; a people descended from the same ancestors, speaking the same language, professing the same religion, attached to the same principles of government, very similar in their manners and customs."[1] That luck, if it were such, ran out a hundred years ago. The reconstruction of "one united people" has been slow in occurring.

No definition of "minority" suits all purposes. I use here a political one, a slight modification of Harlan B. Stone's famous 1938 dictum[2]: "a discrete and insular" racial or ethnic group against which discrimination or prejudice is or has recently been practiced to an extent that makes present political and economic advance of its members very difficult. In the United States today (though not always in the past), under that definition all significant minorities are nonwhite, or of Latin American origin. Except for Chinese and Japanese, American minorities also are, as groups, poor (and recent Chinese immigration has lowered the income status of that group). The minority "problem" facing American government and society is, then, that of persistent poverty attaching disproportionately to nonwhites and Hispanics.*

By no great surprise, that is also the problem of worldwide inequality. But nothing is clear cut, especially not in the relationships of human beings with each other. Ethnic differences abound, ethnic pride can be immense, old ethnic prejudices are slow in dying. To

---

* For the rest of this essay, I may use the term "nonwhite" to include Hispanics. What that implies (beyond convenience) is acceptance of, for the purpose of an essay on the role of government, the majority's perception, which is that Hispanics "are not white like us." In this writer's opinion, no virtue or fault attaches to color; no privilege should either. The terms white and nonwhite have, therefore, no value content. Use of them does acknowledge what is a controlling fact; e.g. that whereas in other countries minorities may be set apart by religion, language, or other cultural distinction, here it is by color, and that the large distinction is of white and nonwhites *as perceived by the whites.*

this day, there are doors in this country closed to Jews, Italian Americans can readily recount harsh social slights, and so on, in a distressing pattern. There are, moreover, throughout the world recurrent conflicts between majority and minority peoples that are not primarily economic, do not in fact necessarily even raise issues of economic equality: Basques and other Spaniards, Quebecois and other Canadians, Ibos and other Nigerians, Belgium's Walloons and Flemings, other peoples in other places.

We shall nevertheless have to say, I think, that though in the United States the "melting pot" has not been the social unifier once bragged of, the American marketplace has become a well-nigh invincible unifier, impossible of escape. Here and there a communal band seeks withdrawal. For all but a tiny few of us, however, the marketplace provides common ends and means, and the political and social sides we take are most usually determined by our function within it and by how well we prosper. As minorities have in turn won their civil rights struggles, the marketplace has become theirs too. This does not obliterate ethnic distinctions; it does render them secondary. The problems between nonwhites and other Americans are become a tangle of economic and racial factors, but the economic are primary. Although the residue of racial discrimination is immense, little can be done by public policy toward either obliterating it or honoring racial differences until economic disparities are greatly lessened, until to be nonwhite does not mean to be probably poor. Leninism and Soviet orthodoxy are insistent that the "nationalities" question, as they call it, is fundamentally a part of the class struggle. They are also insistent that cultural attributes of the Soviet Union's numerous nationalities can and should be preserved. This has the probably intended effect of protecting the "Russian" nation: within the Soviet Union, Russians stand in a position of leadership and preeminence higher even than that of British-stock Americans of our past; to their great credit, they have not found the degradation of the other peoples of the Soviet Union necessary or desirable, as our elite once did here. Perhaps they thereby insure their preeminence all the more firmly.

To make the point as clearly as I can: the primary minorities issue facing American government and society today is economic. That was not the case before the 1960s and 1970s, when basic civil rights had to be won. Formerly, minorities were typically poor and universally discriminated against. Today, they remain typically poor.

No longer, then, does government have its traditional role of "managing" minorities, not at any rate in measure at all comparable to the past. The bilingual issues presented by Hispanics and the complex array of questions regarding Indians do still evoke that traditional role. There is likewise a continuous need for monitoring the federal government's own actions as they affect all minorities, in order to assure fair and nondiscriminatory treatment; such is particularly called for in obtaining fair shares in federal benefits—as in, e.g., the agricultural programs or in the support of higher education and research—and in procurement.[3] Beyond that is, however, the vastly more important question of fair shares in the economy, and to secure those, racially specific governmental policies are not enough.

This is not, of course, to say that old problems of discrimination in all their forms are solved, only that they are in their largest import subsumed now in economics. Until the mid-1960s and for a century and longer before then, the basic charge of every southern state government was to control the blacks and keep them "in their place." We are beyond that, as we are beyond days when, in the name of racial and sectional amity, the federal government maintained segregated armed forces and tolerated the open evasion of the Fifteenth Amendment. One of the extraordinary successes of the civil rights movement is that today in many local governments—big and small —blacks and Hispanics have won executive and legislative offices. These local officeholders, including the mayors of some of our biggest cities, can do little to improve the economic lot of most of their people: ours is a relentlessly national economy. They can, through procurement and appointment decisions, aid significantly in enlarging the minorities' middle class, which is of crucial long-run economic value. What they can also do, and now, is guide and direct the processes of mutual accommodation—of integration, if that may be said—of minorities and whites with each other. At these local levels, where the old issues of discrimination and of whites and nonwhites "getting along" are keenest, minorities now participate decisively in their resolution. In short, the managing of minorities has passed, much of it, to local governments where minority peoples themselves have their greatest influence.

For the national government in this changed situation, what ought to be or can be its purposes and guiding principles? There is no need to look beyond the nation's own social contract, of which we are finally acknowledging that nonwhites are to be an actual part. We once said our purposes were to

- form a more perfect union;
- establish justice;
- insure domestic tranquility;
- provide for the common defense;
- promote the general welfare; and
- secure liberty to ourselves and our posterity.

Fairness toward minorities enters into all those commitments, made by all of us to ourselves. The first two do well enough as conditions for making the social contract real for people long kept by American society at great disadvantage: a more perfect union, and justice.

A MORE PERFECT UNION

The Harvard political scientist Martin Kilson, writing in *The Public Interest,* reviewed data similar to that set out in this book by William Julius Wilson regarding the persistence of poverty among the lowest stratum of black Americans. He concluded by calling on the "American system" to fulfill the goal of life "standards" for blacks equal to other Americans. Toward that end, he approved of vouchers permitting choice of school and "free enterprise zones" facilitating economic development in minority areas. What he saw, however, as centrally important was the need for blacks to forge "cultural patterns conducive to social mobility" and "behavioral change."[4]

No one ought to dispute that mentally normal people in any circumstance can and should try intelligently to help themselves. The conclusion, however, that the general society has little or no primary responsibility for advance of the poor repudiates centuries of western political and moral thought. It reflects the orthodoxy that seems to have descended over our politics and our political theory. Those views have erased, or made very faint, the concept of political obligation painstakingly elaborated by traditional political philosophy and have timidly allowed an acquiescence in the need for "welfare," a mean substitute at best for the principle already arrived at by nineteenth-century liberal spokesmen, of social minimums below which none should fall.

Citizens of a democracy have duties. Representative institutions cannot function responsibly except in a political order where thought is free, informed, and expressed, and where power is accessible to all, both to hold and to influence. A free state requires that each citizen assume care not only for himself but for an area of civic responsibility, however limited and following whatever individual course. This is not likely to occur, nor do we find evidence that it has ever occurred among classes degraded and overburdened by the experience of unmitigated poverty and ghetto living. That kind of experience disables citizenships, a truth known clearly to Aristotle. Perpetual tensions and instability are built within society when discrete classes or groups are, for whatever cause, consigned to social inferiority. Moral agency requires an imperfect universe, and that the poor surely have; but it requires also the possibility of hope.

Historically (and not only in the United States), governments have wanted, when it pleased them, to oppress and discriminate against blacks (and sometimes other minorities as well, such as Jews) *as a group*, but to hold them even while doing so *accountable as individuals*. Blacks' experience in the United States has been one of continual redefining of their legal and constitutional status; indeed, not even yet has the law become clearly settled. Originally, before slavery was grafted onto the common law, theirs was a murky legal standing. From that, they were blanketed into slavery itself. During the first half of the nineteenth century came the possibility of citizenship for individuals, as exceptions to the norm of slavery, but with legalized restrictions not ever applied to whites. After the Civil War citizenship was ordered by the Fourteenth Amendment; then allowable postslavery *and* postcitizenship discrimination *by law*; then removal of such, especially following the Supreme Court's ruling of 1954 in *Brown* v. *Board of Education*; and finally, or at least contemporaneously, the unresolved issue of special assistance through race-conscious law. When legal discrimination was ended, it was as though political power then said to blacks, "in exchange for no longer oppressing you simply because of your group membership we give you now the rank of 'individual,' with the social and political risks, duties, and whatever benefits that entails." In hard truth, short of our "Indian solution," there is probably no alternative. The long American process of defining and redefining blacks' legal status effectively blotted out the capacity of American law and political institutions to treat them other than as individuals. They were made into, as are all the rest of us other than tribal Indians with their semblance of recognized "group rights," bundles of individual rights. Unless there is to be a new constitutional order, they will stay that way.

But does that require, as the Reagan administration would have it, that law cannot provide effective remedies for past denials? Much of the so-called "urban problem" of the contemporary United States, much of the problem of permanent (or, at least, persistent) poverty is bound up in the question of whether that political and legal transformation of blacks from economic instruments into independent individuals will work, and how soon. And the political question is whether American constitutionalism, which was adaptable enough to visit group discrimination on minorities, can now provide special service; and if so, how, a question which Herman Schwartz's essay has illuminated.

Rights have always their other side, duties. Duties without rights are mere obedience to orders, as in the military or in a despotic state. Rights without the self-imposition of duties are barren, socially useless. But duty is of little meaning when the individual is far removed from relationship with the object of duty. (What is *my* duty to the Organization of American States? to the United Nations? What is a Guamanian's duty to the United States?) The resident of one of our urban ghettos probably sees and feels government more than do the rest of us, but the government he sees is an adversary or custodian. It is government in the persona of policeman, welfare worker, court personnel; it is government that has to be coped with, manipulated, avoided, or sometimes implored. It is not government to be loved or even respected, nor to be given its due in return for its acknowledgement of one's status as a self-governing citizen. To speak of that government as empowered by his "consent" is a constitutional fiction that perhaps serves the interests of the government, or the majority that upholds it, but dubiously serves any of his.

The constitutional framers were pragmatically wise, even visionary, in putting "a more perfect union" first among the values of the Constitution. Almost certainly that meant to them primarily a better union of the states. But the men who from the first directed this government were intent on having a national government that dealt directly with individuals. Among the first words of *The Federalist* are:

> It has been frequently remarked, that, it seems to have been reserved to the people of this country, to decide by their conduct and example, the important question, whether societies of men are really capable or not, of establishing good government from reflection and choice, or whether they are forever destined to depend, for their political constitutions, on accident and force.[5]

All political systems admitting of any degree of public participation are hard pressed to elicit genuine "reflection and choice." The United States government has had its own long-time encounter with the task. "Reflection and choice" come hard to an electorate like ours. They come hardly at all among those millions of citizens belonging to an underclass that has neither economic nor civic contribution to make to the policy. To people who are made well aware that they have no talents or skills the economy values, to people who see "government" as merely another institutional power—like the telephone company or the subways or prisons—the concept that they have a right-begetting and duty-requiring "union" with others can only seem another of the social deceptions they have to fend off. To them, government is like the weather: uncontrollable, probably survivable, always to be adjusted to, frequently a big problem.

Democracy is essentially and centrally process, a way of conducting public affairs that satisfies a public's own sense of fairness. It is, however, not enough to say only this, nor would it be enough to say that right methods will safely work to good ends. The voters of 1787–1789 rejected that argument when used to deny the need for a Bill of Rights, preferring to see certain substantive ends and procedural stipulations written directly into the fundamental law. Transient human lives cannot ethically be subordinated to method. It is time for the United States to end its singularity among advanced industrial nations by giving legal force to basic economic and educational rights. If unity is what we want, the path to it is through security of rights, civil, political, and economic.

JUSTICE

Poverty poses three sorts of problems for American policy. First and basic, what rank, what degree of importance, do we give to it; second, how do we define government's degree of responsibility for remedy; and third, what solutions do we shape, assuming we have not concluded that only the poor themselves are responsible for their own condition.

Until the nineteenth century, poverty was hardly even a topic in political theory. In the wake of the French Revolution, one after another writer turned to it, leading to the work of Marx and of the Fabians and English idealists late in the century (of whom the best representative was T. H. Green). Marx can be said to have proposed that poverty, or at least its cause, is the central issue of political philosophy, displacing its typical concern for political relationships and rights. The English writers are less well known to us, but practically meant a great deal more to us than did Marx, even if they had nothing like his seismic force. As John Rawls's book, *A Theory of Justice,* can be described as a justifying statement of American centrist liberalism, so Green's *Lectures on the Principles of Political Obligation* a century before set its directions (and the fact that one writes as a social contractarian and the other wrote from a divergent stimulus does not affect the case).

Politics, Green held, must aid (or else, because it inevitably affects, will distort) the moral development of the members of a society. Its special role is the "removal of obstacles" to self-realization. Green adopted as the measure and criterion of social progress the erasure of barriers separating men from each other (e.g., slavery), thus making possible an ever-widening human fellowship. On this view, the recognition of rights belonging to man *as* man becomes the first mark of historical advance. The end is, however, the perfection of character, and as long as men are merely free from restraints their advance has been only "negative," although necessary. Ethical progress is completed when men in their freedom accomplish moral ends they have imposed on themselves. The free man is thus the emancipated man only in the first step; he is the emancipated man possessed of sufficient education, material means, and social status in the second step; the free man is, finally, the good man. That second step is "positive freedom." It is the purpose and domain of government. Negative rights, Green concluded, make inevitable positive freedom, because the former once acknowledged lead to effective demands for the latter, and because it is socially necessary that all who are politically responsible shall be politically capable. Positive freedom in turn makes possible the fuller development of the negative rights which, as they appertain to the spirit of man, are in the end more important. But it is hypocrisy, Green said, to speak of men as free as long as they remain fettered by ignorance, poverty, or—he added—alcohol. State power has the function of removing such obstacles to the development of self-reliant citizens and persons.

With variations of rhetoric and tone, that was essentially the program of British liberalism prior to 1945 and of the "welfare state" if not nationalization policies of the 1945–1951 Attlee government; of Wilson's "new freedom" and the Progressive movement; and of the Rooseveltian New Deal. All had an unself-conscious moral tone, which has been almost totally missing from post-World War II American political programs except for a brief revival in the 1964–1966 interlude of Johnson's administration. All aimed at enabling citizens to stand on their own feet. All saw the government's role as primarily the "removal of obstacles" through care for the economic security and education of the people. *None* saw poverty as necessary and acceptable, as a condition government could leave to market forces, as the Reagan administration does. As Rawls has written:

> What is just and unjust is the way that institutions deal with [unequal talents and social advantages] . . . there is no necessity for men to resign themselves to these contingencies. The social system is not an unchangeable order beyond human control but a pattern of human action. In justice as fairness men agree to share one another's fate.[6]

To return to our questions, the first—what political priority attaches to the problem of poverty?—has to be answered to the effect that none is higher. Men have debated for centuries the relative values of liberty, equality, order, and justice. There is a large and welcome measure of redundancy among them. There may, nevertheless, be enough distinction to make useful gradations of emphasis among them within a consensual society; i.e., within one where all who are legally held responsible for their acts may be fairly said to have given consent to those laws. But a permanently impoverished class cannot be said to have done so. Our steadily increasing prison population is tacit acknowledgment of this. For a republican society with a huge underclass, there is no feasible course consistent with professed principles and its own stability but to address the problem of poverty, and not turn from it.

From numerous sources the public hears that past governmental antipoverty programs have "failed," and that therefore, none should again be tried. Besides being flawed logic, the conclusion has few analogues in other areas of policy. What ever does work, once and for all? Our foreign policies, based on suspicion of the Soviet Union, have not reduced the USSR's influence or power; they have instead led us into seemingly endless military involvements abroad and have imposed upon us incredibly large expenditures. Yet their failure to achieve their goal—the reduction of Soviet power—is not seen by either Democratic or Republican leadership as a cause for change. Our farm policies have achieved only one of their proclaimed goals —the increase of production. They have failed miserably at any of the others, such as protection of the "family farm" or a better life for rural people, who have instead been propelled in droves by those policies to the slums of the cities. Yet we continue in them, with mere shifts of emphasis. Our policies to reduce use of narcotics have not worked; should we now encourage narcotic use? Goals deemed essential by government are pursued. The abolition of persistent poverty is essential. Hardly anyone publicly denies that. But adequately funded and, above all, sustained policies toward that goal do not follow.

Our policy fluctuations, from one administration to another, are like those in foreign policies: neither affects the larger prevailing patterns of our political economy, which are capitalism and Soviet rivalry. This is not to say that changes of administrations do not matter. They do, often intensely so, as they bring about variations of methods and tactics, of sensitivity to suffering and hardship, and of understanding of rights and liberties. Often these quite important variations revolve about, in terribly damaging ways, our attitudes and acts toward the weak, toward the poor at home and the poorer nations abroad. At home, changes of administration tend to register on a scale of harsher to milder forms of "trickle-down" theories. There have been no end to these, from Charles Wilson's "what is good for General Motors is good for the United States" to John Kennedy's "rising tide that lifts all boats" to Ronald Reagan's "supply-side economics." Without arguing economic merits, the common factor among them all is the subordination of the interests of the poor to other economic goals. Even if that were economically defensible, it is politically wrong.

Our second question—what is government's responsibility?—virtually is answered above. Poverty in industrial societies is a function of low income, and that is the result of unemployment or underemployment more than anything else. By 1983, the officially defined poverty rate included 15 percent of the population, which means nearly 35 million people; and unemployment hovered around 10 percent of the work force, double that for minorities, quadruple that for minority youth. The figures fluctuate from one reporting period to another. They nevertheless creep steadily upward. The causes have been well agreed upon: technological changes that have reduced the number of entry-level, unskilled jobs and have eliminated others through increased productivity; the particular case of agriculture, become now so thoroughly a capital-intensive industry that the farms have been amazingly depopulated; the transference of much labor-intensive manufacturing to foreign countries; the baby boom of the 1950s and 1960s, which has not been fully caught up with by the job market; the great increase in numbers of women in job competition with males; and a hard to measure but certainly large influx of immigrants in the 1970s from Latin America and Asia. These developments have represented *basic*—not transient—alterations of the economy. All or nearly all have arisen with the encouragement, express or tacit, of public policy, especially including tax policies.

The first rule of personal morality is to accept responsibility for the consequences of one's acts; the rule of political morality should be little different. The poverty these governmentally encouraged or tolerated changes have caused requires a public response.

Today's poverty is not something done *to* the poor. It is not caused by policies—slavery or the old British enclosures would have been early examples of such, South African labor laws a contemporary one—framed deliberately to take advantage of the poor, as desired and as power allowed. Some of it, however, results from policies—not introduced by the Reagan administration but gaily carried further by it—to reward the rich. Today's poverty is caused by the way the economy works. Those workings make problems not only for the poor. The poor have less defense, however, nor do they share at all proportionately in the advantages and opportunities that these basic changes also produce; consequently, the gap between the poor and the mainstream widens. Nor, finally, is there much precedent for believing that the approaches society takes and will take toward smoothing out the problems spawned for it by basic changes (rebuilding American industry plans, for example) will have the fortunes of the poor much at heart or in mind; they will be left to the rising tide, though justice would require that they not be.

FROM GROUP DISCRIMINATION TO INDIVIDUAL RIGHTS

The third question—effective solutions—is hard; there can be no dispute about that, at least. Among the possible answers to it can be that government allow the market to solve the problem. That flies in the face of all experience, and all the judgments of the economic and political managers of other countries, but theoretically—and in this case contemporary American electoral politics bends today toward theory, toward ideology, and away from experience—it may be possible.

A more realistic approach is along a line already opened, that of entitlement. The American poverty problem, the seemingly pathological one that will not yield even to upward trends of the general economy, consists primarily of the millions among us for whom the economy has no apparent need: untrained or ill-trained, socially disoriented, culturally misfit, a very large proportion of them young blacks and Hispanics, many who are mothers without mates, many the children of single-parent households.*

Their situation is made more desperate by other complicating factors. First, just above them are millions who are employed at unskilled, low-paying jobs, many in such occupations as fast-food clerks, hotel workers, or other like segments of the expanding so-called "service industries," and who represent almost the only realistic jobs available to those below them. These are jobs that require little or no preliminary training, and consequently provide scant incentive for schooling or special training. A second factor is the large number today of the cyclically unemployed, people who do have skills and are attractive employees, and who compete for such jobs as become available, letting employers choose between hiring them or the perhaps less demanding and more tractable unskilled. A third factor is the ease of entry into and the low risks of the underground economy of drugs, gambling, and sex. A fourth factor is that the system of welfare, including food and medical assistance, does all but guarantee subsistence.

The welfare system is based on entitlement: if stipulated conditions are met, benefits are paid. Those conditions relate to income levels. Other entitlement programs have other criteria: veteran's status, disability, old age, unemployment compensation, etc. So well established and popular are these non-means-tested entitlements that they can be considered now part of the American plan of governing. The means-tested entitlements, on the other hand, become more or less generous as the political winds shift. Their purpose being nothing more than subsistence, the shift is mainly in the levels of poverty included as deserving of this "safety net," more or fewer, rather than in the size of subsistence provision for those included. The welfare

---

* "A major national goal for this decade should be to arrest the proliferation of disadvantaged female-headed black families. Family reinforcement constitutes the single most important action the nation can take toward the elimination of black poverty and related social problems." *A Policy Framework for Racial Justice* (Washington, D.C.: Joint Center for Political Studies, 1983), page 12.

system has no relevance to the ending of poverty; people don't get off welfare, or the need for it, by being on it. At best, it is a bureaucratically, sometimes degradingly, administered and minimally adequate support for those who really cannot work, or a "tiding over" for those out of work. For many, it operates in ways that actually discourage attempts to work, and becomes virtually a permanent arrangement. It is the price America pays to prevent noisome starvation and riotous protest. There are, moreover, many rural and urban communities in our poverty belts where the various forms of welfare —AFDC, Medicaid, food stamps, black lung compensation, etc.—are the principal economic base for everyone in the area, not just the poor.

But however poorly applied, the entitlement principle is a good one. It is also as close as the United States has come to the adoption of "positive rights." The principle could (and should) be extended further, beyond simple subsistence (and essentially that is also what old-age insurance and unemployment compensation are) to cover those things related to making an individual self-sustaining. Such has been the purpose of that largest of entitlement programs, the public school system. The indicated step beyond that is to make job training and entry-level, non-dead-end public service jobs available *as a right*. Mothers who cannot work because of children at home could have the supports they need, either to study at home or have day care provided. And as public schools are compulsory, so should be training and work, of some useful kind, by those not disabled. Between a permanent underclass and the availability of useful work, there is only doubtfully stable middle ground.

The entitlement principle does, in fact, already pervade all the relationships governments, state as well as federal, have toward the economy. Ours is an ideological politics in theory (the ideology of "free enterprise") but determinedly nonideological in application (unless, which may well be the case, the controlling if unstated ideology is simply the protection of vested interests). In recent years we have seen an intellectual revival of "free market" economics, and about it there is a beguiling persuasiveness. Many of us can recall how neatly and ineluctably the demand and supply curves intersected and balanced in our Economics I class, and the blackboard logic of them captures our sometime acquiescence still. The Reagan administration professes its faith in them, and when not inconvenient to its supporters' interests—more to the point, when convenient to its supporters' interests—follows them. In universities, think tanks, and some editorial pages a flock of writers has of late proclaimed them. The classical revival has included, to the good luck of its publicity, some black economists, notably Thomas Sowell and Walter E. Williams, whose prescriptions for ending black poverty consist chiefly of abolishing the minimum wage and curtailing, if not undoing, the strength of labor unions.[7]

Perhaps—who knows?—with a clean slate, free-flowing demand and supply could work. In the tight interlock between politics and economics that history has fashioned the doctrine is meaningless. The American economy long ago claimed the American political system as its own, and has managed it more than it has been managed. The political aims of business are not and have not been primarily derived from creed, but from insistence that Washington and state capitals recognize and observe the *specific* interests of *specific* segments of the business system. The oil industry, the banks, the media, the wheat growers, and all the rest *each* have their welcome in and access to governing circles; and political decisions are made within the context of accommodating their interests, as they each have defined them. In short, they have insisted upon their *entitlements*.[8]

It is an imperfect but not necessarily bad political economy. It resembles and, indeed, draws reinforcement from the constitutional structure of checks and balances: power limiting power, interests adjusting to interests. What has made the system often wretched and brutal is its requirement that interests in order to gain entitlements must have power. The poor have interests, but they have no power.

The remedy is that one that distinguishes constitutional governments from others: law. Where the social contract is not and in the nature of the case cannot be self-enforcing through the approximate equality of powers, law must guard interests. We have recognized this with legal protections of civil liberties. We have after centuries of struggle recognized it with legal protections also of civil rights, notably by the Civil War amendments to the Constitution, the Civil

Rights Act of 1964, and the Voting Rights Act of 1965 and its extensions. The poor have a legitimate interest in not being consigned to poverty. Let the "market" benefit them as it can.* They have not the power to insure that it will, that in the present and the future it will do better for their interests than it has in the past. They require the undergirding of their legitimate interests through legally enforceable claims for education adequate to equipping them for work, and for work itself. They need, in short, firm economic and social rights comparable to those recognized by the juridical norms of most of the western democracies.

Is it realistic to speak of law guarding the interests of a society's weakest? To do so is what, above all, a constitution is for. A constitution, especially a written one, should be and in fact can only be seen as a contract among the people, an agreement by them that they are one political order. We cannot infer or rely upon the consent to that contract of anyone whose political liberty and material security are not valued. The Constitution of the United States has worked because it allowed for general satisfaction of the people who counted. It did that, however, at the price of keeping the millions of its minority peoples outside the circle of those who counted. Those people, the majority of whom are here by reason of original enslavement or conquest, could not prior to the civil rights movement of the 1960s and 1970s have been held to have given their consent. The slow workings of the Constitution made possible the movement. It secured for them after long struggle their negative rights. It is not politically realistic to anticipate that law will now voluntarily proceed to guard their positive rights. The inherent genius of the Constitution is, however, that the negative rights of voting and freedom of speech and freedom from discrimination can exact from law its further necessary protection, for fair shares in the national economic enterprise.

---

* A lengthy two-part article by Christopher Jencks evaluating blacks' recent economic experiences concludes, perhaps not very helpfully: "It is hard to see why blacks should sacrifice themselves on the altar of competition when hardly anyone else shows any inclination to do so." *New York Review of Books,* March 3 and 17, 1983.

A LOOK BACK

It would help to that end if American public opinion would redis-
cover the sense of social obligation which in its best periods it has had
for the conduct of its affairs.

American democracy has lost ground it needs to recover. Ideas
and principles once learned have been allowed to wither under the
thicket of a lately little-questioned moral and political orthodoxy,
which denies social responsibility for the ill-distribution of national
wealth and prophesies harm sure to be caused by governmental intervention to relieve it. Forty years ago, a president of the United States
could say to an attentive public:

> This Republic had its beginning, and grew to its present
> strength, under the protection of certain inalienable political
> rights—among them the right of free speech, free press, free
> worship, trial by jury, freedom from unreasonable searches and
> seizures. They were our rights to life and liberty.
>
> As our nation has grown in size and stature, however—as our
> industrial economy expanded—these political rights proved
> inadequate to assure us equality in the pursuit of happiness.
>
> We have come to a clear realization of the fact that true
> individual freedom cannot exist without economic security and
> independence. "Necessitous men are not free men." People who
> are hungry and out of a job are the stuff of which dictatorships
> are made.
>
> In our day these economic truths have become accepted as
> self-evident. We have accepted, so to speak, a second Bill of
> Rights under which a new basis of security and prosperity can
> be established for all—regardless of station, race or creed.
> Among these are:
>
> · The right to a useful and remunerative job in the industries
>   or shops or farms or mines of the nation;
> · The right to earn enough to provide adequate food and cloth-
>   ing and recreation;
> · The right of every farmer to raise and sell his products at a
>   return which will give him and his family a decent living;

- The right of every businessman, large and small, to trade in an atmosphere of freedom from unfair competition and domination by monopolies at home or abroad;
- The right of every family to a decent home;
- The right to adequate medical care and the opportunity to achieve and enjoy good health;
- The right to adequate protection from the economic fears of old age, sickness, accident and unemployment;
- The right to a good education.

All of these rights spell security. And after this war is won we must be prepared to move forward, in the implementation of these rights, to new goals of human happiness and well-being. America's own rightful place in the world depends in large part upon how fully these and similar rights have been carried into practice for our citizens. For unless there is security here at home there cannot be lasting peace in the world.[9]

Roosevelt was wrong only in saying that "we have accepted" these rights. We had not, and are further from doing so in our ideas and ideals today than we were then. Along our way since, we lost that sense of conviction, that sense of shared social responsibility. If he expounded realism, and this writer believes he did, we have turned away from realism. The excitement of the postwar expansive economy numbed us, our minds as well as hearts.

Poverty became hidden, because we willed ourselves to believe that it was vanishing. We turned our eyes from where it was and it malignantly spread, within minority communities and in the rural ghettos of Appalachia and among the aged. In the great movements for civil rights and social dignity that characterized the 1960s and 1970s we persuaded ourselves that individual rights would usher blacks and other minorities into the rewards of a generally benign economy. The realism of Roosevelt and others forty years ago and more was abandoned for myth. It is not so much visions and dreams that we need to recover, but only common sense, plus the political wisdom that knew then that vast and inbred poverty is inconsistent with political stability and self-government.

The remarkable fact is, nonetheless, that not all minority problems are economic. Hispanics and Indians, in particular, have deep concerns that relate to their determined efforts to preserve communal identities and cohesion. Blacks, on the other hand, have through the long and special processes of their involvement with American law been left in a different situation. The effects—mostly intended—of the law's continual redefining of their status have been both to hold them apart from white citizens—and that ancient separation is not yet fully erased—and yet to force them into the white economy. In degree not similarly true of Indians and Hispanics, they were made to live in the white man's world. Consequently, they were left with little cohesion apart from white feelings about them and their reactions to those. They have been made into lonely individuals, bonded together only by a common resistance. It has been firm bonding, though forged in opposition and not from the materials of a distinctive culture, religion, or language. Black and white people have shared a living here together for a long time, and imparted much to each other of values, aspirations, and manners. Particularly in the South has that been so, but there is not enough difference between North and South to make it untrue elsewhere. In having been made into "lonely individuals" they are like white Americans, in a measure that Hispanics and Indians with their webs of communal supports are not. In that second respect of being forced into resistance they are, of course, unique. It was not merely idealism and sentiment that led the 1960s movement to sing "black and white together"; Hispanics and Indians have never really sought to be "together" with whites. It was an unstated and perhaps unconscious realization that in this land, blacks and whites are alike children of a history that has made lonely and other-seeking individuals of both. Our law, from its individualistic common-law ethos, stumbles and frets when it must deal with Hispanic and Indian claims, with respect for their language or distinctive religious practices or tribal codes. But the blacks' claim is straightforward: it is simply for the protections and opportunities for the exercise of individuality.

Economic and social rights recognized by law would be that:

rights of the individual, rights that derive from citizenship. In that respect, they would differ from First Amendment rights which, in received political theory at least, are rights prior to citizenship, rights that derive from our free personality. Economic and social rights are those that make justice real, perfect our union with each other, make possible an actual government by consent. They cannot be the rights of groups or of classes—only of individual citizens.

We have undertaken in the modern era only one general form of race-specific economic and social policy; that is, of course, the congeries of various programs which we call "affirmative action." They have been temporarily useful, as remedies for past discrimination.[10] It is very much worth noting that the affirmative action programs, although race-specific, have been individualistic at core: they are a means for inserting qualified individuals into positions from which in the past discrimination would have excluded them. Their range is limited. They neither create new opportunities nor do they reach beyond those who, somehow, have prepared themselves for niches in an economy and an educational system which is not providing and in its current capacity cannot provide opportunities for the mass of the poor. We cannot expect race-specific measures ever to reach beyond that limit.

There is no real chance, in politics or in economic policy, of settling at last our minorities problems, of establishing justice for them, except by ending poverty *for all*. The minority poor are a special case, with especially hard features that cannot be neglected, but their case is ultimately rooted in the inadequacy of the American economic system—an inadequacy that has been glaring throughout the whole of the twentieth century except in times of great foreign wars—to provide enough jobs and income for all our people. We are being taught today to accept that inadequacy as inevitable, normal— and therefore a defect neither of the system nor of its political and economic managers, who are also its principal beneficiaries. Seven or eight percent unemployment is natural, we are instructed; in times of inflationary pressures (as in the early 1980s) it must, in fact, deliberately be made even larger in order to hold down prices for the rest of us. It is hard to decide whether such doctrine represents a betrayal of democracy (the ancients described oligarchy as rule in behalf of the rulers) or is simply immoral. Perhaps both. It is a creeping orthodoxy that belies the grand purposes of the Constitution, to achieve unity and justice.

We hear today from authoritative quarters that our public schools and our vocational training methods do poorly at preparing youth, especially minority youth; laymen's observations would bear that out. If those systems don't work well, no jobs and employment policies will either. This writer does not know how to make them work better. What can be insisted upon, however, is the principle, as old as Plato, that education is *the* primary concern and obligation of a state. It is also an obligation of citizenship. A citizen has a right to be educated. No citizen, so far as I can understand, has a right to be uneducated. A person unprepared for socially useful work is heavy baggage, and can be a menace to political stability. These precepts would seem to imply both that the individual's privilege of leaving the educational system before attaining some level of socially useful proficiency should be severely curtailed and that the public's determined care for each individual's educational or training needs be substantially enlarged.

Indians and Hispanics are likewise captives of American poverty, by some measures even more desperately so than blacks. Some Hispanics apparently are not, Cuban immigrants from 1959 to the early 1970s in particular. Critics chide other Hispanics with that example (as they chide blacks of long ancestry here with the example of West Indian immigrants). This is curious for patriots to do, for it is to concede that the far longer experience of Mexican Americans and Puerto Ricans with this society is handicapping. It is another exercise in self-serving logic, in denying responsibility. No learned explanation of Cuban (or West Indian black) economic agility affects the real case, which is that poverty among Hispanics, and discrimination as well, is deeply entrenched and derivative of their place in American history and present-day life.

With Puerto Ricans, there is first of all the issue of the island, where two-thirds still live. We conquered it militarily in the nineteenth century and since have made of it a near total economic dependency, living virtually on handouts from our corporations and our taxpayers. We cannot postpone much longer facing the issue of the island's political status, of whether it will be made a state or granted independence. Not even the pro-Commonwealth party there finds acceptable the present form of commonwealth (a bastard conception, unknown to the Constitution and unadaptable to our political principles). If the answer is statehood, we shall add substantially to all federal welfare costs. If independence, we shall then have to see which way the winds of Caribbean political desperation and volatility blow it.

Puerto Ricans dwelling on the mainland are almost entirely denizens of big-city ghettos. Their economic problems are much the same as those of urban blacks. Their political muscle for requiring that something be done about them is as yet and probably for the future considerably less. Despite similarity of interests, political alliance between them and blacks moves haltingly: the poor are characteristically wary of each other. Recently there have been tentative approaches to political association of sorts with the nation's far largest Hispanic population, the Mexican Americans. The two groups typically are residentially concentrated in widely separated states, and have had different backgrounds. They nevertheless share much: similar attitudes about the family, the same church, above all the same language.

With but small exceptions, Hispanics of every group are concerned to defend the social legitimacy of their Spanish language. Bilingualism has always been an issue for Hispanics and the invigorating civil rights achievements of the 1960s and 1970s enable them to make of it an issue the rest of us have to confront. That has elicited the complaints of the fearful. People never concerned with the past subordination of Hispanic people, their exclusion from any consensual union with the majority, now accuse bilingualism of despoiling national unity. Why, they ask, if the Italians, the Germans, the Yiddish-speaking Jews, if they and others forgot their languages must Spanish-speaking people ask for acceptance of theirs? It is a refusal again to understand the *specifically American* experience, just as the invidious comparison of black economic progress to that of, say, Jews is a shunning of the distinctively American history of blacks. The attachment to their language was forged in long decades of suffering and of holding onto a lifeline of social and personal dignity. How can we not now be a culturally richer society if what they preserved, often with such great difficulty, is brought almost as a gift into our national life, helping open windows of appreciation and communication with the ancient and still vibrant civilizations of Spanish-speaking peoples? How can we be hurt, if in as many schools as teacher availability make possible, there be bilingual instruction and learning?* A unanimous Supreme Court in 1974 ruled that where there are substantial numbers of non-English-speaking children in a school district, instruction in a language they can understand is their right. That is the Court's most authoritative holding yet.[11] We can ponder over the best pedagogical methods, we can debate how far the principle should be extended, we can (and must) struggle with questions of teacher preparation and recruitment. But excitably to see a threat to national unity (which to these worriers must seem a very fragile and vulnerable thing) is intellectual posturing.

Mexican Americans, as Deloria has pointed out, have mostly lost what land base they once had, and are today predominantly an urban people. As such they, and urban Indians, too, share the needs and interests of urban blacks and Puerto Ricans, and like them have a very high incidence of poverty. Probably the worst poverty in the United States (not including the island of Puerto Rico) is on Indian reservations. The paradox is that the mineral wealth and water rights of those reservations are now besieged by immense corporate interests and other powerful developers. Yet they exist still, and tribal religions, customs, and limited ways of self-government are kept alive. It would seem another mark of the providential good luck of the United States. What other western people besides ourselves does not have to travel halfway around the globe for opportunity of instruction in a radically different set of insights into men's relationship to the universe and to nature, and the values that prescribes for our living? The Indian tribes are numerous and differ from each other in many ways. Yet they all share a non-western outlook on the proper place of men in the universe, and consequently on what is of greater and lesser importance and value. It would seem that a nation desirous

---

* I suppose that the principal objections to bilingual schooling are all touched upon in Chapters 7 and 8 of Nathan Glazer's *Ethnic Dilemmas 1964–1982* (Cambridge, Mass.: Harvard University Press, 1983). Later in the book, page 333, Glazer exaggerates, perhaps harmfully so, when he asserts that present law has created "the right to be educated in American schools in language and loyalty to Mexico, in its history, its culture, its customs."

of wisdom would treasure, therefore, the integrity of the tribes as among the finest of its resources.

The history of the many and often conflicting federal and state policies toward the tribes is a source of national shame; there hardly needs to be more documentation of that, the record by now being hardly contested. Each succeeding generation, though, rationalizes its own desires. Governments have done to the tribes or allowed to be done everything that predictably might have destroyed them; yet most have survived, albeit weakly. More than any other minority, Indians are and have been a special care of the federal government. The power of Congress over them has been held to be "plenary," sufficient if so desired even to override treaties once entered into, and is exercised through and under the congressional power to regulate commerce. What the tribes need, in the way of economic assistance from Congress, tribal leaderships themselves can define and press for.[12] But what first of all they have a right to—and the rest of us have a strong interest in—is federal policy that respects tribal authority and the customs and religion of the tribes, and leaves them free to follow their own paths of internal government.

POSITIVE FREEDOM

In what way does governmental action to help minorities and the multitudinous poor among them differ from that traditional "managing" of the minority question that has for so long plagued nonwhite peoples? The life of the law, a wise historian and judge once said, is experience, not logic. To govern is to choose, it has also been said. Our Constitution has given us principles to guide choice, and paramount among them are the search for political unity and for individual justice. The law works best when it is neither regulating nor giving charity, but establishing rights and duties. The First Amendment does not "regulate" the freedom of speech, nor the Fourteenth the equality of persons before the law, nor does the Social Security legislation give alms; they declare rights, as being terms and conditions of our social contract with each other. The recognition of individual rights for economic security and education ought to be the same.

Unlike First Amendment rights, which restrict governmental

action, they would require governmental acts; beyond dispute or denial, that is a vast juridical difference. The difference lies not, however, with established practice in the economic field. From our first protective tariff, American government has *de facto* recognized an obligation to make secure the economic welfare of those to whose power it felt responsive. We can debate endlessly the wisdom of the massive and intricate system of protections, subsidies, and tax structures we have erected and continually remold and add to as power relationships within the society shift. Except for a few theoretical purists, we do not, however, question seriously the government's role as a weighty participant in the managing of the economy. What an economic and educational bill of rights would do is assure that individuals have those minimal securities without which, in any real sense, they cannot discharge the duties of citizenship.

In measured, stop-and-go fashion, we have already moved some distance toward that, with an assortment of medical, food, and welfare entitlements, as well as some job and other protections. We have shied away from placing such in our Constitution, as most western democracies have done, probably because ours is unique in being an enforceable charter but also because the benefits are invariably partial and severely limited. It matters little, perhaps, whether we proceed further by statutes or by constitutional amendment; what does matter is that principles be accepted.

Roosevelt spoke of "the right to a useful and remunerative job" and of "the right to earn enough." One of the ironies of American ideological development since his day is that the "right to work" has been changed to mean, in contrast to the rest of the world's adherence to its old meaning, the right not to join a union; i.e., the prohibition of union shops, an old ethical ideal conscripted and corrupted for ideological service. Ideology does not, here or in the Soviet Union, put people to work. On the evidence of the past, it seems unreal to believe that the situation of our poor will be rectified until we, at long last, do affirm the right of each to do useful work. There is no mention in Roosevelt's statement of a right to welfare (as we have come to know it) or food stamps. Those programs are today necessary because implicitly we have settled for the national goal of merely keeping people alive. The costs of such programs are very large. The costs of putting people to productive work would in the long run be less. We shall always have to care for our aged and disabled. The rest of us are entitled to the opportunity to work.

There is even greater disagreement about how that entitlement can be made actual than with its acknowledgement, great as that is. We typically turn to political inventions made burdensomely complicated through ideological compulsion to protect everybody's interests: business, labor, city government, etc. Most bear some similarity to the old, ill-conceived, and luckily ill-fated National Industrial Recovery Act (the NRA) of the early 1930s; the latest such is the Job Training Partnership Act, a Reagan initiative. These complex programs have never made much of a dent in the unemployment figures; there is no reason to expect JTPA to be different. When they are given up on, after large expenditures, sometimes as high as the cost of a missile or two, the poor are blamed for still being jobless.

Congress will spend extravagantly to protect ideology, in this instance one that requires that we pretend that government is inefficient compared to private business—a doubtful proposition; big bureaucracies whether of government or business are probably equally productive—and that, in any event, it shouldn't *do* anything. It can, of course. Its arsenals used to make weaponry (even the first atomic bombs), its shipyards built the Navy, its Tennessee Valley Authority remade a region. But private business has moved in more thoroughly; government now mainly merely buys and contracts. We keep still the Corps of Engineers, which congressmen find handy for their pork barrels, but even put it out for hire, as in Saudi Arabia.

The fact is that there is much public work to be done in this country, and there always will be. Public works, teacher aides, daycare tending—the list is long and familiar. Government ought to get it done. The national government can be as efficient and economical in managing it directly as can be any big private bureaucracy, and ought unembarrassedly to do it. We ought to stop paying the price for troika schemes, slapdashedly harnessing state and/or local governments with private business and/or labor unions with community groups—and sometimes the hodgepodge gets even denser.

The right to work can most sensibly and rationally be seen as a legally claimable right to a job, or service opportunity, in publicly useful work of the national government.[13] One can urge that without necessary partiality toward any economic theory. Nor is there anything novel in saying it. Keynesians, monetarists, supply-siders—all have had to work around requirements of policy and law, such as equal employment opportunities, safety in the workplace, clean air and other environmental standards. These are ground rules. The right to a job should take its place among them. Unemployment as either an intended or accepted result of national economic policies needs to be, by law, denied our policymakers. Between that and one form or another of the "rising tide" theory, it is doubtful that there is any effective third way; experience does not suggest one, at any rate.

The American poor, and American racial minorities, do not exist in a social vacuum. They are a part of the world's majority of poor, powerless, and overwhelmingly nonwhite people. They are, in fact, the upper level of that global fraternity of marginal lives. America remains an envy of the world's poor, who vote with their feet whenever they can for this society (or like ones in western Europe) over any others. Who has ever heard of the poor of foreign lands seeking entry to the Soviet Union? The African poor are even desperate enough to flock to South Africa, and many of the Caribbean basin not to Cuba but Puerto Rico, where per capita income is well below that in our poorest state. Those are not reasons for excusing or tolerating the reality of American poverty. They do suggest that the methods used to overcome that poverty be drawn from our own liberal principles. By the standards of worldwide needs, the American problem is an easy one. With the responsibilities of world power requiring the judgment of an enlightened citizenry, it is not one we can abide, if our democracy means anything to us. What is urged here is that it can be solved best by traditionally American means, the vesting in individuals of *rights* to basic needs and opportunities. There is no better way to express this than by the old phrase, "removal of obstacles" to individual fulfillment, or by the modern term "entitlements."

The government cannot, of course, guarantee a house if there is not a house to be had, a job if there is not one. We are drawn, therefore, to the necessity of some programs and plans. In a well-ordered society, an obvious method, for example, for putting the unemployed to work in huge numbers could be their training and employment for construction of decent housing for themselves. To legislate comprehensive programs seems today, however, more than our political processes can accomplish. In recent years, we have seen the collapse of one attempt after another: welfare reform, criminal code revision, immigration planning and control, election campaign financing,* tax reform, and others. We have too often preferred to allow ills we all recognize as such to persist rather than adopt less than perfect approaches toward remedying them. Liberals have been prominent in some of those reform-paralyzing defeats. We have too often forgotten that the first business of government is, after all, to govern, i.e., to choose among the alternatives a disorderly world of experience makes possible. One does not, therefore, feel great confidence in the capability of our political system to enact programs that set right the condition of our poorest citizens.

But life has a way, we may still hope, of exacting its own terms. Soon (it will be soon or never) the outraged insistence of people valuing their own lives and civilization will stop governments from their insane arms race. In time, and desperate conditions will not allow it to be a long time, the political societies of the north, of Europe and North America and one can wish Japan, will have to come to some sharing with the impoverished masses of Africa, Asia, and Latin America. And the civil rights—the negative rights—won by our minorities will, as they are now beginning to do, force the case for entitlements in our political system; they will, that is, if the militarism of our government can be curbed before it destroys all of us. If any two words suggested what the movement of the 1960s and 1970s was about, they would be "dignity" and "empowerment"; they are qualities which, once attained, actuate both the impulse for a more just economy and the prospect of achieving it.

The federal government has a continuing heavy responsibility to enforce the antidiscrimination and voting rights statutes created in the 1960s and 1970s. Many state and local governments have similar laws to administer. It is greatly important that this job of en-

---

* When after much labor Congress did in the early 1970s enact a campaign reform measure, bench and bar overthrew much of it, on the astonishing grounds that money is speech.

forcement go on with thoroughness, as long as unequal treatment is otherwise a probability. However, even if every such act on the books were enforced to the hilt—but no other action taken—the effect on minority poverty would not be significant. On the contrary, if that were all, minority poverty as a by-product of the modern economic system could be expected to increase and poverty become, as it now nears becoming, a minority-dominated condition. We shall have then allowed to grow a new type of stigma, disabling generation after generation, as segregation earlier did. It will be a cruel cost to require for the withholding of public action in deference to economic myths.

NOTES

1. *The Federalist*, ed. Max Beloff (New York: Macmillan, 1948), p. 6.
2. *U.S.* v. *Carolene Products Co.*, 304 U.S. 144, 152 (1938).
3. For one description of what happens to minorities as the Reagan administration neglects fair application of benefits, see *Losing Ground: Public Policy and the Displacement of Rural Black-Owned Homesteads* (Washington, D.C.: Housing Assistance Council, July 1983).
4. Martin Kilson, "Black Social Classes and Intergenerational Poverty," *The Public Interest*, Summer 1981. Or see the Op-Ed piece of John H. Bunzel, one of Mr. Reagan's appointees to the U.S. Commission on Civil Rights, *New York Times*, September 20, 1983. To "promote minority advancement" he would seek somehow to persuade unmarried black teenage girls to stop having babies and would study why blacks do not do as well on written examinations as Asians; space limitations notwithstanding, that is a very short list.
5. *The Federalist*, p. 1.
6. John Rawls, *A Theory of Justice* (Cambridge, Mass.: Harvard University Press, 1971), p. 102.
7. Walter E. Williams, *The State Against Blacks* (New York: McGraw-Hill, 1982). The Sowell shelf lengthens. His positions are well enough stated in Chapters 5, 6, and 8 of his latest: *The Economics and Politics of Race* (New York: William Morrow, 1983).
8. For one aspect of this, see Elizabeth Drew, *Politics and Money* (New York: Macmillan, 1983).
9. Franklin D. Roosevelt, Annual Message to Congress, January 11, 1944, in *Franklin D. Roosevelt, Selected Speeches, Messages, Press Conferences, and Letters*, ed. by Basil Rauch (New York: Rinehart, 1957), pages 347–348.
10. Leslie W. Dunbar, "Toward Equality, Toward a More Perfect Union," in *The State of Black America 1982* (New York: National Urban League, 1982).

11. *Lau* v. *Nichols,* 414 U.S. 563 (1974).
12. See Vine Deloria, Jr. *A Better Day for Indians.* (New York: Field Foundation, 1977).
13. It is too bad that the eminent black leaders and scholars who issued *A Policy Framework for Racial Justice* (Washington, D.C.: Joint Center for Political Studies, 1983) propounded yet one more NRA-type invention.

INDEX

abolitionist movement, 141

abortion, xiii, 18

Abram, Morris, 58, 63, 64, 70, 73

accommodation, 184, 194

AFDC program, 44–5, 56 *n*.56, 84, 183; children on, 99; to rural minorities, 182; to teenage mothers, 89; and unemployment, 108–9

affirmative action, xi, 15, 28, 33–6, 93, 111, 211; and black college enrollment, 31, 38; in employment, 34–6, 46, 48, 65, 67; gains (1974–80), 62; and group identity, 69–70; morality of, 66–73; Reagan's policies, 58–67, 72, 73; vs. seniority layoffs, 36, 54 *n*.30, 72

age structure: in cities, 98 and *t*, 101; "critical mass," 99–100; and employment rate, 97–8

agribusiness, 159–60, 167, 173, 174, 176, 178–9

Agricultural Adjustment Administration, 158–9, 173

agriculture, 163, 201, 202; blacks in, 156–60; federal programs, 171, 173–4, 178–80; Mexican workers, 161–2, 163, 164

Alabama, 14–15, 27, 158

Alaskan natives, xvi, 81*t*

alienation, 16

American Indians, 124, 126, 153–6, 191, 194, 197, 210, 212; children, 16–17; in community colleges, 174; crime rate, 81*t*; and criminal justice system, 127; cultural attitudes, 187, 214–15; and government policies, 153–4, 215; heirship lands, 154, 180–3; land leasing, 153–6, 180–2; leadership, 17; political attitudes, 16–17; population, 127; and taxation, 174–5; treaties, 17–18, 215; welfare programs, 182, 183

Anderson, Bernard, 35

Appalachian Land Ownership Task Force, 175, 177

Appalachian Regional Commission, 171, 172

Appalachian whites, 152, 164–7, 168, 174; cultural viewpoints, 186; heirship lands, 181–2; property taxes, 175, 177; stereotypes, 184–5; welfare programs, 166–7, 182

Aristotle, 196

arms race, 219

ABOUT THE CONTRIBUTORS

VINE DELORIA, JR. published *Custer Died for Your Sins* in 1969 and has since been recognized as a primary authority on American Indian affairs. Eight books later, *The Metaphysics of Modern Existence* confirmed the breadth of his concerns. A member of the Standing Rock Sioux Tribe, he was executive director of the National Congress of American Indians from 1964 to 1967, holds degrees in theology and law, and is a professor of political science at the University of Arizona.

LESLIE W. DUNBAR has written frequently on problems of civil rights and American politics. He was with the Southern Regional Council from 1958 to 1965 (executive director, 1961–1965), and was executive director of the Field Foundation, a principal supporter of civil rights causes, from 1965 to 1980. During 1984–1985 he is a "scholar-at-large" with the United Negro College Fund.

DIANA R. GORDON, a lawyer, has been long active in criminal justice reform, most recently as a principal officer, and as president (1982–1983), of the National Council on Crime and Delinquency. Her publications include *City Limits: Barriers to Change in Urban Government.*

CHARLES V. HAMILTON is Wallace S. Sayre Professor of Political Science at Columbia University. He holds a degree in law as well as one in political science, and his teaching career, which early included Tuskegee Institute, has always been combined with active involvement in politics and civil rights issues and with service on numerous boards and study commissions. His latest book is the textbook *American Government*.

HERMAN SCHWARTZ, through a crowded career of litigating, governmental service, private activism, and writings both scholarly and popular, has achieved the unusual distinction of being acknowledged an authority on civil rights, prison law, antitrust law, energy regulation, and wiretaps law and practice. He is now a professor of law at American University and is director of the William O. Douglas Inquiry into the State of Individual Freedom.

WILLIAM L. TAYLOR was staff director of the U.S. Commission on Civil Rights, 1965–1968, and had been with it from 1961. His earlier career included being a staff lawyer with the NAACP Legal Defense Fund, and he now carries on his unbroken involvement with civil rights as director of the Center for National Policy Review at Catholic University Law School. School desegregation has been a particular interest, and he was recently a lead attorney for the plaintiffs in the important St. Louis and Cincinnati cases. He is the author of *Hanging Together: Equality in an Urban Nation*.

WILLIAM J. WILSON is Lucy Professor of Urban Sociology and a former chairman of the Department of Sociology at the University of Chicago. He was a Fellow (1981–1982) at the Center for Advanced Study in the Behavioral Sciences at Stanford University. His books include *Power, Racism, and Privilege: Race Relations in Theoretical and Sociohistorical Perspectives; Through Different Eyes: Black and White Perspectives on American Race Relations; The Declining Significance of Race: Blacks and Changing American Institutions;* and the forthcoming *The Hidden Agenda: Race, Social Dislocations, and Public Policy in America.* His major current research interest is the changing nature of urban poverty.